A
THOUSAND
Sleepless
NIGHTS

ALSO BY
Teri Harman

The Moonlight Trilogy:

Blood Moon
Black Moon
Storm Moon

A THOUSAND

Sleepless

NIGHTS

TERI HARMAN

SWEETWATER
BOOKS

An imprint of Cedar Fort, Inc.
Springville, Utah

ISBN 13: 978-1-4621-2192-2

Published by Sweetwater Books, an imprint of Cedar Fort, Inc.
2373 W. 700 S., Springville, UT 84663
Distributed by Cedar Fort, Inc., www.cedarfort.com

LIBRARY OF CONGRESS CATALOGING-IN-PUBLICATION DATA

Names: Harman, Teri, 1981- author.
Title: A thousand sleepless nights / Teri Harman.
Description: Springville, Utah : Sweetwater Books, an imprint of Cedar Fort,
  Inc. Springville, Utah, [2018] |
Identifiers: LCCN 2017049136 (print) | LCCN 2017053318 (ebook) | ISBN
  9781462128860 (epub, pdf, mobi) | ISBN 9781462121922 (perfect bound : alk.
  paper)
Subjects: LCSH: Marriage--Fiction. | LCGFT: Novels.
Classification: LCC PS3608.A74478 (ebook) | LCC PS3608.A74478 T46 2018
  (print) | DDC 813/.6--dc23
LC record available at https://lccn.loc.gov/2017049136

Cover design by Shawnda T. Craig
Cover design © 2018 Cedar Fort, Inc.
Edited by Melissa Caldwell and Jessica Romrell
Typeset by Breanna Call Herbert

Printed in the United States of America

10 9 8 7 6 5 4 3 2 1

Printed on acid-free paper

For my Grandmas: Mary Jo, Loie, and Roberta.
Thank you for your creativity and humor, your
quiet gratitude, and your sassy spunk.

PART ONE

Matilda

*M*atilda White pressed her Aunt Jetty's withered, skeletal hand between hers. Jetty's normally milky skin was now ashen and parchment-thin over flaccid blue veins. Matilda stared at the veins, which were easier to look at than her aunt's sunken face.

Both the tall, single-hung windows in Jetty's bedroom were flung open to allow the cool air to flow in over the four-post bed, rustling the creamy sheers hung at the windows and around the bed. The air brought with it the sound of crickets and the smell of grass. The room was dark, with one pillar candle burning on the nightstand.

"Don't leave me," Matilda whispered, her throat tight and face wet with tears. "I can't stand it. I won't survive it."

"Oh, Tilly," Jetty sighed, her voice hoarse and dry.

Matilda finally looked up. Jetty's jade-green eyes were clouded, the lids drooping. Her wild ochre hair was gone. About a half hour ago, Matilda had removed the emerald silk scarf covering Jetty's scabbed baldness because it had been itching her. This person was not Jetty. Not the vibrant, unpredictable woman who had raised Matilda since she was six months old.

Jetty coughed, clearing her throat. "The garden starts will be ready for planting about mid-May." Matilda nodded obediently. "Don't forget to prune the tomatoes or all the growth will go to the greens instead of the fruit."

"I know."

"And water the herbs a little extra. You know they are picky."

Matilda held back the sobs rising in her chest. "Don't talk like that."

"Like what?"

2

"Like you won't be here."

Jetty laughed, which quickly turned into a racking cough. "But I won't be! Fate has spoken."

Matilda couldn't laugh about this. More hot tears tracked down her face.

Jetty grew quiet, and Matilda's gaze went immediately to her aunt's chest to be sure she was still breathing. She was, but it was a Herculean effort. "What can I do?" Matilda asked.

Jetty smiled, weakly squeezed her hand. "I never told you about Frank."

Matilda looked up, sniffed, intrigued despite her despair. "Who was Frank?"

"Frank Mitchell. He was the man I was supposed to love, but didn't." Jetty paused to breathe. Matilda moved her chair a little closer, keeping a comforting grip on Jetty's hand. "He was so handsome: tall, broad shoulders, thick chocolate-brown hair, and the eyes to match. He was witty and suave. He wanted me to marry him. I said yes and made the biggest mistake of my life."

Matilda had never heard even a whisper of this. Jetty had always been so open about her life, sharing stories like cookies, but not this. "What happened?"

Jetty wearily closed her eyes and shrugged. "I didn't love him, not really. A year into our marriage, I felt like a prisoner in my own tedious fairy tale. I was pretending to be someone I wasn't, and nothing kills a person quicker." She opened her eyes, and a bit of her usual spark was there. "Except maybe liver cancer."

Matilda scoffed. "Stop! That's not funny."

"Oh, sure it is." She closed her eyes again, but the smile remained. "So I left Frank. Best thing I ever did. 'Cause a month later, I met Enzo Amara. I ran away from my marriage, ran all the way to Florida, and found the love I had always dreamed of. I found my life."

"Enzo Amara? Another man you never mentioned?"

"It hurts too much." A tear slipped down her wrinkled cheek. "Enzo was everything. Devastatingly handsome, but not in that Ken-doll way that Frank was. Enzo had rich character written in the cut of his jaw and eyes filled with a thousand stories. He was quiet and kind, but fiercely passionate. He was a talented stonemason. Oh, you should have seen his hands!" A smile full of memory. Jetty looked at her own

3

hands and the smile slipped away. "He was also Italian and could cook like nobody's business."

"Is that why you love to cook?"

"Yes, he taught me. I feel close to him when I cook. It's all I had after he was gone." A small sigh. "Every time I cook pasta, I can feel his hand on my face."

Matilda's heart fell. "What happened to him?"

Jetty's tears flowed more freely now, and her breathing grew loud, ragged. "He fell. Off a ladder. Just a normal day at work and then . . . it wasn't. It was the end of everything. I got only three blissful years with Enzo. A blink of an eye, really."

"I'm so sorry, Jetty." Matilda matched her aunt's tears. "He sounds amazing. I wish I'd known him."

"I've never been that angry. It was a *desperate* kind of anger, that helpless kind that eats away at you." She took a hard breath. "Twice I woke up with the curtains on fire 'cause of that nasty grief."

Matilda rubbed Jetty's hand. Jetty loved to embellish, to add magic to the ordinary. "Really?"

"Truly."

"What did you do?"

"I came to Silent Fields; they needed a kindergarten teacher. I bought this house. No one in town knew what I'd been through. I couldn't stand the idea of sharing it. I told your mother, of course, but no one else because speaking his name sliced open my heart." She sighed. "It felt like I was bleeding to death. *Slowly.* I buried that fiery grief and parts of me turned to ash. I never got them back."

Matilda began to worry about how upset Jetty had become. Her breathing and heart rate were irregular. A cold sweat had formed on the back of her hand and across her bare forehead. "Jetty . . ."

"I'm okay." She took a slow breath. "If you had not come to me, I may not have loved anything or anyone again." She touched Matilda's cheek with her cold hand. "I lived in a fog of grief until you came. And that's not to say I didn't grieve my sister and your father—their deaths hurt something awful—but you gave me a reason to live again. You need a reason to live after a tragedy."

Matilda kissed the back of Jetty's hand. She knew that her aunt was trying to teach her something, to help her deal with what was to come, but Matilda didn't want to think about it. She didn't want to plan for a life without Jetty. "I wish I had known Mom and Dad. I wish they were here."

"They'd be very proud of you, Tilly." Jetty tucked Matilda's long black hair behind her ear. "You look so much like your father: the dark hair and dark eyes, perfect olive skin. But your shortness—that's all Ivy. She was the shortest person I knew until you." Jetty gave her a teasing smile. "Sweet, short Ivy." An extra strain appeared around Jetty's eyes. "Your poor mother. Please don't be angry at her."

Matilda frowned. "Why would I be angry at her?"

Jetty's brow lowered. She looked at Matilda for a moment as if ready to say something, a struggle in her eyes. "I think I need some water," she finally mumbled in a rough voice. She coughed weakly.

Matilda turned away to grab the cup and straw. When she turned back, Jetty had her eyes closed. She took a tiny sip of water and then, "You know, Parker reminds me of Frank," Jetty whispered.

Matilda's stomach tightened. "What? No. I love Parker."

"I don't doubt that, but Tilly . . . is he your Enzo?" Jetty looked at her straight on, her expression serious. "Remember when you were learning to swim? It took you a long time to get comfortable with it, but even once you knew what you were doing, you were extra cautious. Do you remember?"

Matilda nodded, her mind filling with the sound of lapping water and excited children. "That pool seemed as big as the ocean."

"You would sit in the shallow end and watch the kids jump off the diving board. You watched them with such *fierce* longing. You wanted to do it, but you never talked yourself into it. You chose the safer road."

Matilda recalled with stark clarity that feeling of *wanting*. Wanting but fearing. And fear winning over. It hadn't been only swimming. There had been many moments in her life of fear and wanting, including this moment of watching Jetty slip away. "It scared me," she mumbled meekly.

Jetty closed her eyes and nodded. "I know, my girl. I think you have too much of both your practical mother and your crazy aunt in you. Those two sides are at constant war. But you're about to face a hard time. You'll have to wrestle with your own grief. You'll need someone to help clear the fog. Can Parker do that?"

Jetty was right, of course. Matilda had fought a battle of practicality and spontaneity every day of her life. Craving to fly but scared of heights. "Parker is a good man. He'll be there for me."

"That's not what I asked. I think maybe he's a Frank, a shallow end. I haven't said anything because I kept waiting for you to decide on your own. But I'm out of time and can't go without speaking my piece."

Matilda blinked. Her heart raced as her mind fought Jetty's opinion. She didn't know what to say. Mostly because she was afraid Jetty might be right.

Jetty went on, her voice low and tired. "I'm not saying he's a bad choice. Parker *is* a good man, like you said. He's been a wonderful friend to you. Marrying him is a very practical choice. But the question is this: Are you sitting in the shallow end wishing you could dive?"

"I don't . . ."

"I don't want you to live like I did, first with Frank and then after Enzo's death. I don't want you to live weighed down by sadness or paralyzed by fear. I want you to be *happy*. The kind of happy that borders on insanity. Playful and emotional and barefoot in the rain and kissing in the moonlight at three in the morning. Not he reads the sports section while she reads the travel section over breakfast, and pantsuits, and perfectly clipped hedges in the front yard. That insane kind of happy is far more interesting and fulfilling. I don't want you to deny yourself that kind of joy because of practicality or because you've suffered tragedy."

"Jetty, I don't know. That doesn't really sound like real life. It's sounds like a story. It sounds—"

Jetty started coughing violently. Matilda moved onto the bed and slipped her arms around her aunt's frail form. She held as tightly as she dared as Jetty hacked.

A splatter of blood fell across the white sheets.

Matilda wanted to scream.

Once the coughing eased, she tried to offer Jetty another drink, but she wouldn't take it.

"Just hold me, Tilly-girl."

"Okay, okay," Matilda answered softly, and a little desperately. She leaned back into the headboard and cradled Jetty in her arms. Jetty didn't speak; her breathing was enormously difficult. Matilda felt she should answer Jetty's questions about Parker and herself, explain how it was all right, but found she didn't have anything to say. She didn't know how to answer. And that made a knot form in the back of her neck.

Jetty stirred. "I'm so sorry . . . I won't be . . . at the wedding. Don't . . . let this . . . ruin it."

"Shh," was all Matilda could say. She didn't want to think of the empty chair at her upcoming wedding. She didn't want to think about the wedding at all.

"And . . . Tilly. Be careful . . . with your grief. It's powerful; it's a . . . terrible thing. And you still . . . carry so much from your . . . dear parents. I'm sorry . . ." Jetty coughed painfully.

Matilda held her until it passed; her own eyes pressed shut, tears leaking onto her cheeks. "Shh, now. Rest. Don't worry about me. Just rest." Matilda put her cheek against Jetty's cool head. She didn't want to think about grief. Just the idea of what was to come made her bones shake and her mind rattle into panic. Jetty's fate—and her own—sat in her gut like a sleeping beast.

Matilda looked over Jetty's head to the bedroom windows. A quiet, moonlit night lay beyond. "It's a full moon, Jetty. Your favorite." Jetty's body relaxed a little more into Matilda's. "The yard looks like I'm seeing it through an antique mirror. The trees and grass are silver. There's a breeze in the treetops. It smells like life; spring is almost here. The clouds don't dare touch the moon for fear of hiding its brilliant light. I think it's shining just for you."

Jetty sighed quietly.

Her last breath.

Which rose from her cracked lips in a lacey white puff.

Henry

*H*enry Craig sat at a table at the back of the Detroit Public Library Main Branch, bent over a blank sheet of paper. It was cold in this corner, by the large window. Henry was bundled into a hooded sweatshirt, ink stains on the cuffs. He tapped his pen on the table, nothing in his head. No words. No ideas. Nothing.

I'm supposed to be a writer.

He looked up from his page at the shelves and wandering patrons. *Of course, sitting at this table every day doing nothing doesn't really qualify as writing.*

Throughout his terrible childhood, as he was passed from one awful foster home to the next, all he'd ever wanted was to read and write. To write like the authors who swept him away from his own pitiful tragedy. He felt their passion as keenly as anyone; he felt the words roaring in his veins. And yet here he sat, nothing but frustrated scribbles on his page—again.

He shoved the page into his tattered backpack and stood, scraping the chair back loudly enough to solicit a harsh, faceless shush from among the stacks. He frowned as he stomped down the stairs and out into the noisy city street.

The cold air hit him like shards of glass, penetrating his thin sweatshirt. He flipped his hood up, pulling it low over his freckled face, and plunged his hands into his pockets.

He was late for the night class he taught at the community college. *Creative Writing.* Henry shook his head and nearly laughed out loud. True, he nearly had a PhD in creative writing, but that didn't make him feel like a writer. He wouldn't feel like a real writer until he could unleash the passionate words trapped inside him. Like an obsessed treasure hunter, he knew they were there somewhere.

He just needed to find a way to dig them up.

Matilda

*M*atilda's first day back to work at the Silent Fields Library after Jetty's funeral was not going as well as she hoped.

The whole town had turned out for the untraditional funeral. Jetty had never attended church, though she'd donated money, food, and clothes to all three of the local congregations when they were in need. Many neighbors had ignorantly whispered behind her back about her quirks. *That silly old maid, Jetty Oliver, with her jars of herbs and obnoxiously colorful house. Her wild hair and even wilder gardens.* But underneath the gossip everyone loved Jetty; it was impossible not to. Many had passed through her kindergarten classroom, young minds set on fire with learning and discovery, or learned to draw at the community center under her tutelage.

So the town had dutifully gathered in the Silent Fields Cemetery, around Jetty's simple reclaimed-wood casket, the surface carved with a sun, a moon, and a sky of stars. There were mountains of flowers, pale lavender lilacs, and bold yellow tulips mostly—Jetty's spring favorites. Matilda read the last chapter of *Bridge to Terabithia*, Jetty's favorite book. Matilda doubted anyone had been able to understand what she read through her tear-tight voice.

Then, with the sun shining and the air cool, it had been over.

Done.

Jetty gone.

And the beast in Matilda's gut had rumbled awake with a bitter growl.

Huddled in the medieval basement of the library, Matilda tried to get control of her tears. Lately, they unexpectedly attacked, fierce and demanding. She'd barely made it to this dark corner behind several shelves of forgotten books before the sobs exploded.

An orphan for a second time, Matilda felt Jetty's loss deep in her bones. Her parents had died when she was too young to grieve them, too young to understand the loss. Now, it felt like Jetty's death was also theirs all over.

She was alone.

Matilda slapped the stone wall and felt a ping of pain where the ring on her finger connected with the hard surface. She blinked at the simple single diamond gold engagement ring.

I'm not alone. I have Parker.

It didn't bring her any comfort. Jetty's words had attached themselves to her thoughts, digging holes in what she'd once thought was solid logic. *Is he your Frank or your Enzo?* Jetty had whispered on her deathbed, leaving Matilda not only alone but also confused.

I love Parker. We are getting married. Everything will be all right.

More tears welled in her eyes.

She brushed them away and turned to look at the shelves. Most of the librarians hated coming down into the basement with its one-hundred-year-old stone walls that smelled faintly of dirt and decay, its eerie shadowy corners that watched everything, and the poor, forgotten books. A book graveyard, creaky and damp. Some in town even whispered stories to the children about ghosts that shuffled the library basement on dark, moonless nights.

Matilda loved it. The thrill of the bizarre, the mystery of things time had forgotten. She'd never admit it, of course, but sometimes coming down to the book graveyard was as exciting as things got in her small town life.

But today she found no thrill or comfort. The walls and shadows only seemed to pull her deeper into her despair.

"Matilda!"

Matilda jumped at the gruff sound of Beverly Wilson's voice. Beverly came around the shelves. She was wide, tall, and her feet pounded too harshly when she walked. Atop her broad shoulders sat a too-masculine face, square and made more severe by the way she pulled her dull brown-gray hair back into a bun. *The forbidding fictional librarian in the flesh*, Matilda often thought.

"What are you doing down here? I've been looking for you for ten minutes." Beverly crossed her arms over her large chest.

"Uh . . . yeah. Sorry," Matilda stumbled, trying to wipe the tears away as casually as possible.

"Well, you know I don't tolerate sneaking off when it's not break time."

Matilda nodded slowly. Her eyes were puffy and no doubt as red and veiny as plum flesh. "I just needed a quick minute."

Beverly scowled and then raised her eyebrows. "What are you waiting for? Your minute is over. It's Saturday, and the line at the circulation desk is like Estelle's when the donuts come out."

Matilda jumped. "Sorry." At least Beverly wasn't coddling her like everyone else in town. As if her grief had turned her to thin glass. Even if it were true, something about Beverly's gruff normalcy was bolstering. Matilda gave one last sniff before marching past Beverly and up the stairs.

"Is Parker picking you up today?"

Matilda didn't hear the question. For the past fifteen minutes, she had been sitting at the circulation desk staring at the cover of *A Secret Garden*, thinking about Jetty's garden, which she would have to plant alone this year. Her eyes ached. She felt new tears brewing.

"*Hello?* Matilda!" A thin, long-fingered hand waved in front of her face. "You look like you want to eat that book." A bubbly laugh.

Matilda blinked several times and looked up at Thea Nichols, the lowest librarian on Beverly's totem pole, directly under Matilda. Thea laughed again, a tinkling sound, and sat in the chair next to Matilda. "Haven't you read that already?"

Matilda blinked once more. "Uh, yeah. A few times."

Thea pursed her pink glossy lips. She leaned forward to look at the book again as if to determine why Matilda found it so fascinating. Thea was nineteen and had white-blonde hair cut into a choppy pixie, which matched her slight build and Greek-goddess face. She wore ripped jeans and painted her nails black—about as rebellious as was tolerated in conservative Silent Fields, Kansas. "You were supposed to re-shelve it, like, a while ago," Thea pronounced. Then after looking at Matilda for a moment, her expression softened. "Want me to do it?"

"No, no. It's fine." Matilda picked up the book and stood. "Be right back."

Matilda rounded the half-moon mahogany circulation desk, which sat in front of a fan of ceiling-height shelves, several deep and fat with books. The library was an impressive specimen, built when money was easy for the small town, in the days when the limestone quarry was the biggest, most profitable in the state. Carved double mahogany doors, taller than a man and extra wide, opened to the large main room with its polished limestone floors and grand Victorian chandelier. The chandelier had come all the way from London. And every two years, the library closed for a whole day so that the librarians could polish every crystal and every inch of gold plate. Matilda loved that chandelier. It had a presence, like a dragon watching over the castle.

To the left of the circulation desk stood an elegant dark-walnut curved stairway, which led to the second floor where more books resided. This library was the jewel of Silent Fields, Kansas, placed right in the center of town, and every resident treated it like a chapel. To Matilda it had been a second home, an escape, a haven from the first moment Jetty led her toddling self into the children's section, hand in hand, to snuggle in a quiet corner and turn the pages of picture books.

When Matilda returned to the desk, Thea, picking nail polish from her thumb, asked, "So is Parker coming or not?"

Matilda looked up at the clock, her eyes pulling wide. *Where has the day gone?* "He'll be here in about five minutes." The thought made Matilda even more exhausted than she already felt. But why would it? She should be excited to see Parker.

"It's cake today, right?" Thea asked, still focused on her thumb. "I think it's good you are getting back into planning the wedding instead of dwelling on . . . other things."

Matilda looked at her. Thea was so carefree, so confident, and more often than not completely lacking in tact and sensitivity. She walked around the library with the hip-swinging stride of a diva, unfettered by the minions around her. Next to her, Matilda often felt like a fatally shy Hobbit, but when she said stuff like that Matilda remembered Thea was just a naïve girl. "Uh, oh yeah. Cake. At Estelle's." Matilda had nearly forgotten she and Parker were picking their wedding cake today. *Wedding cake . . . Jetty was supposed to make the cake.*

"Sounds so fun. And free samples of Estelle's cakes—to *die* for. Can't wait until I get married."

Matilda looked at Thea like she'd said something unintelligible, but soon turned away, her grief tugging hard on her attention. She fingered the edge of the desk. Picking out wedding cake *should* be exciting and a good distraction. She should be antsy to get to Estelle's. *Right?* But all she could think about was crawling under the covers of her bed.

"And the handsome prince arrives." Thea finally dropped her thumb and looked to the main doors.

Parker strode in with his wide smile, wind-blown hair, and flushed cheeks. Matilda often thought he walked that line between handsome and too good-looking. He could have been a movie star if he'd been born somewhere other than the forgotten east corner of Kansas. In high school, his wheat-colored hair, always a little too long, and radiant blue eyes, clear like water, had made him the object of every girl's attention and desire. Matilda had admired from afar as well, never imagining that the school heartthrob would one day fall for the girl who was only five feet tall and always carried a book. Sometimes two books, just because it made her feel safer somehow.

Parker had never said a word to her in high school. They'd gone to different colleges, and both had returned to Silent Fields to start their careers. The first real interaction they ever had was when he'd strolled right up to her at The Mad Hash Diner two summers ago and asked her to dinner. They were twenty-three then, but when he'd smiled his dashing, square-jaw smile at her, she'd felt as giddy as a sixteen-year-old. Matilda couldn't help but feel a sense of triumph, like she'd won some kind of contest.

Did she still feel that way? Was that the right way to feel about the man you chose to spend your life with?

Parker had his hands in the pockets of his Dockers, the collar of his black peacoat turned up like Cary Grant, and a red knitted scarf at his neck. He sauntered forward. Matilda and Thea both stood. Parker offered his smile first to Thea. "Hey, Thea," he said easily. Matilda frowned. Why did it suddenly matter who he said hi to first? He was simply being polite.

"Hey, Parker. Still snowing?"

"Yep. I don't think it's ever going to stop."

Thea laughed, a little too loudly. "So much for spring."

Parker turned his attention to Matilda. "Ready to go?"

Matilda tried to stop frowning. "Yeah," she said, looking away. She corralled her things into her purse. The bag was a vintage piece: 1960s Chanel, black quilted leather, found at her favorite antique shop. She put the gold chains over her shoulder and stepped around the desk.

"Have fun picking a wedding cake," Thea called, her eyes still on Parker. Matilda frowned again. Thea's confidence made her a serial flirt, but it had never bothered Matilda until this moment.

Parker put his arm around Matilda's waist and called over his shoulder. "Thanks! We will." Turning back, he kissed her temple. "Hi."

"Hi."

"How are you feeling today? Was it hard to be back or was it helpful?"

"I'm okay," she lied. "It was good to be back and have things to do. How was your day?"

"Great day. I came up with a new slogan for the mill. Should really help with sales." Parker worked as marketing director for Wood Craft, a custom cabinet mill and Silent Fields's largest employer. When the quarry started to lose business to other quarries in southeastern Kansas, the cabinet factory had moved in and saved the town. Parker was determined to keep it growing.

"Good. That's great," Matilda said numbly. She felt the weight of grief, felt its strange heat inside her rib cage. She wanted to cool it by running away, by hiding from it in sleep. But she couldn't cancel the wedding cake decision; she'd already put this off twice because of Jetty's illness. And Jetty wanted her to move forward.

Isn't this forward?

A few minutes later they were brushing the snow off their heads and shoulders in Estelle's warm bakery. Estelle, a gorgeous African-American woman in her mid-fifties ran over from behind the counter. Her braided hair was slightly dusted with flour and her apron dark with chocolate. "You finally made it!" She hugged them both. No one smelled as good as Estelle. "Come on back to the wedding room."

Estelle led them to a small office where there was a short desk, three chairs, and pictures of cakes covering every inch of wall space.

She flopped open a giant binder. "Now, you two go through and look at all the pictures. We can recreate anything you see or mix and match for something custom. Take your time; I'll check back in a bit. And bring samples!"

Matilda sat in one of the chairs, keeping her purse on her lap. Something about the weight of it felt necessary at the moment. She frowned at the cakes on the walls. Parker started to turn pages.

"So what are you thinking?" he asked. "This one's nice." He pointed to a white three-tiered cake with silver lace fondant around the edges.

Matilda leaned in to see it. "Very pretty, but a little traditional."

"I thought you liked traditional." Parker flipped more pages.

The comment annoyed her, but when she thought of all the decisions they'd made so far, Parker was right. White church, June date, princess gown, long veil. All the safe, predictable choices. "How 'bout that one?" She pointed to a chocolate ganache cake with three tiers, but pentagon shaped and suspended on a spiral stand. "We could put real roses on it. White ones."

Parker frowned at the picture. "A chocolate wedding cake? I don't know."

"It's beautiful. And . . . fun." Suddenly, she wanted nothing more than that cake.

"It's a little out there. Don't you think?"

"No. What's wrong with something a little different?"

"It's not our style." Parker turned the page.

Matilda blinked, anger rising in her throat. She wanted to yell at him, or maybe claw each of the stiff cake photos from the wall and rip them to shreds. She wanted to storm out of the shop.

Whoa! Stop it.

She'd never been mad at Parker before, never wanted to destroy something beautiful. *What is wrong with me?* Her head began to pound, her purse felt like a stack of rocks on her lap. *Stop it. Get control.* But she couldn't seem to calm her heart and the pounding in her head only increased. She stood abruptly; Parker jumped. She said in a rush, "Uhh . . . the white with silver lace. That's fine. I really have to go."

Parker stood, putting a hand on her arm. She looked over at him. Parker was only five foot six, short for a man, but people never noticed because of his looks. "Hold on. What's wrong?"

"I'm sorry. I thought I could handle this, but I can't. I don't feel good. I'm so *tired*. I just need to go home and sleep."

"Is this because of Jetty?"

Matilda pressed her teeth together. She hated him for asking that. She met his eyes and knew he could see the anger spark in hers. He blinked and leaned away slightly. "I need to go home," was her only answer.

Parker picked up his coat. "I'll drive you. My car is at the library."

"No, no," she said, stepping to the door. "I'll walk. You stay and get things arranged with Estelle. This needs to be done. I'm sorry."

"Okay," Parker said, eyes narrowed in concern and confusion. "Want me to come over later?"

Matilda avoided his eyes. "Not tonight. Okay?"

"Okay." He didn't hide his disappointment.

Without another word, Matilda was gone.

Matilda

atilda woke at two-thirty in the morning to the smell of smoke. She flipped over and sat up, breathing hard and choking on the cords of smoke rising off her quilt. The quilt Jetty had made her years ago out of a kaleidoscope of red fabrics.

With a strangled yelp, Matilda beat at the blanket. But there was no fire. Only smoke. She watched it dissipate and tried to reason where it had come from. She looked around the room—nothing out of place. It was chilly, as it always was this time of year since the radiant heating in the old Victorian cottage wasn't the most efficient source of warmth. But nothing was on fire.

Did I dream it? She sniffed the air, the smell almost gone now. *A nightmare? All imagined?* And yet, she remembered what Jetty had told her about her grief for Enzo starting the curtains on fire. Of course that wasn't real, that was just Jetty's colorful way of describing things, of telling stories. *My burning grief . . .*

Matilda pulled Aunt Jetty's favorite threadbare shawl from the bottom of the bed and wrapped it tightly around her shoulders. The shawl smelled like Jetty—sage and vanilla—and it made Matilda feel empty inside. She turned to a picture on her nightstand of her and Jetty sitting on the porch swing, laughing. It'd been taken the summer after high school. Jetty's wild, curly orange hair was blown away from her round face by a hot breeze, her head thrown back and mouth open wide. Perfectly Jetty. Photo-Matilda looked up at her, her long, straight black hair pulled into a high ponytail, her dark eyes adoring. They both wore cut off shorts and tank tops, no shoes.

"I wish you were here," Matilda whispered, her throat tight. "I don't know what to do." Matilda closed her eyes with a sigh. Because she did feel like she needed to do something, to act. Jetty's death had left her feeling not only alone, but trapped. Nothing felt right. Not Jetty's crazy Victorian house with its tiny rooms, Jetty's paintings hung on the walls, and colorful exterior. Not the library Matilda loved so much. Not her beloved little town of Silent Fields. And not Parker, the man she was supposed to marry in a month and a half.

Everything was wrong.

"What do I do?" she asked the picture again as she set it back in place.

Matilda slipped out of bed, put her feet in her slippers, and went to the window. The snow was still falling. A late-spring snowstorm.

Jetty's story about leaving Frank to find Enzo played in her head. What a brave thing Jetty had done. To leave in search of something more. To leave the shallow end to jump off the diving board.

Could I ever do that?

I should do that.

A frightening feeling swelled in Matilda's gut, a potent desire to jump from the high dive. The air left her lungs. She leaned forward to grip the wooden window frame. It was foolish, childish, to think running away would solve anything. Her grief would not stay behind. She couldn't leave.

Matilda turned slowly to look at her red-and-white patchwork quilt, made by Jetty's hands. She couldn't think clearly; suddenly she wanted too much. She wanted those things Jetty had talked about. Running in the rain. Seeing new places. New people. A love that made the grief go away. A love that filled her with passion, not polite friendship.

I want that.

The statement was simple, but the ramifications sadly complicated. Leaving the shallow end had consequences. So many things could go wrong with an impromptu dive into the unknown. You could drown in all that want for more.

She wanted things, things she denied herself. All her life, she'd held back, acted cautiously. Was it because she'd survived the car crash that killed her parents? She'd always felt an undercurrent of need to be careful for their sakes. But Jetty hadn't been afraid to jump, and she'd found Enzo. She'd been happy, if only for a brief time. So was it real or fiction? Was it possible there was a man somewhere in the world she could feel that way about? Her own Enzo? Jetty had advised her to find someone to love. Was he out there? Someone better for her than Parker?

Could leaving Silent Fields help cleanse her of her grief?

Or did she settle for Parker and forget these foolish dreams? Bury the grief. Trudge forward.

She turned back to the window. The snow fell in heavy folds of fat flakes, as it had been doing for almost twenty-four hours. This kind of storm was usual for this late in April. A freak storm. A sign, as Jetty might say. *Sometimes the weather wants to tell us things,* she'd said once or twice during a torrential downpour or too-hot day. *Sometimes it's a sign.*

Matilda peered out, looking for that sign.

Sudden purpose and unusual bravery seized her by the throat. She pulled her old suitcase from under her bed—the kind women carried in black-and-white movies—and tossed it open. She threw in clothes, a random stack of books from her shelves, and the picture from her nightstand. She ran into the bathroom and grabbed her toothbrush and shampoo and brush. After throwing those on top of the clothes, she snapped the case shut.

Click, click.

Breathing hard, she kicked off her slippers and lowered her feet into her snow boots. She shrugged on her coat over her pink cotton nightgown and Jetty's shawl.

Logic and fear tried knocking at her door. *Knock, knock.* But she managed, for the first time in her life, to ignore them. She went with the daring.

Down the stairs, out to the car. Kicking up wakes of powdered snow.

Suitcase tossed in back.

Keys in ignition.

Driving out of town.

As the snow finally stopped falling.

Henry

*A*gain he sat. At his table. In his spot. The brilliant spring sunlight poured in the tall windows, falling in white lines over his page. And again, he had nothing to write. With a huff, he stood and began to pace up and down the stacks. Sometimes a walk in the books helped a little. Afterward, he might eek out a half-decent sentence or two.

As he walked, he punished himself.

A year away from a PhD in creative writing with only a few decent short stories and a pathetic attempt at a novel to show for it. What is wrong with me? Did I pick the wrong career? Maybe I'm not a writer after all.

Maybe . . .

Henry stopped walking, he stopped thinking. Ahead of him, at the end of the hall of shelves, a woman was reaching up to replace a book. Surprisingly short, she needed to lift onto her tiptoes to reach the spot. Long black hair—*like spilled ink*, he thought—fell down her back, nearly to her hips. As she settled back to the ground, she tucked the hair behind her ear, in a swift, gorgeous movement that Henry felt in his chest.

Henry blinked twice and then turned to run back to his table.

The words!

So many words raged at the tips of his fingers. The kind of words he'd always prayed for. He snatched up his pen and wrote as quickly as he could manage. Briefly, he wished he had a good typewriter. Maybe something old fashioned and reliable. It'd be so much faster than a pen.

He knew the landscape of her body. He knew the peaks of her soul. He knew the caves in

21

her mind. He knew her. And yet, each day he marveled at her as if she were an enigma. She was not what he had dreamed for—his dreams had never been this astonishing. She soothed his pain; she stirred his passion. Their love was not like the love of fairy tales. This was real. Connection, attraction, commitment, marriage. Real. Holding her hand, walking down a foggy street. Smiling at her across a room. Watching anger spark in her eyes. Feeling the cool touch of her forgiveness.

Every moment of every day was real. As it should be.

Henry's heart raced, his chest moving irregularly. People were glancing at him with wary looks, but he didn't notice. The words were burning his page and sparking his soul to life.

Finally!

He looked up, a goofy grin on his face. Marveling.

Then a thought: *The girl.*

Henry scrambled out of his chair. There were still words unearthed and waiting to be catalogued, but he needed to find her first. He went to the right row of books. She wasn't there. *Oh, no. No.* He hurried down the next row and the next, panic edging up his throat. *What if I don't find her?*

He stopped.

What if I do?

The woman stood only a few feet away, a fresh stack of books in her arms. An ID tag dangled from her neck, but he'd never seen her before. *A new librarian?* He could see her face better this time. Dark eyes, thick lashes, and sadness. He'd never seen anyone look so beautiful and so tragic at the same time. *Like an outcast goddess.* She looked lost and yet right at home. She carried the books like a newborn lamb and took a moment to look at each cover; a few made her smile.

Henry wanted to talk to her, but just the thought made his freckled cheeks burn with shyness. He'd never had a girlfriend in high school and only once since he started college. Penny Goodman. A sweet girl, almost as shy as he. But in the end, more a friend than a soul mate. He'd certainly never looked at her and felt his gut burn like this. He'd never wanted to describe her skin or her hair with words that could melt candles.

Henry was ready to run back to his table when the woman turned. She looked at him and he didn't look away. Couldn't. She blinked several times and then smiled. He felt that smile in every bone.

His feet took him forward.

"Can I help you find something?" she asked, her voice as soft and light as meringue.

Henry smiled, his cheeks on fire with blush. "You're new?" He pointed to her ID.

She touched it. Something passed through her eyes. "Yes. Just started." She lifted her chin to look at him properly; Henry was six foot five.

"I'm Henry."

She smiled again, looking a little confused. "I'm Matilda."

Henry said nothing. He listened to his heartbeat and resisted the urge to touch her. The words raged in his head.

Matilda shifted her books, pressing them into her hip. "Was there something you needed?"

Henry blinked. "Uh, no. I just thought I'd say hi. I'm here a lot. I write. Over there." He pointed dumbly and wanted to disappear.

But Matilda smiled. "You're a writer?"

Henry shrugged, looked away. "Today I am," he answered truthfully. He needed to get back to his table to let the words fly, but he didn't want to leave her.

Matilda nodded as if she somehow understood. "Well, good luck, Henry." And she turned and walked away.

Henry smiled as he watched her. Then he hurried back to his table to throw words at the world.

All thanks to Matilda.

Matilda

May 1, 1998, six years later

A lacework of sound moved through her sleep. Matilda floated among the black-and-white patterns, content. The effulgent clack and ding of the typewriter bounced on the edge of her consciousness like a lullaby. In the last six years, those sounds had forever imprinted on the tissue of her heart, the fabric of her soul. Those sounds were Henry. They were words, passion, life.

The only other sound she loved more was that of Lucy laughing.

Matilda woke slowly, pulled out of her lacy dreams by Henry's mad, midnight typing. She fluttered her eyes, allowing for time to adjust to the cone of yellow light from his desk lamp. His tree-tall frame hunched over the black machine, fingers bouncing like raindrops on the surface of a lake. In the dim light, back curved, head dropped, Henry crouched over his desk, his work, like a ravenous predator. Matilda often thought he looked more animal than human when he wrote. Such ferocity, such a desperate need for survival.

She sat up, looking over at Lucy's crib, a small antique thing from the 1920s made of delicate dark wood spindles. It'd been nearly impossible to find a mattress that fit the crib. Matilda loved it.

At eighteen months, Lucy slept peacefully—for once—petal-pink lips parted as she breathed deeply, her cheeks flushed, and dark-brown bobbed hair a mess across her forehead. Normally, the child woke at least three times a night, still wanting milk to lull her back to sleep even though Matilda had weaned her six months ago. But not tonight. Perhaps Lucy sensed the importance of a good night's rest before a long and busy day.

Matilda stepped out of bed, maneuvered around the packed and taped brown boxes, and slipped her arms around Henry's neck. She kissed his cheek. "Noisy words tonight?"

"Boisterous, raucous even." He smiled. "Had to get them out before these things get packed away for a few days." Fingers still plunking away, Henry nodded to his twin set of Remington Rand typewriters, circa 1937. Matilda wasn't the only one with a quirky penchant for old things. Henry had stumbled upon the set at a garage sale shortly after they started dating. One morning run, a couple hundred bucks, and he'd never written on anything else. He'd written his first book, a collection of short stories, on these typewriters. When Matilda asked him why he bought both of them, Henry had merely shrugged. "It seemed sad not to, like separating siblings at an adoption. Plus backup and all that—they are really old after all."

The first thing he'd written on them was a love letter to her. She remembered the way he'd blushed and turned his chin down shyly when he handed it to her, the plain white paper folded in thirds. She'd smiled, a giddy thrill in her gut. And then the words he had written her had taken her breath away and filled her with a deep emotion she couldn't name. She knew every line.

```
Love has been compared to so many things. Grand
things, beautiful things. But I won't compare you
to anything. I don't want to make my feelings less
than they are with an inadequate metaphor. So I
say simply that you make me feel in ways I never
thought possible. There was nothing until there
was you standing in the books. I sit beside you
and I breathe more air. I look at you and I see a
universe. I touch you and I connect with everything
that has ever lived. I kiss you and I exist.
    I choose to love you from this day forward and
never stop.
```

She'd never read such perfect words. Until his next letter, and the next. There were now two shoeboxes full of Henry's love letters.

Matilda looked around the drafty apartment with its now-bare shelves and naked walls. "I hate having all the books boxed up. Feels . . . wrong. Do you think the characters are suffocating?" she asked teasingly as she ran a hand through his mussed dusty-blond hair. When he didn't answer, she added, "We're going to have to build more shelves in the new place."

Henry nodded. His face had that look of far away focus, only half hearing as the words demanded his attention. She smiled to herself and kissed the side of his mouth, right where three freckles gathered together like a cluster of succulent berries. He smiled and continued typing.

"Lady Lucy, your chariot awaits!" Henry grabbed the child under her arms and swung her up into the air. Her delighted screams echoed back on the cold spring, Michigan air. Henry strapped Lucy into her car seat in the back of their 1955 Chevy Bel Air. The car Jetty had given Matilda on her sixteenth birthday. The car Matilda had fled Silent Fields in. Henry ran his hand over the bulbous frame, painted Tiffany Blue, as he went around to the driver's side. The gesture made Matilda smile briefly; Jetty would have loved Henry. She still felt the loss of her aunt as keenly as the night Jetty had taken her last breath. She'd never really faced it or accepted it; it still made her hot with anger if she allowed herself to focus on it. So she didn't think about it. She had Henry and Lucy now.

"Are you sure we have everything?" Matilda asked, still standing on the steps of the old row house. She looked into her purse, feeling a sense that something wasn't right. *What am I forgetting?* Wallet, Lucy's snacks, diapers, wipes, sunglasses, and the only two books she couldn't stand to pack away. She stared at the matching edges of the two copies of Henry's first published work. As a playful joke, they'd given each other a copy as a gift on their last anniversary, only a couple months after the triumphant publication. It'd been quite the year, 1997: Henry's book, Lucy's birth, and their fourth wedding anniversary.

"The trunk is full of books, the back is loaded with clothes, type-writers, and the kid," Henry said casually. "That's all we own."

Matilda looked at the sagging back tires of the Bel Air burdened with all that word weight. All those books they had bought together, and all of Henry's from before. Her own books, of course, were still on the shelves of Jetty's house. She didn't think about that either.

She pursed her lips, checked her bag again. "I have that feeling." A breeze looped down from the sky, smelling of thick, wet snow. Matilda frowned as she looked up at the clear azure sky.

Henry crossed over to her. At six foot five, he towered over her five foot nothing, and so stopped a couple of steps below her to position himself at eye level. He gripped her hips. "Just moving jitters. We have everything."

Matilda tried to push aside the worry. She knew they had everything. *Just nerves. Just the newness.* She sighed. "Okay, yeah, I know."

"Hey, do you remember what today is?" He smiled at her.

For a moment, she didn't know what he was talking about, her mind so muddled with this strange feeling. But then, "The day we met." She couldn't help but smile back.

"Exactly. Our lucky day. So everything will be fine."

"Of course." Matilda wanted to believe it.

"Let's go, yeah?"

"Yeah." Matilda leaned forward and placed a kiss on Henry's lips. He wrapped his arms around her waist and held tight for a moment.

"Here we go," he whispered.

"Kansas City, Kansas—watch out!" Matilda smiled, trying to let humor lighten her anxiety. Not only did she have that forgetful feeling, but also something about moving back to Kansas made her uncomfortable. She hadn't been back since the night she fled in her nightgown and snow boots. She'd never even called Parker to explain or apologize. She'd picked up the phone a hundred times over that first year, but could never face the sound of his voice on the other end. So she'd written a letter, a note really. *Parker, I'm sorry. Matilda.* She'd paid a courier service to deliver it so there'd be no postmark. The shame of it turned her stomach now, making it all so fresh. But Kansas City was hours away from Silent Fields, and their new house in a quiet neighborhood was perfect for raising Lucy and for Henry to finish work on his next book. It would be fine. Once they were there, the memories would subside back into their designated corner of her mind. This was a new beginning, a fresh phase of life with Henry and Lucy. Matilda didn't want the mistakes of her past to taint it.

Lucy called *Mama* from the car, and they crossed over. "Ready to go, Lucy?" Matilda asked.

"Yeah," Lucy said in her baby-voice, her round cheeks lifting in a smile. She offered that same yeah to nearly any question she was asked.

Henry started the car, the solid old engine roaring to life. Matilda handed Lucy a small cup of Goldfish crackers as Henry pulled away from the curb. The first thrill of moving flopped in Matilda's stomach. They were really going. Leaving Detroit and the apartment they'd lived in since they were married. Leaving behind life before they were parents. Now they would be small town folk, a regular family. Henry would write and teach at Kansas University. Maybe Matilda would volunteer at the local library. Lucy would be free to run around barefoot in a backyard with grass and trees and a garden. Just as Matilda had as a child under the care of Aunt Jetty.

"Think this old beast can handle the two-day drive? Maybe we should've gotten something new," Henry asked as they merged into traffic on I-94.

"Let's hope so 'cause it's too late now. But it was making a funny noise yesterday when I went to the store."

Henry laughed. "It's always making weird noises." He looked at the gages. "We're gonna spend a fortune on gas."

Matilda nodded. "We should learn to like *new* things." She glanced back at Lucy, happily kicking her legs and shoving crackers into her mouth, one pudgy fistful at a time. Half of the food would end up a gooey mess in her seat. Her little eyes, finally changing color from the deep blue she'd been born with to a mixture of brown and green, much like Henry's, watched intently all things out the window. Matilda had tried to brush her short hair this morning, give it some semblance of order, but like Henry, Lucy liked to run her hands through her hair and so now it looked like she'd stood in the wind. The little purple flower clip Matilda had put in was predictably missing.

Matilda smiled.

Next to Lucy on the seat were the two typewriters locked away in their black hard-leather cases. Matilda smiled at them too, thinking of Henry's neurotic writing. "It's all your fault," he often told her when she found him up at night or missing a meal. "Until I saw you, the words wouldn't come. Now they won't stop." Now there was one published collection of short stories and a half-finished novel. And a happy Henry. *It's all my fault,* she thought with an inward thrill.

She'd never loved anyone like she loved Henry. It was instant and almost overwhelming. When they first started dating, she thought she might drown in the sea of feelings he stirred in her. To this day, six years later, he could still make her feel that way—deliciously and deliriously lost. But he also made her feel calm and at home. Satiated. That feeling everyone looks for. He was her Enzo.

Henry looked over at her now and smiled, his freckled face bright with the sun spilling in the window. He put his hand on her thigh, and she placed hers on top of his.

The first day of the drive went smoothly. They stopped every couple of hours and let Lucy run around in the first park they could find. For the most part, she seemed content to watch the scenery buzz by and nap sporadically. They ate homemade cookies from dishwasher faded Tupperware and tuna sandwiches wrapped in wax paper. That night they took a room in a cheap but surprisingly clean hotel; Lucy snuggled into the bed between them.

Matilda didn't sleep at all.

Though she was warm and comfortable, the sound of Lucy and Henry's breathing the perfect lullaby, sleep could not break through the whirlwind in her mind. She still felt as if she'd left something behind. She ran a checklist of every item they owned down through her mind, from each and every book to the plastic baggie of bobby pins in her makeup bag. It was all there, tucked into the Bel Air. So what was this feeling?

And she could still smell snow—sharp and crisp.

Like the night she fled Silent Fields.

Jetty had always urged Matilda to listen to her instincts. But Matilda wasn't sure what they were telling her. How did she decipher this tightness in her chest, the shudder in her stomach? Though she did her best to dismiss it as nerves, part of her knew better.

Part of her knew it was more.

Henry

Henry stood outside the hotel. The trunk of the Bel Air was open, waiting for the bags, but he turned away to look at the sky. Dark gray clouds roiled in the distance, the corners swept upward as if by a broom. The road to Kansas City was in that direction, under those threatening clouds. Their new home was only a few hours away.

The wind was calm now, but he wondered if they would drive right into that mess. Not that it mattered—the Bel Air, thick and heavy, was a champ in storms. But still. Lucy didn't like thunder or driving in the car when it rained. A couple weeks ago, they'd been caught in a mad downpour while driving home from dinner at their favorite burger place. Lucy had screamed, shaking in her seat, fat tears making her big eyes look bigger. She hadn't calmed down until they'd ducked into the apartment and closed all the blinds.

Henry shut the trunk. Descriptions of the clouds invaded his mind, all the ways he might put it down on paper. *Rebel clouds, impending storm, noxious thunder.* He shook his head and tried to push the words away before he unburied a typewriter.

Back in the hotel room with its beige walls, maroon bedspread, and bad nature watercolors, Henry found Matilda standing at the window, shoulders tense. She was such a small thing, but he never realized it until a moment like this when he could observe her quietly. Only when her body was still and she wasn't talking did he see how little Matilda was. He knew something was bothering her; she hadn't been able to hide an emotion from him from those first moments in the library. But *why* she felt something often remained hidden from him. She'd never spoken much about why she left home after Jetty's death. She refused to go back and visit. Henry worried that moving back to Kansas had stirred up some emotion or memory which had put her in this funk.

He crossed over, smiling down at Lucy who sat on the floor playing with a mangled plastic Slinky. The newness of her, this little person, part him, part Tilly, and part her own, had not left him yet. He didn't think it ever would. He'd never had a real family, and the marvel of it struck him multiple times a day. The permanence and comfort of Matilda and Lucy settled a fight deep inside him he once thought would rip him to pieces. This was what Henry had always wanted, always needed, but feared he did not deserve.

Matilda didn't turn as he approached. He ran a hand down her long, silky raven hair. "We didn't forget anything."

She sighed. "I know. I'm fine." She let the dusty curtains fall back into place. "This is the right decision. Right?"

Henry's brow furrowed. This was the first time he'd heard her express doubt about the move. "Of course. It's perfect for us."

Matilda nodded slowly, looked away. "Everything in the car?"

"Is this about Jetty? Are you worried about going back to Kansas?"

"No, I don't think so."

He reached out to touch her face. Her eyes were almost as dark as her hair—dark but so bright. Sometimes blinding. "Just a few hours and we are *home*."

She tried to smile. "Good. It will be nice to get there." She stepped around him and scooped up Lucy, still intently chewing on the neon orange Slinky. "We're gonna drive into a storm."

Henry felt a wave of cold as she said it. Something in her tone. "I saw it."

"Let's hope Lucy is asleep."

As they neared Kansas City, about an hour out, the storm growled to life. The sun retreated, throwing the sparse country into slate darkness. An eerie stillness hung in the sky until the thunder set the rain free. For a few minutes it was sideways, pelting rain, but a downdraft of cold air soon turned the rain to snow. Snow so thick Henry had only about a foot or two of visibility off the hood.

"Man, this is ugly." Henry glanced back at Lucy, thankfully asleep in her seat, head fallen at what looked like the most uncomfortable angle possible. Henry's pulse quickened. As someone from Michigan, he'd driven in snow numerous times, but this came on so quickly that he worried about black ice. And it was getting hard to see the lines on the road.

"Should we pull over and wait it out?" Matilda gripped the door handle so tightly Henry wondered if the metal had indentations yet.

"Maybe. Or we might drive out of it if we keep going." He wasn't sure what was best. He wanted to be safe, but pulling off the road had its disadvantages. If the storm dumped too much snow they might get stuck and he'd have to dig out the car. Or another car might slide off and hit them. And if he stopped, Lucy would probably wake up. Even moving slowly felt safer than stopping. "We're close. We can just plug along."

Matilda nodded stiffly. "It's snowing."

Henry frowned at her wistful, worried tone. The temperature in the car had also plummeted and he reached to turn up the heat. That's when he felt the slippery shift of the car, like the first dip of a rollercoaster. His stomach clenched and he flung both hands back to the large steering wheel.

Matilda gasped. "Black ice! Did we hit black ice?"

Henry fought the urge to slam on the brakes. The car was gaining speed, slipping, sliding. At first the Bel Air stayed straight, but then the fat, weighted backend started to swing out. Henry's heart leaped into his throat. He turned into the skid, keeping his foot off the brake, trusting physics and gravity, but it wasn't helping.

Matilda was breathing fast. A mighty scream came from the back seat; Lucy was awake. Matilda twisted in her seat to look at Lucy. "It's okay, it's okay. Just some snow." She turned back and Henry felt the pressure of her eyes, felt the desperate begging in them to keep them safe.

The car was now sliding like the tires were made of silk. He tried to pump the brakes, but it didn't slow them down. His hands were white on the wheel. "We're not slowing down," he whispered.

Lucy's crying grew louder and louder. Acid anxiety burned the back of Henry's throat. *I have to keep them safe.* He pumped the brakes, he fumbled with the wheel. Still, faster they slid.

Matilda's fingernails dug into his thigh. "Henry . . ."

The road started to slope downward, adding to their speed. Henry peered out the windshield, hoping there would be a flat patch of shoulder to slow them down, help them stop. He found instead a steep drop-off. All he could see was the knife-sharp edge of the road and an abyss of snow.

I can't lose them. Then, darkly, *Maybe I never deserved them.*

"It's okay, Lucy," Henry said as calmly as he could, but at the shaky sound of his voice, the child's cries only increased.

Matilda turned around, took Lucy's little hand. "We'll be okay. The road is just slippery. Daddy will slow us down. It's okay."

Henry felt sick. It wasn't okay. The backend betrayed him and swung out to the right. They spun in a full circle. Matilda screamed. Lucy cried louder. Henry felt the weight of the car slop to the side. The car spun again, whipping hard. The wheels caught a patch of gravel.

A rough tug, a squealing whine.

The world turned upside down.

The crunching of the metal and crackling of glass drowned out Lucy's cries. Henry's head knocked into the side window; the steering wheel was too close to his chest. He thought he said Matilda's name, but wasn't sure if he only thought it. The car flipped again and again.

Henry couldn't feel the pain because Lucy's crying had stopped and Matilda's body was a rag doll in his side vision. He lost consciousness before the car stopped tumbling through the snow.

Matilda

It's my fault. My fault. My fault.

Matilda felt far away from herself, like being lost in a dream. But something was tugging at her. Sensations of cold and wet registered partially, soon replaced by a burning, breath-taking pain. She inhaled loudly and opened her eyes. A world of white. Stars showing through holes in the gray clouds.

Panic edged aside her pain. "Lucy? LUCY!" Matilda tried to turn, but found herself trapped against the dashboard, pebbles of windshield under her face. "Henry? Lucy?" *Oh, it hurts. It hurts!*

Matilda shuddered, kept her eyes closed. *The snow. The black ice.* The memory of the car spinning and rolling attacked her mind. She tried again to lift up to see Lucy or Henry, but couldn't move; her seat had her pinned. She turned her head to the left, the glass cutting into her face as it slid along the dashboard.

Henry lay over the steering wheel, his face bloodied. The sight took her breath away and black spots appeared in her vision. Panic tasted foul in her burning throat. "Henry! Wake up!"

Henry did not move, did not open his eyes.

"No, no, no. Please don't. Please!" Matilda swallowed bile. "Lucy? Can you hear Mama? Lucy!"

Matilda had never heard such silence, like the cold stare of an accusation, like a death sentence. She started to cry, which only made the pain worse. *This is my fault. I should never have run away. I'm being punished. I'm finally drowning in my deep end.*

Matilda blinked her tears away, trying to see clearly whether Henry was still breathing. She needed to get to Lucy. Struggling, Matilda managed to get her hands on either side of her head, pressing hard into the dashboard. She shoved with all her might, screaming with the effort and the pain it caused. The first time nothing happened, but a wave of anger made her try again and this time her seat gave way and she collapsed back.

Free.

Surprised, she could only lie for a moment and breathe in gasps of wet, cold air. Then she turned over, howling in agony at the wallop of pain from her left leg. She looked down at the white and red exposed end of a bone. Her vision went gray and she nearly fainted, but she turned away. When her eyes fell on Lucy, Matilda no longer felt her own pain.

Lucy's precious little body was askew in her car seat, her dark hair wet with blood. Her tiny round face white. Matilda felt the earth shift. "Lucy . . . baby?" She scrambled toward her, ignoring the glass and metal cutting into her and the movement of the broken bone in her leg. She reached out a trembling hand to touch Lucy face. Cold. Too cold.

"*No.*"

Matilda's hand dropped to her child's chest. Silent and unmoving. Great, powerful sobs swelled in Matilda's own chest. "No," she cried loudly. "Lucy!" A hot black grief sprung to life in Matilda's gut. The air filled with smoke. *My parents. Jetty. Lucy and Henry. I am cursed.* Her whole body began to tremble with anger. This was more grief than anyone should be asked to bear. How could she possibly survive its murky weight?

"Matilda?" Henry called out weakly.

She couldn't turn to look at him, did not register any joy that he was alive. "She's gone."

"What?" Henry shifted, yelling out in pain from his injuries. "No, Tilly—"

"Yes. Lucy's gone." Matilda fought a wave of dizziness. "It's my fault. I never should have . . ." *Did I bring this on us? Jetty, you were wrong.*

35

"Matilda?" Henry's voice was desperate, tight with pain, but also commanding. "Look at me!"

Matilda slowly turned her head. "I wish I had never met you."

Then, blackness.

PART TWO

Henry

$\mathcal{H}$enry woke with his face on the table in the Detroit Public Library, sun burning his cheek. He blinked several times, disoriented. Then he sat up sharply, heart thudding.

This isn't right.

"Hey, man, are you okay?"

Henry turned toward the voice attached to a hippie-looking guy in loose jeans, a grubby black shirt, and long, nasty dreadlocks. The hippie's eyes were pulled wide with worry, his body slightly leaning away as he looked at Henry.

"Uh . . . yeah," Henry mumbled. "I just . . . fell asleep? Weird dream . . . *I think.*"

Hippie nodded. "Looked like you might be having a heart attack or something."

"No. No, I'm fine. Thanks." *But I'm not fine. I don't remember coming here. I don't . . .*

The hippie nodded once again, "Cool typewriter," he added and then strolled off.

Henry frowned. *What typewriter?* His eyes dropped to the table.

A blank piece of paper, his pen. Just like always. But also more. A book and a sleek black typewriter. It was obviously old, with ribbon and keys, no source of power other than fingers pounding those shiny letters. It sat low and long, like a cat, the exposed grin of typebars shining in the light. Along the bottom frame in silver letters it read *Remington Rand.* Something about it sent a nervous chill through him. He looked around the library as if someone might explain to him the appearance of the items. Had someone left them while he slept? *Was I really asleep?* But both the typewriter and the book faced him, waiting patiently at his elbow. His fingers itched to touch the round keys, to slide the platen until it *dinged*. But touching it felt dangerous, so instead he moved his attention to the book.

A Thousand Sleepless Nights by Louis Winston.

Henry read the title three times, hoping it would sound familiar. It didn't. And in all his extensive reading, he'd never heard of an author named Louis Winston. The only connection he had—which seemed meaningless—was that his middle name was Winston. Heart pounding, it took Henry several minutes to gather the courage to pick up the book.

The cover was dark blue, with mountains, a field of grass, and a big full moon. Henry opened it. The air suddenly smelled of snow. His chin jerked up to look out at the warm spring day beyond the window. He turned a page and nearly dropped the book.

On the title page, in a round, elegant, feminine hand, the words: *For Henry.*

For Henry. This is my *book? But . . .*

The smell of snow grew stronger and the room felt like it would close in on him. He looked from book to typewriter to window, feeling flustered and antsy. Henry thought about leaving the two anomalous things behind, but found he couldn't. Quickly, he shoved the book into his backpack, scooped the typewriter under an arm, and fled. Standing on the steps of the library, he tried to catch his breath. The typewriter felt like a cinderblock in his grip, the book an anvil on his back. He turned to look up at the massive gray Italian Renaissance–style building. The many large arched windows looked the same, the big trees rustling in the breeze were the same. He scanned the street, Woodward Ave. It all looked the same and yet slightly different.

Confused, and moderately dizzy, Henry slowly descended the steps. He stopped next to a row of newspaper bins. His eyes focused on the one closest. The date caught his attention and the street seemed to quake under his feet.

Sunday, May 3, 1998.

He tried to swallow the knot in his throat. He looked around, frantic, heart punishing his ribs now.

That's not right!

To Henry, it was Friday, May 1, 1992.

Matilda

Matilda sat bolt upright in her bed in Jetty's house.

Breathing hard, confused, she looked around. Everything was wrong. Her dresser and armchair were brown with thick dust. The windows were grimy, the corners filled with cobwebs, the sills littered with fly corpses. The many books on her shelves were shrouded in dust and webs as well. The air smelled stale, unused.

Like the room hadn't been lived in for years.

Matilda shut her eyes and shook her head. *A dream. Another dream. I dreamed I left town in a snowstorm and now this . . .*

She opened her eyes to the same scene. Turning, she looked to the place on her nightstand where the picture of her and Jetty should be, but it wasn't there. An empty space. Her heart pounded harder, her head felt tinny.

This isn't right.

Matilda's head snapped up when she thought she heard a baby screaming, but the sound faded too quickly to be sure. Goose flesh rose on her arms and as she moved to rub the skin, she noticed the book and the typewriter. Sitting at the foot of the bed, spotless and clean.

The book was thin, trade paperback size. "*A Thousand Sleepless Nights* by Louis Winston," she read aloud, her whispered voice loud in the grubby room. On the cover, a pearl-white full moon rose over a generic set of jagged mountains, skirted by an indigo expanse of open land. There were tall grasses around the edges, bent as if by a stiff wind. The moon made Matilda think of Jetty, and her stomach tightened. The pages were rippled from being wet at some point.

She picked it up.

Thousands of books had passed through Matilda's hands. Hundreds of thousands, perhaps. But none like this. Never before had a book made her fingertips burn, the skin on her neck grow cold, or her heart struggle to pump blood into her arteries.

This is not my book.

Compelled by a strange feeling, she opened the book. In black ink, written on the dedication page were the words *For Matilda*, in a slanted, broad-stroked handwriting, like a man's. Water had made the ink lines puffy, bleeding into the paper. Bleeding.

Everything went cold.

A blackness roiled in the back of her head, a crushing sense that something was wrong. *But it's not my book . . .* She flipped another page, thinking, *My middle name is Louis, after my dad's grandfather.* The dedication caught her attention. She read it out loud in a cautious whisper, "'For my wife, who breathed life into these once-pathetic stories and awakened my shy heart with her shining brilliance and sublime beauty.'"

Tears came to her eyes, emotions she didn't understand stirred up by the words.

Lowering the book to her lap, she surveyed the typewriter. It was beautiful. Something about it made her want to smile, but how could she be happy about it? It was certainly old, but well kept. Someone had cared for this machine. The dust-free keys gleamed in the sunlight. Another sound made Matilda startle—this time the clack of keys— but it too faded before she could lift her head.

I'm hearing things and hallucinating.

Matilda looked around her ruined room again and suddenly needed more clean air to breathe. With the book locked in her hand, she fled the room, leaving the typewriter resting on the bed. Running down the stairs, through the derelict living room, kitchen, and out into the wild backyard. Jetty's lovely yard laid half dead in overgrown chaos. Weeds chocking the flowers, the thin, papery grass grown to shin-height. The garden beds a mess of more weeds. The sight made tears roll down Matilda's cheeks. *How could this happen overnight?*

Matilda spun in a circle and then stopped. She closed her eyes and gripped the odd book to her chest. "This is a dream," she whispered. "Wake up, wake up."

"Matilda?"

Matilda spun around, realizing for the first time she was in her pink nightgown and barefoot. Thea stood at the fence. Jetty's house stood on a corner lot and the backyard chain-link fence faced the side street. Matilda blinked and then frowned. Thea was at least six months pregnant.

"Oh my gosh! It *is* you!" Thea's eyes went wide.

Matilda's head pounded so hard she couldn't see clearly. She took a couple steps toward Thea. "Thea?" She'd grown her hair out into a soft bob, curling just under chin. She looked older, different.

"Yeah, yeah. It's me. Plus one, of course." She placed a loving hand on her swollen belly.

"But . . . but how?"

Thea threw back her head and laughed. "Well, I won't give you the *intimate* details, but about two years after you left . . ." She paused awkwardly, like she had said something forbidden. Quieter, she finished, "Parker and I started dating. We've been married for a little over a year." Her brow furrowed as her hand rubbed absently at her stomach. "Matilda, are you okay? You look . . . sick."

Matilda put the heel of a hand to her forehead and pressed hard. The book in her other hand felt extremely heavy. *After you left* . . . But she hadn't left. She'd wanted to, but woke up in her bed. She hadn't actually done it. This was the next day after that night. The morning after . . . *Isn't it?* Her eyes lifted to her dirty bedroom window.

Thea married Parker . . .

"Do you want me to get Dr. Wells?" Thea called out. "Are you gonna faint or puke or something?"

Matilda pressed her eyes closed. "Thea, what is the date?"

"Huh?"

"The date! What day is it?" Matilda yelled.

"Good grief. You don't have to be *rude*!" An impatient huff and a sideways glance at Matilda who felt ready to attack Thea, despite the baby bump, if she didn't hurry up and answer the question. Thea frowned. "It's May 3, 1998—*of course*. Sunday. I was just going to church—I'm late, as usual . . . Tilly?"

The earth shifted and then nothing.

"Well, there she is! Welcome back—in more ways than one."

Matilda blinked up into the wide, rectangular face of Dr. Richard Wells, Silent Fields's physician. The familiar sight of his droopy gray eyes flooded her mind with memories of annual office visits, shots and lollipops, and one broken finger after a fall from the school monkey bars.

"I'm a little worried about your blood pressure, Tilly." Dr. Wells held out a hand and helped Matilda sit up. She was still in the overgrown backyard of Jetty's house. He pulled a cuff off her arm and folded it into his black bag. "Can you tell me what happened? What brought on your panic attack?"

Panic attack? Yes, there had certainly been that. But what was she supposed to do when she woke up in Jetty's ruined house and it was six years later than she expected it to be? She looked up at Dr. Wells, hunched over her, his giant-like frame shading her from the morning sun. "I . . . I'm not really sure."

His eyes narrowed in concern. "How did you get back into town? Did you drive? Did you sleep last night?"

"I . . ." Matilda looked passed the doctor's shoulder. Thea was still there, watching nervously as she chewed her thumbnail. Her pregnant belly. Parker's baby. Parker, the man Matilda was going to marry, and then . . . "I think I had a nightmare. Or something. I'm really disoriented."

"Have you been sick? Any illnesses in the last six years? And what are all these scars from?" He pointed to her arms, left leg, and right cheek.

Matilda shook her head, dizzier at the sight of her own body. There were pink slash marks on her forearms and a long nasty gash on her left shin. She touched her face and found a few small indentations near her jawline. She couldn't pull in a breath. Those weren't her forearms or leg or face. That wasn't right. She'd never been hurt like that.

"Matilda?" Dr. Wells lifted her wrist to check her pulse. "Take a slow breath, dear. Your pulse is racing. What's wrong?"

"I don't . . . I don't know." She couldn't take her eyes off her left leg. Suddenly, it hurt, a bite of pain strong enough to make her cry out. She grabbed at the limb, but the pain had already gone.

Dr. Wells put a hand on her back. "Take some breaths. Breathe for me."

Matilda tried to breathe, but nothing in her body worked right. Nothing in her head made sense.

"It looks like you broke your leg. Here." He pointed to her scar. "And it didn't heal very well. How did you do that?"

She didn't have an answer. *How can I not remember breaking my leg?* She couldn't look at the scars anymore. She felt violated. She looked around the yard instead. "What happened to my house?"

Dr. Wells furrowed his brow even further. The look made Matilda nervous. "Matilda, you left town, remember? Without a word. None of us knew what to do. Greg Flounder had a yard crew come by the first few years, and I think he still pays the utilities, but he hasn't been in good health lately, so some things have fallen to the wayside."

"But I didn't leave . . ." Matilda clamped her mouth shut when the concerned look on Dr. Wells's face deepened. *He's going to commit me. Maybe he should.* Matilda hurried to stand up, which became an awkward exchange of Dr. Wells trying to assist her and then her assisting him when his old knees stiffened.

He cleared his throat and brushed at his blue dress shirt and red tie. "Why don't you come back to my office with me? We can figure things out."

Matilda swallowed, looked at Thea, and then back. "No, no. I'm fine really. Just a bad night. I got back late and went right to bed and was just a little disoriented when I woke up. It's a little weird to be here." Not a lie. "I'm sorry for the trouble."

"It's no trouble. Are you sure? I gotta say I'm more than a little concerned." He placed a large hand on her shoulder, turned her, and pointed a small flashlight in her eyes. "No signs of neurological problems. Did you hit your head?"

"No, I don't think so." Bad choice of words.

Dr. Wells nodded. "Are you sure you won't come back with me?"

"No, I'm fine. Sorry to scare you. I'm fine. I'm home, aren't I?"

Dr. Wells smiled. "Yes. And it's real good to see you again. We've missed you. We've worried. And Jetty would be so happy to have you back in the house."

The emotions in his words made her want to run, to scream, but she smiled and mumbled, "Thank you." She looked around nervously. The mysterious book was on the grass. She picked it up and tucked it to her chest.

"Well, if you insist on staying here, please take it easy. Rest, eat something hearty, and call me if you don't feel any better. Okay? Promise?"

Matilda half smiled. Dr. Wells said the same thing at the end of every examination. "Yes. Promise. Sorry if I pulled you out of church." She took a few steps toward the back door.

He laughed. "Don't be. You did me a favor. Reverend Claude was going on and on like he does. I was half asleep when Thea tapped on my shoulder." He smiled over at Thea and then back to Matilda. "I'll call you later to check in." He retrieved his bag from the dead grass and then, with a wave, went out the gate. Matilda watched him walk down the street, ignoring the weight of Thea's stare.

"Are you *sure* you're okay?" Thea called out. "You're limping." She looked pointedly at Matilda's left leg. "And what are you doing here? I mean, it's your house, of course, but we were all beginning to think you'd never come back. It's been *so* long. And the way you left . . ."

Matilda met her eyes and then looked away. *It's been so long.* "Thanks for getting Dr. Wells, Thea." Then she opened the screen door and went inside without looking back.

Henry

Henry sat right down on the front steps of the library, typewriter on his knees, and did not move for several minutes. He couldn't. Not until he understood why he thought it was 1992 and the world was busy living in 1998. He held the newspaper in his hand and read it from front to back three times.

Did I hit my head?

Am I sick?

Am I dreaming?

Nothing made sense, each possible explanation weak and unsatisfactory.

Should I ask someone? Tell someone?

Dramatic visions of white coats and padded cells convinced him to keep his mouth shut for now.

Bill Clinton was president and accused of having an affair with an intern. The tech geeks were all buzzing about Windows 98. Across the street, there was a billboard advertisement for the season finale of a television show called *The X-Files* on the FOX network. The fifth season.

But none of that was right. George Bush was president. The computers at the University of Ann Arbor—where he was earning his degree—ran on Windows 3.1. He watched plenty of TV, but *X-Files* didn't sound familiar.

It's 1998. It's 1998. HOW?

Henry set the newspaper beside him on the step and looked at the typewriter. He ran his fingers loosely over the cool keys. Words started to form in his head, words that wanted to be written. He lifted the typewriter and put it aside.

He took the book out, thinking that would be easier to examine. *A Thousand Sleepless Nights.* He opened it and looked at his name. *For Henry.* Not only was this apparently his book, but *someone* had given it to him. But who? He didn't have any friends close enough to give him books. He didn't have parents or relatives. It wasn't a library book—no numbers for shelving or plastic to protect the cover. But something about it made his blood move faster.

Henry couldn't retrace his steps. The last thing he remembered was sitting at the table and trying to write, with pen and paper, not a fantastically old typewriter. It was supposed to be a Friday. Normally, he'd be teaching his creative writing class at four this afternoon. Then, as usual, he'd grab dinner at the Indian place by his apartment, browse the used bookstore until it closed and go home to his apartment with an armful of new books. *Normally. Usually.*

He should call the community college.

Henry bent the book back and forth, the pages creaking.

What happened to me?

He hefted the typewriter and stood, heading back into the large library. The whole place was done in fine cream- and gold-toned marble and decorated with huge, vibrant murals and frescos. He didn't recognize the receptionist. "Excuse me," Henry said quietly. She looked up—blonde, big blue eyes, pretty—and smiled, her eyes moving briefly to the typewriter. "Is there a phone I can use?" he asked.

"Sure." She picked up the receiver of the desk phone and leaned forward. "I'm supposed to direct you to the pay phones outside, but you look like a nice guy. Cool typewriter too." Her smile grew, she brushed her hair off her shoulder.

Henry blushed fiercely as he took the phone, careful not to touch her fingers on the exchange. "Thanks."

He dialed the college English Department, unsure exactly what to say.

"English Department," a bored female voice said.

"Uh, yes. Can you tell me if Henry Craig still teaches any night classes on creative writing?"

She sighed quietly. "Let me see." Computer keyboard noises. Henry's heart pounding against the earpiece. "It looks like Dr. Craig stopped teaching for us recently."

"Okay. Do you know why?"

"Nope, sorry. All I have are dates."

"What date exactly?"

Another sigh. "April 25, 1998. Anything else?"

"You said, *Dr.* Craig?"

"Yes, he has a PhD in creative writing."

"Okay. Thanks." Henry handed the phone back to the smiling receptionist and turned away before she could commence flirting. The date the secretary had given meant nothing to him. It only confirmed that things had happened that he could not remember. Including finishing his PhD.

Standing on the outside steps once more, Henry closed his eyes and fought back a harsh surge of emotion. After several agonizing moments, he opened his eyes and looked down at his hands. They were trembling at the edge of the typewriter. He tilted the machine to one side and found a pink scar on the back of his right hand.

That's not right.

He sat down, put the typewriter on the step, and then pushed the sleeves of his sweatshirt up, revealing more scars he didn't remember. He touched his face and found a deep ridge on his forehead that he didn't know. *I'm scarred. I have scars. These aren't my scars.*

Henry looked out at the busy street; he heard nothing but a heavy silence. It smelled like rain or snow or something wet. He pulled his sleeves down as far as he could.

Slowly, typewriter back in hand, he went down the steps and headed for home.

Certain the home he expected wouldn't be his anymore.

Matilda

Standing in the dusty living room, Matilda held Louis Winston's book in her hands as if it were an anchor to dry land. Everything around her was exactly the same and yet completely transformed. The blue gingham couches. The steamer trunk coffee table, now home to the anomalous typewriter. The red-brick fireplace surrounded by bookshelves. Even the small vase of daffodils she'd put on the mantel after Jetty's funeral. Except they were dead and decayed to almost nothing, a spider crawling in the remains.

Wake up. It's time to wake up. WAKE UP!

The doorbell rang.

Matilda screamed, dropping the book. It hit the floor in a puff of dust. Numbly, she went to the door, opened it. Parker stood there. Handsome as ever, but with shorter hair and more lines around his eyes.

He blinked several times and then let out a long breath. "It really *is* you," he whispered. "Thea said, but I didn't really . . ."

"Parker" was all Matilda could say. Part of her wanted to hug him, but she suddenly remembered that he wasn't hers anymore. And that she'd been planning to leave him anyway. *Last night—but not last night.* She had left. She . . .

"Are you okay? What happened?" Parker stepped forward, studying her from head to toe. "You don't look good."

Matilda looked away from his curious examination. "I'm fine." She folded her arms over her thin nightgown, wishing she had on pants, a thick sweater, some makeup. Anything other than this old thing that made her feel so pathetic and out of place. She didn't need to feel that way any more than she already did.

49

He narrowed his eyes and leaned his head a little to one side. "You don't look fine. You look . . . scared."

The words brought a flash of tears to Matilda's eyes. She wanted to tell him everything. Have him fix it, explain it—*something*. "I just . . . I'm not feeling too good. Just need some rest."

Parker slipped his hands into the pockets of his tan Dockers. He wore a white golf shirt to match. His shoes were made of a more expensive material than she remembered. Things at the cabinet mill must be good. He had a look on his face, like he wanted to say something more. He nodded slowly. After a tense moment he stepped forward. He touched her arm and Matilda felt incredibly shy. "Tilly, what happened?"

He never called her Tilly. Everyone else had adopted Jetty's pet name, but he never had. She didn't like the way he said it. A sudden breeze blew through the weeds in the front yard. Emotions stuck in her throat.

"You married Thea?"

He blinked. "Yes."

Matilda nodded. "That's good. I'm glad. And a baby?"

"In July. A boy." He took another step closer and Matilda retreated two.

"Good. That's good."

He caught her eyes; his were full of sadness. "I looked for you."

Matilda bristled. *I did leave. I left and I can't remember.* "I'm really sorry."

"That whole first year. I looked for you everywhere. I did . . . *everything* I could think of. I waited for you to call. Every time the phone rang . . ." His jaw tensed, and Matilda saw the anger under the sadness. Emotions clouded his voice now. "I worried. I worried *every* second of *every* day. I didn't sleep. I went to the police, but they said it looked like you'd left on your own. Missing suitcase, missing car, house locked up tight. But it didn't make any sense to me." A breath, then quieter. "I thought you might be *dead*."

Matilda couldn't fight the tears anymore. "That's so horrible. I don't know . . ." What could she say? "I don't know what to say."

"Then that note came." He took a slow breath. Matilda didn't remember a note. Parker went on, "That stupid note. But at least it was something. At least—"

"I'm sorry!" she interrupted. She couldn't stand it anymore. *Please stop. Just stop. I don't remember! How could I do that to him? What happened?*

Parker ran a hand back through his sunny hair, quiet for a long moment. "Are you staying?"

Matilda nodded. What else would she do?

Parker reached out again, but she pulled away. He dropped his arm with a sigh and turned away. "I'm glad you're okay," he said as he looked out at the porch. Then he walked away.

Matilda shut the door and collapsed to the floor, sobbing into the filthy wooden planks.

Henry

enry spent the entire day researching himself, the book, and the typewriter. Nothing gave him answers. The young man living in his apartment had no idea who Henry was and could offer no clues. The university could only tell him when he'd graduated and when he'd stopped teaching. Nothing about what came after. An ER doctor told him his head was fine, no signs of trauma or malfunction. He didn't have any friends, and coworkers only shrugged, saying he never mentioned anything to them. *And this is what comes from being a loner,* he thought as he checked into a cheap motel. At least he had some money in his wallet. Not much, but enough for a few days.

The room was sparse, and not incredibly clean. Henry put his things on the bathroom counter and stood to stare at the bed. It looked hard, uncomfortable, and empty. Instead of sleeping, he went to the small desk by the one window over looking the parking lot. He was tried and hungry. On the desk, he found a stack of random old newspapers. He snatched the top one off the pile and started to flip pages. A distraction, a simple task.

When he came to the classified ads, his eyes snagged on a small listing at the bottom of the page. *Wanted: Editor/Writer for Weekly Newspaper. Silent Fields, Kansas. Writing experience preferred.* A jolt of energy went through him. Before he realized it, he had the phone in his hand, and was dialing the listed number. As the phone rang, Henry checked the date on the paper—almost six months ago. He swore and nearly hung up, but the line answered.

"*Silent Fields Post.* This is Ronnie."

"Uh . . . hello. I'm sorry. I just came across an ad for the editor position and didn't realize it was so old. I'm sure you've filled it."

"I haven't. Are you interested?" Ronnie's voice had the dusty sound of an older gentleman.

Am I? What am I doing? "Yes, very."

"Your experience?" The old man sounded excited.

"I have a PhD in creative writing from the University of Michigan. But I haven't done much with newspapers."

"When can you start?" Even more excited.

"Really?"

"Yes. I've been running this paper for almost fifty years now. I'm ready to retire." A raspy laugh. "Heck, I was ready ten years ago. If you want the position it's yours. The pay is good, the hours not too bad. It's a good job. And our town is a great place to live."

Henry blinked, sat up straighter. He looked around the room. "I'll be there tomorrow night. I can start Tuesday."

"Excellent. Oh—guess I ought to ask your name?"

"Henry Craig." *What am I doing?*

"All right, Mr. Craig. Let me give you directions to our little town."

Matilda

After an hour of sobbing and hating whatever it was that had happened to her, Matilda found the strength to get up off the dirty floor. She desperately craved sleep, a way to avoid this nightmare, but a sense of survival took her to the bathroom instead.

Fighting more tears, she set to cleaning it. She lit the pilot light on the water heater and let the taps run to clear the pipes. She put a load of crusty towels in the washer, grateful that Greg Flounder, Jetty's lawyer, had all the utilities still working. He must have kept paying the bills out of Jetty's estate. She'd saved a great deal of money, the house was paid for, and he was the kind of man who wouldn't let things go completely to waste, as Dr. Wells had said. *Of course, he shouldn't have had to do all that. I should have arranged the upkeep and care. Why didn't I?*

Once the bugs and dust were gone, and the towels dry, she took off her nightgown, threw it in the trash, and got in the shower. Standing under the warm water, she thought many things. And thought some more. But still nothing came. Digging frantically into her head, she found not a single memory after the night she and Parker chose their wedding cake.

What she did find was a sucking sense of being lost. A blackness in her head that told her she'd lived those six years and now they were gone. Six years didn't just pass in a blink. They happened, things happened. A lot of things.

It had all been taken.

But why? And how?

Rinsed clean, Matilda took a fresh pair of sweatpants and a T-shirt from the dryer. She switched the laundry and stood with her hands on her hips in Jetty's beautiful gourmet kitchen. Jetty would have died of shock to see it like this, grimy and smelling strongly of decay. Matilda opened the large French doors of the fridge and immediately stumbled away, choking and coughing on the rank smell of rotten food.

How could I leave like that? Since apparently I did. How could I just abandon this place to this mess?

Feeling guilty and in need of more to do, Matilda emptied the putrid contents into a large garbage bag. She scrubbed the inside shelves with bleach from the laundry room. She emptied all the cupboards and the pantry until there was a mountain of black garbage bags on the back porch. Every surface was sterilized and all the dishes run through the dishwasher—twice.

Exhausted, Matilda collapsed onto one of the metal stools at the white marble island. Head in her hands, she closed her eyes and listened to her stomach growl ravenously. The normalcy of needing to feed herself gave her a strange feeling. *I can't remember six years, but I still need to eat. I'm here. Everything is normal, except what's in my head.*

But getting food would mean she'd have to leave the house. The idea of venturing out into town quickly swept her hunger aside to make room for nausea. How could she face the questions? The looks of amazement and confusion and accusation? She could very easily imagine what had been said about her after fleeing, leaving Parker with no word. Abandoning everything.

Matilda tried again to reach into the swatch of blackness in her memory. Chills rose on her forearms and her head started to pound. A horrible sense of dread filled her gut. This was not a happy place. Feeling like the blackness might consume her, Matilda quickly stood up and forced her mind into the present. If she couldn't eat, she could sleep. But not before her room got a good cleaning.

Matilda was just remaking her bed with the now freshly laundered sheets and red quilt when the doorbell rang. She stopped, the quilt suspended in her hands. Briefly, she had an image of all her neighbors standing on the porch, arms folded, mouths hard, ready to throw rocks and run her back out of town. Nervous and dizzy from hunger, she went slowly down the stairs.

One lone figure stood behind the panel of fogged glass in the door.

Matilda almost decided to ignore whoever it was, but finally, curious, opened the door.

"Parker?"

Parker held up a casserole dish. "Thea sent me with this. She said you'd need some food."

Matilda looked at the white dish. She smelled garlic and cheese; her stomach clenched uncomfortably. "Well, honestly, she's right."

Parker nodded, gave her a nervous half smile. "Can I come in?"

"Uh," Matilda looked behind her. She hadn't had a chance to clean the living room. "Sure. Yeah. I haven't cleaned everything yet."

Parker stepped passed her. He smelled of cologne, something deep and woodsy. He hadn't worn cologne when she'd known him. He headed for the kitchen. She slowly shut the door, and then followed. Memories of Parker went with her. They had spent so much time together in this house: sitting on the couch talking with Jetty, lying together watching a fire die in the fireplace, laughing in the kitchen over cinnamon rolls or brownies.

"Thea's good with pasta, and I know you like that," he said as he set the dish on the island. "Wow. I'm not sure this kitchen was ever *this* clean." He smiled and met her eyes, but quickly looked away. He took the foil off the dish and pulled a plate from the dishwasher.

Matilda stepped closer. "You don't have to . . . I'm sorry about before . . ."

Parker scooped a generous portion onto a plate, pushed it to her. "Just eat. I can hear your stomach growling. It's kind of pathetic." Another half smile.

Matilda tried to return the smile, but her face felt oddly stiff. She sat at the counter and forked slightly overcooked but well-flavored pasta into her mouth. She was happy to chew instead of try to talk to Parker, who didn't seem in a hurry to leave. She wondered if he still liked to wear that old Royals baseball cap. She'd always liked the way the ends of his hair flipped up under it.

He leaned back against the sink. The late evening light poured in on his shoulders from the window. "The whole town knows."

Matilda swallowed. "When's the hanging?"

Parker laughed. "Dawn, I think. You're expected to make a long, dramatic apology before they let you swing."

Matilda smiled before filling her mouth with more food. A moment later, "So . . . how are things with you?" The question sounded stupid, but Parker relaxed a bit more.

He shrugged. "Really good, actually. The mill has steady work. More than we can take on, which is always good. We've done some high profile jobs in Kansas City and St. Louis. Thea's still at the library. We live over on Kenwood, Rich Owen's old place."

"That's a nice house."

Parker nodded. "Yeah, yeah it is. We've remodeled here and there. Thea likes doing that kind of stuff."

Matilda's plate was empty. Parker's eyes were lowered and she took a moment to examine him. He was still as handsome as a 1940s film star, but a bit of his arrogance had deflated. There was maturity in the set of his shoulders. Something tugged at her. Not regret that she hadn't married him. Even without remembering the last six years, she knew not marrying him had been right. Maybe just the regret of hurting him so badly.

Pushing her plate away, she said. "I know I said it earlier, but I really am sorry. You didn't deserve what I did. I wasn't in my right mind."

Parker met her eyes. Emotions passed over his face. Sudden tension filled the room. "Are you in your right mind *now*?"

Her cheeks flushed and she had to drop her eyes to the grain in the marble. "I don't . . ." A powerful urge to tell him everything cut off her words. "I'm a little lost at the moment."

He pushed away from the sink to stand directly across from her, leaning over the island. "Did something bad happen to you? Did someone hurt you?"

She knew he referred to the scars on her face and arms, the limp. Matilda thought of the blackness in her mind. She shook her head. When Parker's hand came to her arm, she froze. Lifting her eyes, she met his and felt embarrassed by the emotion she saw on his face.

"Matilda, seeing you again . . . like this . . . it brings back a lot. A lot of hurt and confusion, but also regret. I'm sorry about how I talked earlier; I didn't mean to push all that on you. Just the shock, you know?" He met her eyes and she nodded slowly. He went on, "I think I'm partially to blame for how you left. You lost Jetty. You were

57

hurting. And I wasn't there for you like I should have been. I didn't understand how much you needed me."

Her eyes burned. "No, it wasn't—"

"It was. I was immature. Stupid. I'd never lost someone. I didn't understand how that can change you."

Matilda saw the pain on his face. "Who did you lose?" she whispered.

"My dad. Six months ago. Heart attack. All that heavy food finally caught up with him." Parker drew back his hand, looked away. Outside the sun slipped away, welcoming night.

Matilda's stomach clenched. "I'm sorry. I know how close you were."

He nodded slowly. "Yeah." A beat of weighted silence. "So anyway . . . I understand better now. How you felt and why you left."

Matilda folded her arms, suddenly cold. "I'm not sure *I* understand it."

"Where did you go?"

Where did I go? Do I lie? "Uh . . . I traveled around a bit."

Parker nodded, his expression telling her he saw the lie.

Matilda stood, uncomfortable and exhausted. "Thanks so much for the food. Tell Thea she's very sweet to think of me."

Parker watched her too closely. "Yeah, of course. Do you need anything else?"

Matilda ground her teeth together, a rush of annoyance tightening her throat. "You don't have to be nice to me."

Parker looked hurt. "I'm just . . ."

"Sorry. I didn't mean that how it sounded." She looked at the now spotless wood planks of the floor and sighed. "I only mean I don't deserve it, and you're not obligated in any way."

"Why not?" There was a demand in his tone.

Matilda put her hand to her forehead. *Just go away.* She opened her mouth to try to explain, but Parker rounded the island and stood right in front of her. His cologne filled her nose. For a moment they only looked at each other, a strange energy passing between them.

Parker touched her face. Matilda closed her eyes. "Parker . . ."

"I missed you."

She didn't want him to say that. His touch, though a small comfort, felt wrong. She reached up to pull his hand away. "Go home, Parker."

He nodded, his jaw tense. His eyes moved once around the room and then he stepped back. "I'm not trying to . . . I love Thea," he tried awkwardly.

"I know. I didn't think . . ."

"I want to help. I couldn't then; I can now."

Matilda briefly closed her eyes. She knew she needed help, but still felt so uncomfortable and shy. "Okay" was all she said.

Parker looked at her for a moment. "Good night, Tilly."

"Good night," she whispered as he left the kitchen.

Long after the front door clicked closed, Matilda stood in the kitchen looking out the window at the darkening sky and gathering clouds.

Henry

It was senseless, but what else was he supposed to do. He had to have a job, a place to live, something to do other than wonder. Maybe if he slept in a new place, had a new job, a new town, a new life—then maybe those six years wouldn't matter anyway. Much of his life had been years he wished to forget. What were six more? Or maybe they'd come back to him. He had no idea; he only knew he couldn't stay in Detroit.

He'd rented an old beat-up Buick and headed south to take the job as the editor of the *Silent Fields Post*. A nothing newspaper in a small town he'd never heard of. *Perfect.* He'd been driving for nearly twelve hours, with only a few quick breaks. He didn't want to stop until he was there. It was important that he *just get there*. A little after two in the morning on Tuesday, he was only thirty miles out of Silent Fields.

And it was raining like it would never stop.

Henry felt the bald tires of the wasted old Buick slosh and slip on the wet road. He managed to keep the car under control for a while, but then the backend swung out badly. He turned into the skid, but nothing happened. Hands fumbling on the wheel. Heart pounding hard in his chest. *Slow down, slow down*, he begged. But the heavy car only gained momentum.

The car spun. Once and then twice, whipping around like a carnival ride. Henry could hardly keep his eyes open—mostly from the panic—but also from the bizarre feeling that he'd done this before.

I shouldn't have come here. This is what I get for running away.

Another spin and then the tires caught the lip of the shoulder. Before Henry could cry out, the car slipped down an embankment, falling fast for several terrifying seconds, and then slamming hard into the ground. The sound of crunching metal and smashing glass. And pain. Hot, razor-edged pain in his head, arms, chest, and legs as he was jerked with the momentum of the impact.

The sudden silence pressed down on Henry's throbbing chest. For a moment, he could only breathe against it, shock numbing his reactions.

I've been in a car accident.

What do I do?

The question broke the surface of his shock. He was miles from Silent Fields. It was the late hours of the night. Another car hadn't passed him for a good half hour before the accident. Had he seen a house? Any mailboxes? He closed his eyes. His right leg twitched with lightning pain. *Please don't be broken.*

Henry opened his eyes. Fierce rain fell on the shattered windshield, illuminated by the one headlight left working. It was oddly peaceful. Which scared him. *Get out of the car. No one is coming for you.* Resolved to walking out of the ditch and dragging himself to the nearest house—if there was one—Henry tried to move.

He screamed, something between a bellow and a moan.

A wave of pain rocked him back in the seat. Glass crunched under his thighs. He tasted blood in his mouth. He sucked down cold air, trying to breathe and fighting the dizziness in his head. A sound made him still.

Is that a child crying?

The thick rain took all sound and deadened it, pulling it down into swampy puddles. Perhaps he hadn't heard crying at all.

Just try the door.

Henry slowly lifted his left arm, which didn't seem to be injured. He found the door handle. After a steadying breath, he pushed. The door creaked, but didn't open. Leaning into the door, he held his breath and gave a heaving thrust with his shoulder. The door flew open forcibly; Henry yelled out in pain as his body flopped to the side.

Maybe someone heard that.

Doubtful.

Henry looked out his open door at the wet landscape, black beyond the small circle of light where his car rested. *Get out. Good grief, it's cold.* A biting cold that went straight through his wool coat and jeans, along with the icy water.

A wave of dizziness forced him to close his eyes and breathe. He lifted a hand to his forehead; his fingers came back with bright-red blood. *More scars . . .* He didn't look at it very long. He moved his hand down his right leg, praying he didn't meet exposed bone. No bone, but more sticky blood.

After unclipping his seatbelt, which amazingly hadn't become stuck, Henry took a long breath. He tried to move his right leg. It hurt like mad, but it moved. Assisting with his hands, he pulled the leg toward the door. Left leg out, boot in snow. Right leg . . . gritting his teeth, Henry yanked on the leg. His boot hit the snow with an unnatural drop and a punch of pain.

He had to lean into the steering wheel and wait for the spots in his vision to disappear. *Now stand. Stand up.* Using the door as a crutch, Henry pulled himself out of the car. Next came the big test. If he couldn't put weight on his right leg, he might as well crawl back into the car and wait to freeze to death. Or drown. He pictured the car filling up with rain, like an aquarium tank.

Kansas is trying to kill me.

Briefly, his mind strayed to the words, as it did so easily. What words would he use to write this scene? Hopeless? Stranded? Facing his mortality? "Stop it," he hissed out loud. *This isn't fiction. This is real. Don't write. Save yourself.*

Henry eased weight onto his right leg. The pain came from his ankle. Awful, twisted pain. But it took a little weight. Henry hopped backward, using mostly his left leg. He angled himself toward the light. There was an ugly gash in his shin. Something in the underside of the dash must have shattered and cut into him. Blood trickled into his eye now, and his chest felt tight, like a weight had been strapped to it.

At least I will know the cause of these scars. Maybe I was in an accident before. Head trauma? Amnesia? The idea made him feel even colder, so he shook it off. He needed to help himself now, not worry about before. He needed a doctor. There could be internal injuries, more head trauma.

Walk.

But it wasn't really walking—it was spastic hopping crossed with dragging.

And how it hurt!

Once away from the car, Henry found the darkness not quiet so black. The rain seemed to glow with its own light, pearlescent and beautiful. The words tried to come, but Henry pushed them away.

Back on the road, he stared for a whole minute at his chaotic tire tracks. Gouges in the gravel, like tracks of wounds. *How did this happen?* An edgy flare of panic raced up his throat.

Henry turned away and headed in the opposite direction. The rain swallowed him; the wet wind pushed him forward.

After walking for an interminable amount of time, the pain growing worse with each step, and the rain turning his skin to soppy mush, Henry finally saw a single square of yellow civilized light tucked into a gathering of trees. He pushed forward, turning off the road, and trudged down the long driveway. He kept his arms pressed close to his body, his coat collar turned up. His ears, nose, and fingers burned with the cold.

Finally, he collapsed on the weathered porch steps of a small farmhouse. In the darkness, the clapboards looked sickly gray, the paint peeling like sunburned skin. Lamplight filled one curtained window, but there was no sound or hint of movement in the house.

Pulling in air, trying to ignore the throbbing pulse of blood at every injury, Henry bit his bottom lip in hesitation. A sudden shyness stalled his onward attitude. What would these poor people think when he knocked on their door in the middle of the night, beaten to a bloody pulp, soaking, and nearly helpless? Would they help him? Or call the police? Introduce him to the end of a sawed-off shotgun?

After another moment of pointless debate, he stood, climbed the stairs, and confronted the door. He took a deep breath and knocked quietly. His ears strained to hear a response. None came. Forced to knock again, he did so a little louder this time, Henry grimaced at his intrusion.

A shuffle of movement behind the door, the thudding of feet, possibly angry feet. Henry swallowed, stepped back. The door flew open to reveal a gruff figure hunched behind it. The man swore under his breath at the sight of Henry and then asked angrily, "Who are *you*?"

"I'm so sorry, sir. I know it's late—" Henry shivered so hard his words bounced around on his tongue.

"Late? Boy, it's three in the morning!" The older man, dressed in faded flannel pajamas, straining at the buttons over his generous belly, frowned sternly.

"I really do apologize, but I . . . my car slid off the road. I'm hurt." Henry swallowed and then added quietly. "I need help."

"Well, that's what you get for driving in this freak weather." The farmer squinted in the dark, narrowing cold, wrinkled eyes at his unexpected visitor. His eyes changed as he finally saw the extent of Henry's injuries, but there was no softening. The man opened his mouth to say something, shifting slightly as if to shut the door, but was cut off by another voice. "What's going on, Gill?"

A short woman, round and soft in all the grandmotherly ways, appeared behind her bald husband. Her hair was raincloud gray and hanging in thin long wisps around her kind face. She took one look at Henry and put a hand to her heart. "Oh, you poor thing! What on earth happened to you?" She pushed passed an annoyed Gill.

"Abby, we don't have any idea who this guy is," Gill protested. "You can't . . ."

"Oh, shut up, you old grump," she shot back. "The boy needs help. And I can tell just lookin' at him that he's good through and through. Be a decent Christian for *once* in your miserable life." She frowned reproachfully, but then turned a bright smile on Henry. "You a thief?"

Henry blanched, blinked. "No, ma'am."

"Ax murderer? Annoying salesman? Fugitive? Nail biter?" She smiled as she said the last one and the tension in Henry's gut eased slightly.

"No, ma'am."

Abby nodded and reached for him. "Then you come in now, out of the icy night, and let's see what we can do."

Henry looked to Gill, who huffed and stomped away. Abby gently took Henry's arm, pulling him forward. "Come on. That old dog won't bite, he just likes to bark and act tough." Gill's scoff was loud, but Henry sighed with relief and almost smiled at the older couple's banter.

Abby tucked a crocheted throw around his shoulders and pulled him into the small house. He looked down on the top of her head; she was short and waddled when she walked. She gestured to the sagging couch in the living room that appeared trapped in the 1960s.

Henry sat heavily and promptly passed out.

Matilda

Matilda spent the next day cleaning and cleaning some more. The house was done except for Jetty's room. She couldn't bring herself to go in there yet. She'd done some stuff in the yard, but running back inside at the sight of any person really slowed progress. She'd eaten most of Thea's pasta and tried to keep her thoughts from wandering into the blackness.

Now, desperate for sleep, she lay in bed, unable to get comfortable or to turn off her anxiety. At midnight, rain pouring outside, Matilda finally abandoned the effort to fall asleep and picked up the strange book that had been sitting on her bed with the typewriter. Perhaps reading it would help her memories surface.

At two-thirty, Matilda turned the last page of *A Thousand Sleepless Nights*, breathless and uneasy. Such words! Words that agitated things deep inside her: longing and ideas that had always been there, but that she pushed down. That pernicious craving for *more*. So much more. She lowered the book to her bed and pressed a hand to her aching chest. She wanted to cry, but fought it. There had been enough crying.

Something about Winston's effulgent words frightened her. Even holding the book made her heart beat irregularly and her mind spin with questions. Reading it had felt essential. But now what? It hadn't brought back any lost memories, only unidentifiable emotions.

She set it down carefully on the bed. Bent from hours of reading, the pages of the book would not lay flat, like a door that would not close. An open door. An invitation. A shouting mouth. Matilda turned away to look at the black eyes of her bedroom windows. The glass was now scrubbed clean and the laundered sheers were drawn, but she could still make out the shape of the large oak trees in the front yard, the curtain of rain. The lightning and thunder were frequent and flamboyant. The book yawned at her, like a demanding cat. *You didn't help me remember*, she scolded it silently.

"Jetty," Matilda whispered, desperately needing to talk to someone. If only her aunt could answer back from wherever she was now. "What does it mean, this beautiful book? Where did it come from? Why does it make me feel like this? What happened to me?"

The romantic stories in *A Thousand Sleepless Nights*—the imagery, the metaphors, the characters—all felt real, as if she were remembering them instead of reading them for the first time. They opened a closed door inside her, a longing she didn't have a name for. And didn't want to know.

The phone rang.

Matilda jumped, but turned to pick up the receiver.

"Are you awake?"

"Thea, it's two-thirty in the morning."

"So? I'm not sleeping 'cause I have a little ninja in my belly and I had a feeling you weren't 'cause, well, you're all mysterious and tortured now."

Matilda frowned at the body of her old-fashioned rotary phone, black with a white dial. "That doesn't mean you should call me in the middle of the night."

"It's raining."

"I know."

"Remember how it snowed the night you left? Something about this rain reminds me of that. Not sure why, but it's creeping me out."

Matilda looked over at her windows. Thea was right and the point was not lost on Matilda. She pushed down the cover of *A Thousand Sleepless Nights*. The book and the rain. This feeling in her chest. "It's just rain."

Thea hummed a half-hearted consent. "Was the pasta all right?"

"Delicious. Thanks so much." Matilda thought of Parker touching her face.

"You're welcome. I figured you wouldn't want to venture out yet."

"You figured right. I'm not sure I have the guts to leave this house even though Parker said everyone already knows I'm back."

"Don't worry about them. It's just something to talk about. There's never anything to talk about." A shuffle on the phone. "Good grief.

Even rolling over is a major effort." Thea grunted. "What are you going to do? I talked to Beverly today. She said if you want your job back you can have it."

Matilda sat up straighter. Go back to the library? She hadn't even thought that far ahead. "Really? I don't know . . ."

"It's better than sitting around that house or darting in from the yard like a scared cat the second you see someone. Yeah, Rosie Silverton saw you run away as she came around the corner." Thea sighed. "Anyway . . . come back to work. Beverly said she's still mad about how you left without giving her any warning. That was incredibly inconvenient for her, of course"—Thea's tone was thickly mocking—"so you would be on probation. One single, teeny-tiny mistake and she will fire you on the spot. And enjoy it—a lot. Possibly heft you over her head and throw you down the stairs." Thea laughed; Matilda smiled. "Of course, she can't really fire you once I have my baby or she won't have enough minions to do her bidding."

Matilda shook her head. "Thanks, Thea." Go back to the library? It felt strange. But what didn't now? She couldn't sit around the house wondering—she might go truly insane. If she couldn't remember, she could only move forward and hope that answers would come soon. Pray that soon she'd know why she couldn't remember six years, why her arms and face had scars, why she now walked with a limp, and why there was this pressure in her chest.

Thea went on, "You're quite welcome. It'll be nice to have you back. Especially if I can wear you down and get you to spill all the secrets of the last six years."

Thea's tone was playful, but Matilda's gut twisted painfully. She rubbed at the sudden throbbing in her temple. "When can I start?"

"Wednesday. Eight sharp."

"Wow. Okay. Soon." It was Tuesday morning. "But I'll be there."

"With bells on."

"Unlikely."

A long yawn. "Well, suddenly, I'm very tired and ninja boy has settled down. Go to sleep, Tilly."

"Thea, are you mad at me for leaving?"

"Yes."

Matilda blinked. "But . . ."

"But why am I being so nice?"

"Yeah."

"'Cause you looked so lost yesterday. So you ran off—good for you. I've wanted to do that a million times. But you're back now. And you need someone on your side."

This was not the Thea Matilda remembered. This was a thoughtful woman, not a silly girl. "That's pretty amazing."

"I know." Another grunt of movement. "But, Matilda . . ."

"Yeah?"

"Don't steal my husband. You left him."

"I know that. He's all yours. You are better for him than I was anyway."

A relieved sigh. "That's true, of course."

"Go to sleep, Thea."

"I will, hopefully." She laughed. "Night."

"See you tomorrow."

Matilda hung up the phone. She looked at the book, her pile of pillows. Instead of lying down, she went to the window to watch the rain. Memories came of the last time she'd stood here looking at the snow. *What really happened that night? And every night since?* A curious feeling wormed in her stomach, that kind of feeling like something is going to happen. She'd felt it that night too, while gazing at the heavy snow. That time she'd left town. What should she do now? What would tomorrow bring?

She touched the rain-cold window, tracing the rivulets of water. "It's a sign," she whispered.

Henry

"Time to wake up, handsome."

The voice sounded so far away. Henry didn't want to leave the comfort of sleep. Though he'd had dreams, horrible dreams.

"Come on. I got bacon and hash browns and fresh coffee. And drugs. You'll definitely want those."

A twinge in his stomach. Henry blinked hesitantly. His whole body ached fiercely. Nothing about this place was familiar. He was naked expect for his boxers. A spurt of panic flared in his throat. When his eyes popped wide, the woman said, "Whoa! Easy. You were in an accident. Remember that? Your car went off the road in a rainstorm. You walked—God knows how—a few miles to my house. I'm Abby. Abby O'Nell. I've got a grumpy husband called Gill; he answered the door. Remember any of that?"

Henry looked at her, her eyes the color of weak tea and her shoulder-length gray hair hanging in a braid. She wore a stiff-looking royal purple blouse and bright-yellow pants. "Abby?"

"That's right. You passed out right after I brought you in the house. Scared the *life* out of me. I called our Dr. Wells, who came right over." She motioned for him to sit up and put a hand under his arm to assist. Sharp stabs of pain answered every movement, but he managed it. Abby pulled a large plate heaped with food from a simple wood nightstand and set it in his lap. "Eat while I talk. You need some nourishment."

Henry picked up his fork. The sight of the eggs made him both ravenous and nauseated. He looked around the small bedroom with wood-paneled walls, a rickety twin bed, and an oak dresser. "Am I still at your house?"

Abby sat on a chair that looked like it'd been brought in from the kitchen, fifties-style with metal frame and red vinyl cushions. "Yes, our spare room. Dr. Wells didn't think it wise to move you. Your ankle is pretty bad, and you knocked that head around a bit. Doc splinted the ankle and wants to get x-rays as soon as you're able. He cleaned and bandaged up your nastier cuts. He also said several of your ribs are bruised, but not broken." She looked at his arms and forehead. "Looks like you're no stranger to cuts and scrapes."

Henry wanted to hide his scars, but didn't want to put aside his plate of food. In his head, he heard crunching metal and shattering glass. The excruciating walk in the freezing rain came back to him, every awful, hopeless moment. He cleared his throat. "How long did I sleep?" He took a bite of the hot food; it was divine.

"About six hours. It's nine in the morning now. Tuesday." Abby handed him a cloth napkin. "Is there someone I can call for you? I looked in your wallet—hope you don't mind—and didn't find any pictures or phone numbers."

Henry swallowed a mouthful of bacon, looked down at his plate. "No. It's just me." He felt Abby study him.

"And where were you headed last night, Henry Craig, from Detroit, Michigan? That's a long ways from the forgotten corner of Kansas."

Henry looked up to see her smile, an encouraging expression that somehow made him feel at ease when he shouldn't. "Silent Fields. I'm the new editor of the *Silent Fields Post*." His eyes widened. "I'm supposed to start today. I'm supposed to be there right now."

Abby laughed and slapped her knee. "Really? Ronnie finally gets to retire? Oh, he must be tickled pink with joy. We all thought he'd die sitting at that cluttered desk." She shook her head, laughed again. "Don't look so worried. I'll call over and tell him what happened."

Henry nodded, some of his panic easing. *What a way to start a new job.*

He finished the last of his breakfast and Abby easily pulled the plate away, replacing it with a mug of steaming coffee. "So you're a journalist?"

"Uh, sort of. I'm a writer, anyway."

Abby put her head to the side, evaluating him again. "So why take a newspaper job in little ole Silent Fields? Not much chance for prestige or wealth."

Henry sipped his drink, avoided her eyes. "It's a good job. A steady paycheck. Those are hard to come by in my profession."

Abby said nothing. Only looked at him as if she could read the truth under the partial lies. She nodded. "I did my best to clean you up last night. Sadly, your clothes were a loss, but I pulled out some old stuff of Gill's. It won't fit great—you're much taller and he's much fatter—but we can pick up your things at the police station. They fished them out of your mangled car." Henry's stomach lurched. His things. A fleeting relief came to him. His things were fine. His copy of *A Thousand Sleepless Nights* and the typewriter. He couldn't stand the thought of losing either one. He needed them, even if he didn't know why.

Abby was still talking. "Also, it was pure delight to find all those freckles under the blood." She pointed to his face and he blushed. "I'd guess you'd like a long hot shower?" She reached for a bottle of ibuprofen on the nightstand, dispensed two into his hand.

"Yes, Mrs. O'Nell. Thank you."

"Call me Mrs. O'Nell or ma'am again and I'll slap you silly." She smiled mischievously. "Abby is just fine."

Henry actually laughed. It hurt his ribs, but it also loosened something wound into a tight knot behind his heart. "Yes, ma'am." He grinned back.

She playfully slapped his shoulder before picking up his empty mug. "Towels are in the linen closet in the hall. Hot water lasts about a half hour. There's an old set of crutches behind the door from about fifteen years ago when Gill broke his leg riding his stupid horse, Mator." An eye roll. "Once you're decent, I'll take you to the clinic for those x-rays."

Henry sat forward, wincing at the protest in his ribs. "Abby?" She turned around, the bedroom door open. "Thank you. Really. You didn't have to . . ." Sudden emotion made his voice waver. Few people had showed him kindness in life. His mother, a crack addict, had dumped him on the stairs of a police precinct hours after his birth. From day one in The System, he'd had rotten luck, bounced from bad

71

house to bad house, experiencing little of empathy and compassion. That Abby gave him all without question surprised him greatly.

Abby smiled, her eyes soft and warm. "You're welcome, Henry."

"Well, it's not broken. Which is good and bad." Dr. Wells, a giant of a man, loomed over Henry in the small exam room of the Silent Fields Medical Clinic. The town was so small there wasn't a real hospital, only one doctor, it appeared. "A bad sprain takes a lot longer to heal than a break. I'm afraid you'll need to be off it for at least two weeks and then only minimal activity after that for about four weeks."

"Really? That long?" Henry looked down at his foot secured into a bulky black boot cast. Normally, he ran three to six miles a day, six days a week. He went for walks in the evening. He visited bookstores religiously. To be laid up with only his obfuscated thoughts . . . it might drive him mad. He came here to be distracted, to get better. Not worse. "But my new job . . . and I still need to find a place to live."

Dr. Wells shook his head. "I'll talk to Ronnie. I'm sure he'll be okay with waiting another two weeks." A deep laugh. "Heck, he's waited this long!"

Henry exhaled in annoyance. He rubbed his forehead. "Um . . . okay. Is there a good hotel close by?"

"Oh, no you don't," Abby spoke up. She'd sat through the whole appointment with him, which made him feel awkward and comforted at the same time. "You'll stay with us, in the spare room."

"No, Abby, I can't do that. I've imposed enough. You don't even know me."

Abby frowned like he'd insulted her. "Do you have a mother? A wife? A sister or even an aunt? A friend here in town?"

Henry blushed and looked down at his hands. "No, ma'am."

"Well, I don't have any sons of my own. God brought you to my door so someone could help you. What kind of Christian would I be to toss you out with little more than a 'fend for yourself' pat on the back?" She nodded once. "You'll stay with me for the two weeks, and then we'll find you an apartment. I think there's one open in the Mayor House. I'll find out. And don't worry about Ronnie."

Henry didn't know if it was God or fate or plain old luck that had led him to her door, but he didn't want to be a charity case. He'd always been able to take care of himself. She kept saying *we*. He wasn't used to that. He opened his mouth to protest again, but Abby cut him off.

"Oh, I know. You can take care of *yourself*. You're a big, strong *man*. But you can get over that for a couple weeks and let an old lady help you." She adjusted her purse on her lap. "Besides, you'd be doing me a favor. Farm life can be lonely and Gill ain't much for talking. So can we just skip the macho debate?"

Henry looked over at Dr. Wells, who was grinning from ear to ear. "Sounds reasonable to me," the doctor said, trying to keep the laugh out of his voice. "The ankle and the ribs will make it tough to do much of anything. You'll need help, whether you want it or not. Abby's the perfect nurse, I promise you."

Henry's cheeks were hot, no doubt as red as apples. He turned to Abby, who smiled like the fox in the hen house, knowing she'd won. "Yes, ma'am," he said.

She slugged him in the shoulder. "I told you to stop that ma'am crap."

Abby had Henry settled into bed with a full belly and a teetering stack of books by his nightstand by nine that evening. The awkwardness of being waited on itched under his skin. Henry's shyness, not his ego, made it so difficult. The attention was too much. As a kid, he'd trained himself to be as invisible as possible, to fly under the radar of his foster parents, especially the ones who liked to hit. He'd done everything for himself so he didn't have to ask for anything. Now, here he was confined to a bed while the ideal grandmother tutted around him, taking care of every need like he deserved it.

"Abby, really, go enjoy your evening. I'll be fine."

"I know. But I got one more thing. Hold on—I'll be right back."

Henry dropped his head back to the pillows with a frustrated sigh. He cursed the rain and slippery road and his stupid ankle. He cursed the weakness that had brought him here.

A moment later, Abby was back, a large box in her arms. She set it on the end of the bed and disappeared out in the hall again. Loud scraping on the floor preceded her dragging in an ancient card table with an ugly green top. Lastly, she muscled in one of the kitchen chairs.

"What's this?" Henry asked.

"You'll see," she sing-songed. She set up the card table and placed the chair. From the box she lifted his black typewriter, low and sleek. "Ta-da! Penny Dobbs—that's the secretary over at the police station—brought over your things. I thought you'd like this all set up. This is a beauty of a typewriter."

Henry lowered his brows. His heart beat strangely at the sight of the machine. He wanted desperately to touch the keys. "Yes, it is," he said, trying to sound casual.

"Where did you find it? Most people your age use computers."

"Yeah, umm . . . I just sort of stumbled upon it. It's a Remington Rand, from 1937. It was Agatha Christie's favorite model." Those were the only solid facts he could give her.

Abby touched the keys appreciatively.

Henry tried to keep his expression neutral. The words were already pounding on the inside of his skull. Words that wanted out, but that he couldn't seem to release since waking up in the library with six years missing. "Thanks."

Abby nodded. "You okay?"

"Yeah, fine." He pulled his eyes away from the typewriter.

Abby watched him for a moment. He tried to keep his emotions hidden under the surface. A longing rose inside him, so powerful he suddenly found it hard to breathe. And a fear, twice as bad.

Abby reached into the box again. "Here are some of your books." She set a small stack next to the one already on the nightstand. *A Thousand Sleepless Nights* lay on top. The others he'd bought on the drive down. There'd been a used bookstore by the gas station outside Kansas City that he hadn't been able to resist. It didn't feel right not to have books. He'd walked out with a whole box and only a few dollars left to get him to Silent Fields.

Abby looked back in the box. "Where are your clothes?" She lifted her eyes to him and his stomach tightened.

"I like to travel light" was his pathetic excuse.

Abby nodded slowly, knowingly. "Well, then I'll go into town tomorrow and get you some things. You can't keep wearing Gill's ugly hand-me-downs."

"Abby, you really don't—"

"And in case you want to do any writing on that typewriter . . ." Abby cut him off and hurried out of the room. Henry took long breaths and forced himself not to look at the typewriter or the books. Abby strolled back in and plopped a stack of white paper on the table. "I look forward to the soothing sound of the keys. Soothing and also inspirational. My mom took in typing when I was young. I love the sound of a good solid typewriter. Those new computers just don't have the same sound."

Henry could only nod as he listened to the sound of keys in his head.

Abby paused for a beat and then went to the door. "Good night, then."

"Good night. Thanks."

Abby hummed her acceptance and shut the door.

Henry rolled over, away from the typewriter. How would he be able to sleep with all the words in uprising? And all the questions that came with them. The same ones that echoed in his head nonstop.

He shouldn't have come here. How could he have thought he could run from his problems? From his mystery?

So stupid. You are a stupid man.

Yet he'd been unable to do anything else but come.

Run away, start over.

Henry felt certain it was the right thing to do, but he had no evidence to support this feeling. So far it wasn't going well at all. Certainly, nothing like he'd imagined as he drove.

And now, the typewriter at his back, begging him to write and *A Thousand Sleepless Nights* beside him, begging to be read. But he didn't have the strength to read Winston's book, and he'd given up writing his own words. He was done. Henry switched off the bedside lamp and closed his eyes.

I'm done.

Matilda

Matilda stood under the grand chandelier in the library foyer gazing straight up into the crystals, like looking up at the star-filled sky. If she listened closely, she could hear them tinkle in the airflow from the heater. The rain had stopped before dawn, and the sun was quickly working on erasing it, but the air remained crisp. Sunlight danced over the crystals. She had the urge to spin in a circle.

For a moment she felt whole.

A very brief moment.

"Well, well. I almost thought Thea was making the whole thing up."

Matilda lowered her chin, erasing her smile to greet Beverly with due humility. "Hello, Beverly."

Beverly only raised an eyebrow. The head librarian looked exactly the same: matronly and severe. "Can I trust you?"

Matilda folded her hands contritely. "Yes, ma'am. I apologize for my leaving without notice before." It still made her uncomfortable to admit to something she didn't remember but she had to keep up the act.

Beverly's eyebrow climbed higher. "Not much has changed. The computers have been updated, but I trust you'll be fine with that."

"Yes, ma'am."

"And I assume Thea informed you about your probation. Not one mistake, Miss White."

The sound of her last name tugged at something in her head. Why didn't it sound right? "Yes, of course."

"Well, then get to work. There's a cart that needs shelving."

Matilda nodded and went to the circulation desk to stow her things. Pushing the cart down through the stacks gave her an unsettling sense of vertigo. *This is right and yet . . . it isn't.* Matilda shook the thought away and focused on her work.

Thea found her a half hour later. It still surprised Matilda to see her friend with a pregnant belly. Thea wore a long blue knit dress, stretched tightly over her bump. Her fingernails were painted pink, no longer black. "Has Beverly been horrid?" she asked.

"Nothing more than usual. I see time has not softened her."

Thea laughed. "The opposite, if anything." Thea picked up a book from the cart and shelved it. "You doing okay?"

Matilda slid a book into place. "Yeah." It was mostly true, as long as she didn't allow her thoughts to wander into the blackness.

Thea nodded. "Want to go to lunch at The Mad Hash? It's still as good as always."

"I don't know if I'm ready for that. Plus, I brought the last of your pasta to eat."

"Is that all you've eaten for two days? I could have brought groceries. But really, you need to stop hiding."

"I know. I'll go to the market tonight—I have to. Not only do I need food, but things like toilet paper, deodorant, shampoo, toothpaste. A tooth*brush*, actually." Thea made a face, but laughed. Matilda went on, "I wish there was a way to keep hiding—"

"Good heavens!"

Matilda had spoken too soon. Rosie Silverton stood behind Thea with a hand on her chest, as if the sight of Matilda had given her palpitations. Rosie was tall and thin, in her sixties, and always wore tailored pantsuits; she had one in every color. Her auburn-gray hair was tied into a neat chignon, not a hair out of place. Her family owned the mill, which made her Silent Fields royalty, especially in Rosie's own mind.

"Matilda White. The prodigal child returns."

Matilda winced and Thea rolled her eyes, her back to Rosie. "Hello, Rosie," Matilda said quietly.

Rosie stepped closer. "I have to say I'm shocked. Just shocked. I didn't think you would come back after what you did to poor Parker."

"Parker is fine, Rosie," Thea interjected.

Rosie waved a hand at her. "Oh, I know. I just mean . . . well, that was quite the drama, wasn't it?"

"It's nice to see you, Rosie," Matilda said, trying to diffuse the woman's curiosity. "How are Sid and Katie?"

"Oh, the kids are fine," she glossed over the question and dove into her own inquisition. "What brought you back? Where have you been? Did you apologize to Parker? I'm surprised Beverly took you back. I'm not sure I've ever seen her as mad as when she found out you'd disappeared. And the way Parker moped around town. His heart shattered . . ." Her manicured hand came back to her chest.

"Rosie, come on now," Thea started.

Matilda put her hand on Thea's arm and smiled at her. Then looked to Rosie. "It was just time to come home."

Rosie frowned at this vague answer, but seeing the expression on Matilda's face held back further questions. She, no doubt, was concocting her own story to spread around town. "Well, yes. Everyone likes to come home. Who wouldn't want to come home to our perfect little town? You shouldn't have left. I suppose you finally realized that."

Matilda smiled stiffly and picked up a book to signal she was ready to get back to work. "It was nice to see you, Rosie." Rosie frowned at her again, followed by a judgmental head to toe examination. Matilda was glad she'd worn a long skirt and long sleeved shirt to hide all her ugly scars. She hated to think what kind of rumors would come from people seeing those. She fought the urge to cover the tiny ones on her cheek with her hand and thanked the bad lighting in the stacks.

"You too," Rosie finally said and turned on her heel.

Matilda and Thea exchanged a look. After a moment, Thea said, "Oh, yes. Perfect little Silent Fields."

Matilda smiled weakly, thinking she'd also need to get some makeup for the scars on her cheek. Or maybe she should just disappear in the night again.

By the end of day, Matilda was blue in the face from answering—or rather *not* answering—questions about where she'd been for the last six years and why she'd come back and why she'd left like a thief in the night. It seemed people were coming in the library solely to pepper her with *why* and *how* and *what*. And to see Silent Fields's lost child returned in the flesh. Matilda wasn't the only one annoyed. Beverly had been steaming from the ears all day, put out to have her schedules and rules compromised for such petty drama. Several times, Matilda thought Beverly might fire her just because of the disturbance.

When Matilda locked the front doors, she heaved a long sigh of relief. "This town," she muttered. No one had actually asked her how she was doing, if she needed anything, if they could help. All they wanted to do was gossip about her scars and her limp, which everyone seemed to know about despite her clothing. She guessed she had Dr. Wells to thank for that. One woman, Cindy Block, a baker at Estelle's, had leaned close and asked if a man had given her the scars and limp. "Did he beat you? Is that why you're back? You're running away from a man." A tongue click and head shake. "Honey, it happens all the time."

Matilda had blinked in shock, unable to answer, which Cindy probably took as a yes. But the truth was, it was possible. Maybe it'd been so bad that the trauma of it had blocked her memory. But Matilda couldn't imagine herself ever being with a man who beat her. What if it had happened against her will?

Matilda couldn't let herself wander down those slimy thought paths.

With the library now closed to the curious, she put her head on her arms on top of the circulation desk. "I hate everyone."

Thea was there, shuffling papers. "Well, don't feel too bad. They hate you more." Matilda heard the smile in her words.

"I hate you most of all."

"I know." Thea closed a drawer. "Come on. Let's go to The Mad Hash and eat fries until we explode."

Matilda lifted her weary head. "Are you kidding me? It'll be a public flogging. Rocks might be thrown."

"Maybe a hamburger or two."

Beverly interrupted, stomping over from out of the stacks. "Doors locked?"

"Yes, ma'am," Matilda reported.

"I trust tomorrow will not include such an intrusion from your personal life, Miss White." Beverly took her small purse from a drawer and tucked it under her arm.

"Oh, how I hope so."

Beverly only frowned, and then turned on her heel to leave.

Thea giggled quietly. "She's just jealous she never had a personal life."

Matilda rolled her eyes. "I'm going home. I need to recover before I go to the market."

"Want a ride? Think of the floggings possible walking down the sidewalk. Lots of readily available rocks."

"Yeah, you're right."

In Thea's red Honda Civic, Matilda leaned her head against the cold window. The sun was shining and flowers were blooming, a lovely spring.

"Oh, did you hear about the mystery guy?" Thea gossiped.

Matilda closed her eyes, suddenly annoyed by the high-pitched tone of Thea's voice. "No."

"*Well* . . . apparently he crashed his car in the storm Monday night and walked like ten miles on a broken foot to Abby O'Nell's house. And Abby being Abby—she took him in and is helping him recover from the accident. Dr. Wells saw him yesterday."

"I'm sure Gill is thrilled."

"I'm sure they are best friends by now, Gill and the new guy."

Matilda smiled at the idea. "Drinking beer and yuckin' it up. Swapping farm war stories." Thea laughed. "Good for Abby though," Matilda added. "She's actually someone I'd like to see. Does she still come to the library every Friday?"

"Like clockwork. Dr. Wells told my mom that the guy is here to take over for Ronnie at the paper." Thea switched the radio station.

"Really?" Matilda lifted her head. "Ronnie's *still* running the paper? And now he's giving it over to an outsider? I'm shocked." She put her hand to her chest sarcastically.

Thea laughed. "He's been campaigning for a successor for like ten years, but no one *here* would take it. He finally had to lure in someone from the real world. Going well for the guy so far, don't you think?"

Matilda laughed. "Splendidly, indeed."

"And someone told Edith he's *really* good looking."

"How is Edith? Is she still in town?"

"My sister is the same as always: quiet, refined, and alone. I swear she's never gonna allow a man into her life. No one is ever good enough. It's getting pathetic. I'm two years younger and look at me." Thea gestured to her belly. "And, yes, she's still in town. She runs Old

Mill Antiques now. Edith and her old junk. It's a good thing she loves it so much because it's the only thing she has to keep her company."

"I love that store. I'll have to go see her."

"Just don't try to set her up with anyone."

Matilda laughed. "Not really my thing. I'm sure she'll find someone when the time is right."

Thea pulled into Matilda's driveway, sat back in her seat, and rubbed her belly. "Yeah, maybe. Who knows? I've never really understood Edith, but she's my sister and I love her, so I guess I should stop bad mouthing her."

Matilda smiled as she looked out at the faded white clapboard, aspen green shutters, and violet gingerbread trim of Jetty's Victorian cottage. Matilda had cleared most the weeds yesterday. She still needed to touch up the paint where it had peeled. It had a long way to go to get back to Jetty standards. If she hurried, in the summer there would be roses and wisteria hanging from the porch.

I always wanted a storybook house, Jetty had said. *So I made one. Decided against making it out of candy though. That would probably attract too many bugs.*

The memory made Matilda smile. But then she frowned. *And I abandoned it.* She relished every moment of the chore to repair it. *Atonement. Punishment. For crimes I can't remember committing.*

"Want me to hang out with you? Beat back the heathens that come knocking?" Thea offered.

"No, thanks. I'll survive. You should go home and put your feet up. I'll see you tomorrow for more 'accost Matilda' fun." She opened her door. "And thanks for the ride."

"Of course. See ya!" Thea waved.

Matilda stood in the kitchen. Only the small Tiffany pendant light over the sink was turned on, casting a colorful soft glow. She stared, hands on hips, at the three pies and platter of cinnamon rolls. *What do I do with all that?* Cooking to avoid thinking about the upheaval in her life had its problems. Of course, Jetty would be pleased her gourmet kitchen was back in action.

The trip to the market after Thea dropped her off had been like surviving an obstacle course. She'd dodged people left and right, sprinted down aisles at random to avoid being seen, and crouched behind her cart more than once. But the checkout line had been her undoing. Kathy, the cashier, had a question for every item she scanned.

But at least Matilda now had food. Plenty. Too much. She could hole up in her house for at least two weeks, if it came to that. Or maybe a whole month. *Don't be dramatic,* she told herself, still staring at the baked goods.

Randomly, she thought of Abby O'Nell and the injured new editor.

She found a box, put two pies into it, and carried it out to the small, detached garage. Jetty's old tangerine-orange Volkswagen Bug slumbered under a thick blanket of dust. Matilda could walk to the library and market, and most places in town, but Abby's place was a half hour outside of Silent Fields. Matilda's beautiful Bel Air was not there, not in the garage or driveway. Missing. *Along with six years.* Matilda set the box on the workbench and focused on the car that was there. *Will it even start?* She found an old rag and scrubbed off the windows, making plans to wash it properly tomorrow night after work. She yanked open the door, which gave a grinding squeal of protest. The inside was nearly as dusty as the outside. With a sigh, Matilda sat in the driver's seat, slid in the key, and prayed. The engine sputtered, died. She tried again. After a guttural gasp, the engine turned over.

"A miracle," she whispered. She smiled at the blue lace agate stone dangling from a string from the rear view mirror. It had always been there. As a child, Matilda had been thrilled by the smooth surface of the stone, adored the early-morning-blue color lined with white, and loved what Jetty said about it. "I put it there because it's supposed to have calming energy. I hate to drive. It's like being trapped in a metal box and thrown down a hill. So the stone is there to *calm* me. But really it's there because it's pretty."

Matilda touched it now. "It's still pretty, Jetty." She retrieved the pie box, wedged it carefully in the passenger seat, and then headed out of town toward Abby's farm.

Abby had always been a good friend, a regular at the library. She had read almost as many of the books on the shelves as Matilda had. Each time Abby came in, they'd hide far away from Beverly's tyrant eye and talk books. Their favorite new cheap romance or a character they couldn't stop thinking about or how they had cried at an ending.

Matilda parked outside the old farmhouse. Looking through the murky windshield, she wondered how Abby would receive her. Suddenly nervous, Matilda looked over at the pies and almost turned around to go home. She forced herself out of the car.

Careful not to upset the pies, she balanced the box up the steps and rang the doorbell with her elbow. It was almost ten o'clock; something she probably should have thought about before she was standing on the porch.

Thankfully, Abby opened the door, not Gill. Abby blinked twice and then smiled. "Matilda! Is that you, sweetie? Well, bless my soul! I'd heard you were back. What are you doing here?"

"I made some pies. Thought your invalid might want some comfort food. And I wanted to say hi."

Abby laughed. "I wondered how long it would take until that news got 'round." She pushed open the screen and Matilda stepped in. "I bet it was Dr. Wells. He's the worst gossip of them all. Not sure he cares much for the whole doctor/patient privacy thing. He was the one told me *you* were back."

"I'm not surprised. Seems he's been very talkative lately." Matilda followed Abby to the kitchen and set the pies on the stove. "Apple and pumpkin. Hope you like those."

"Thanks, sweetheart. Want coffee, tea? A stiff drink?"

Matilda laughed. "No, I won't stay. It's late."

"You sure? I'd love to catch up." She stepped closer. "I've sure missed our book talks."

Matilda half smiled, glad for Abby's kindness. "Yeah, me too. Sorry that I left." Matilda looked back at the pies.

Abby must have read something in her expression. "You've had to say that a lot lately, huh? The 'I'm sorry.' I can only imagine the reception of this town."

Matilda continued to look at the pies, trying to hide her emotions. "Yes, I have. I went back to work at the library today."

Abby whistled. "Brave girl. Well, you don't have to say sorry to me. Everyone's allowed to go crazy and do what they need to do. Our goofy town should mind its own business." Abby stepped next to her and nudged her arm with her own. "You okay? Looks like you've had a rough go."

Matilda felt the weight of Abby's examination. She tugged her long sleeves further down to hide her scars. "A little."

"That why you came back?"

The warmth in Abby's tone and her standing close made Matilda want to break down into her arms like a little child. Like she would have done with Jetty. "I think so."

Abby nodded sagely. "Sometimes you just need to come home." She stepped away, to the stove, and Matilda exhaled in relief. "You sure I can't make you a hot beverage? You can sit for a bit. I won't feel as guilty about shoveling pie into my face if you do it with me."

Matilda smiled. "No, thanks. I better go. It's late and you have the new editor to take care of."

Abby looked to the hall again. "I'd introduce you, but I think Henry is sleeping."

At the sound of Abby's guest's name Matilda felt a sharp pang in her chest. She flinched, confused. To cover the reaction, she said quickly, "No, of course. That's fine. I'm sure I'll see him sooner or later." She moved out into the hall and toward the door. "You'll be in town Friday, right?"

"Of course. I'll find you. I've got six years' worth of books to tell you about." Abby touched her arm. "Thanks for the pies, dear. You are sweet."

"My pleasure."

Abby opened the door. "Hang in there. And if you need anything, Tilly . . ."

Matilda stepped past her with a shy smile. "Thanks, Abby." She went down the steps, trying her best to hide her limp. It was obvious Abby noticed it, watching her closely, but the old woman smiled kindly, completely without judgment or curiosity.

"Good night," Abby called as Matilda got into her car.

Abby waved as Matilda turned and drove away.

Henry

Henry stood in the hall leaning on his crutches as Abby walked someone to the door. All he could see was long black hair, shiny and rich, and the swish of a long black skirt as the woman walked. And how short she was. His heart took off in an unnatural gallop, his mouth went dry.

Abby turned, startled. "What are you doing up? Thought you were sleeping."

"Who was that?"

Abby blinked at him, stepping closer. "You are *mighty* flushed." She pressed a hand to his forehead. "I think you might have a fever. That can't be good."

Henry heard nothing. "Who was that?" he repeated, staring at the door.

Abby followed his eyes. "Just a neighbor. Brought you some pie. What's wrong with you?"

Henry shook his head. *What is wrong with me?* "I . . . I think I got up too fast."

Abby hummed a suspicious *mmhmm*. "Want some pie?"

He blinked twice, looked away from the front door. "Sure. Yeah, sure."

Henry sat on the bed, staring hard at the typewriter. He'd just eaten the best pie of his life. He wanted to write about the woman who'd made it, about a woman he'd seen for no more than three seconds.

And he hadn't *really* seen her. Just her hair, her short stature, the swing of her hips as she walked. He couldn't stop thinking about the swing of her hips, the color of her hair. In his head, this partial image was surrounded by words, like a flock of pesky black birds.

He wondered what her face looked like.

Henry hopped over and dropped into the chair in front of the sleek machine. He lifted a paper from the stack and slipped it into the paper table. Rolling the knobs, it came into place. *A blank page. A writer's greatest fear.* He exhaled, the paper rustling in the sudden rush of air.

Violently beautiful words, sensual and lovely.

Hands hovering over the keys, Henry's heart raced.

"No," he whispered to the typewriter. "Stop it."

He was an addict; he needed to resist the craving. Especially one that wanted him to write about a woman he didn't know. Henry threw himself back in the bed. Tomorrow he'd ask Abby to take away the typewriter.

Matilda

*E*very night for two weeks, Matilda had nightmares. Tangled in the quilt, her pretty brass bed squeaking as her body jerked and thrashed, she dreamed of spectral, terrible things.

A voice calling out her name in panic. Someone crying, maybe her. Snow. Endless drifts of frigid snow. And the pain, like nothing she had ever felt. Pain in her head, in her racing heart, and in her left leg.

Matilda woke at dawn, chest heaving and left leg burning. She threw back the quilt to examine the leg. There was nothing wrong with her leg, except for that four-inch jagged scar. Rubbing the aching muscles, she tried to shove away the nightmare.

She flopped back to the bed. *What is wrong with me?* She'd always been a vivid dreamer, but not nightmares; those were rare. She'd had a few in the last days of Jetty's life—dark visions of being left alone—but nothing like this. These dreams lingered, staying with her all day, mucking up her mood and thoughts.

But what did she expect? Of course a mind as broken as hers would produce nightmares.

Matilda shook her head. *These desolate dreams.* Maybe she should call someone and tell them the truth. Abby? Thea? Parker? If she got it out in the open, would that ease the pressure in her chest? The desire to talk was always there, right on the edge of every thought.

Turning, she lifted Winston's book from her nightstand. The pages were well-bent now, the binding loose. She flipped to the page she wanted and read.

> I want to find comfort in my loneliness. I want to crawl under it,
> a childhood blanket fort, and stay there always. And yet, even as I

embrace my solitude, I wish it away. I crave what everyone craves: a house, a family, security, safety. A house full of love, laughter, arguments, the smell of food. I want someone in bed beside me, a hand on my chest late at night. But do I deserve it? I don't think I do and so I must accept this curse.

I want to be lonely.

But I hate it.

"I hate it," Matilda repeated out loud.

When Matilda had been about eight years old and able to grasp that her parents were dead, she'd spent a lot of time crying.

"Listen to me, Tilly," Jetty had said, holding her close in that same bed. "You are never alone. Your mom and dad watch over you. The ones we love never really leave us." She hugged a little tighter. "Always, always remember that." A moment of silence. "They are dead, but not gone. You are here. You are them. Don't cry anymore."

Now, with washy sunlight creeping in the widows, Matilda closed her eyes, her heart heavy with grief. *I'm so alone. I'm cursed.* The blackness in her mind threatened to overwhelm her. She took a long breath. "Are you here, Jetty?" she whispered. "I can't get rid of this grief. I miss you."

Matilda sniffed and shook her head. "Stop it." She got out of bed, leaving the confusing emotions to wither on the pillows. It was Saturday and she had the day off. A whole day of hours that needed filling. So first a long bike ride. While cleaning up the yard, she had found her old bike in the small garage, dusty and tires flat, but otherwise ready to ride after a little care. She'd started riding in high school and had loved it. It was only natural to start again when she had so much time to fill. The best thing about gliding along in the saddle of her road bike was that the world got lost in the slipstream of quickly passing scenery. She could switch gears, push her muscles harder, be in control, and forget. She could move fast and not limp.

Maybe she could out-pedal the feelings in her chest or ride down some answers.

The ride had helped.

Matilda stepped out of the shower feeling lighter, free of her nightmares. She dressed in jeans and a black V-neck Tee and pulled her hair into a ponytail. There was one more room that needed cleaning. The last thing. The thing she'd put off long enough.

Jetty's room.

Matilda opened the door, which squeaked in protest, having been shut for so long. The smell of dust was strong, but the memories were stronger. They hit Matilda full in the face. Instantly, there were tears on her cheeks.

Across the hall from Matilda's room, Jetty's bedroom had always owned a sense of wonder. It was a magical place. Jetty had painted a large mural of the beach and the ocean that covered all four walls. It was the same picture on each wall—a strip of sandy beach and the rolling ocean beyond—but each one had a different feeling. One was sunny; one was cloudy and gray, churned up during a rainstorm; one was a peachy sunset; and the last was sparkling under the full moon.

Each stunningly real.

Standing there now, Matilda swore she could hear the surf.

As a child, Matilda had often wondered why Jetty had chosen to fill her room with the ocean. They lived on the dusty plains; the ocean was so far away. But knowing now about Enzo and Florida, it made perfect sense.

Jetty had a four-post bed, draped with silks of all different colors. When Matilda was in eighth grade, Jetty had become obsessed with birdcages. The room was filled with birdcages, all shapes, sizes, and colors. And Jetty had filled them with her books, getting rid of her traditional shelves, as if to keep the words from flying away.

Matilda walked over to one cage nearly as tall as she and touched the cool metal. On the top of the stacks of books was Jetty's favorite: *Bridge to Terabithia*. Memories of the funeral, of Jetty reading her the book nearly every summer of her life, flooded her mind. It was a story about losing the person you love most in the world. That vibrant, amazing person who showed you the world. So like Jetty's own life, and now, so like Matilda's.

Sniffling, Matilda stepped back and put her hands on her hips.

Time to work. No more tears.

Henry

"This place is just right for you!"

"It's nice."

"Nice? This is one of the best apartments in town. You're lucky it's available."

Henry smiled as he shook his head. Abby walked slowly around the space while he leaned into the white quartz island in the small kitchen area. His new apartment was two blocks over from the library, where his new office was, and one of four built into an old colonial mansion that had once been the mayor's residence. This unit was on the top floor, the east side. He appreciated that the owners had transformed it to look like a New York loft with exposed gray brick, tall windows, and an open studio floor plan.

"I am lucky and I'll take it."

"Of course you will. I already picked up the keys." Abby dug into her purse and threw the key ring to him. He caught it easily, looking down at the single brown key. *A new apartment. This is serious.* A rush of nerves tightened his throat. He slipped the key into his pocket.

Abby crossed over to him. "You got any money for furniture?"

"Yes, ma'am, a little. Ronnie gave me an advance on my first check. But all I need is a bed."

"And a couch, coffee table. And a desk. Can't write without a desk."

"Abby, I told you . . ."

"Blah, blah. I know what you told me. I'm still bringing that beautiful typewriter over here first thing tomorrow."

Henry pressed his teeth together. He knew she meant well, and after all she'd done for him, he couldn't hurt her feelings with a protest.

"Okay. Well, where does one buy a desk, a bed, and a couch in Silent Fields?"

"Clive's Furniture on Main Street. But first, I'm starving. How about some dinner?"

Abby stopped outside the large picture window of a small diner. "Welcome to The Mad Hash," she announced. "Best food in town. It's owned by Bob Meekam, a retired banker turned biker turned chef. So please ignore all the cheesy motorcycle memorabilia."

Henry laughed as he hobbled over to the door, his big boot cast making his steps awkward. He opened it for Abby. The small eatery was decorated with brushed-metal tables and chairs, a black-and-white tile floor, and an odd collection of vintage motorcycle memorabilia, just as Abby had warned. It all felt a little out of place for what Henry had seen of Silent Fields, but he liked it instantly. He smiled at the smell of deep-fried goodness. A young hostess dressed in a tank top and mini skirt flashed them a big smile. "Hey, Abby, nice to see you."

"Hey, Pam," Abby answered.

Pam's heavily painted eyes moved to Henry. "And you must be Henry, the new editor." Her smile grew. "Sit anywhere you like."

Henry smiled shyly, nodding without actually looking at the hostess. "Thanks," he mumbled. Her smile increased, and she flipped her long fake-blonde hair off her shoulder.

Henry led the way to a table near the back. Abby grunted as she eased her body into the booth. "That pretty young hostess has got her eye on you, son."

Henry shook his head, color rising to his freckled cheeks again. He opened his menu to hide his face. Abby had taken to calling him son more and more over the last weeks. At first it made him uncomfortable, but now Henry found it endearing. She and Gill had never had any children of their own, and since Henry was an orphan, he enjoyed the way she treated him like family, like her own. It was nice to feel owned.

Abby's bulbous, stout fingers appeared over the top of the menu, pulling it down. "So?"

"So what?" he said, laying the menu on the table.

"You gonna ask her out?"

"No, ma'am. I am *not*." His face was now as hot and red as sunburn.

Abby smiled knowingly. "There's nothing wrong with a little fun, Henry. If anyone deserves it, it's you. And you live here now. Gotta get to know people, right?"

Henry moved his eyes to the front of the room where Pam was vigorously wiping a table, bent forward, certain personal items almost falling out of her tank top. Turning back, he said, "Not really my type." And how could someone as broken as him take anyone into his life? There was also the worry that there had been someone during those six years. The woman who had written *For Henry* in Winston's book. Where was she? Was she looking for him? He wanted to look for her, but didn't have a place to start.

"And what *is* your type? Every single gal in this town will soon be panting on the sidelines. What's wrong? Someone back in Detroit?" Abby raised her gray eyebrows, opening wide her weak tea eyes. She hadn't pressed him much about his life before knocking on her door and for that he was grateful.

"Not that," Henry said flatly, trying to keep his emotions out of his voice. He looked at Pam again. "I'm sure Pam's a nice girl, but nothing about her is attractive to me."

"Well, keep those dazzling eyes open. Maybe one *will* be attractive to you and you can start doing more than reading and watching TV with an old woman."

Henry blushed again, offering a noncommittal shrug as his only answer. "Speaking of all the time we've been spending together," Henry deftly changed the subject. "I'm sure Gill is happy to have me gone." Gill had not warmed to Henry in the least. In fact, Henry was pretty sure Gill hated him more now than the night he knocked on their door. The cantankerous old man wouldn't even look at him without scowling. He wondered how someone as sweet and giving as Abby had ended up with someone as brash and nasty as Gill.

"Oh, he's thrilled. But don't let that get to you. He's . . . Gill." A resigned shrug. "Nothing makes him happy." Abby frowned and looked down at her menu.

An older waitress named Pearl stopped at the table to take their orders. As Henry handed her back his menu, his eyes caught on a woman sitting at a booth in the opposite corner. Her face was hidden behind a paperback novel, an empty plate on the table in front of her. Under the table, her short legs were crossed, the one on top bouncing lazily, her long white lacy skirt fluttering. She was alone.

Abby said something, but her voice sounded far away. Henry's chest suddenly ached fiercely, contracting and expanding all at once. He bent forward, trying to pull in a breath, but the air felt as dense and scratchy as sand. The woman lowered her book to take a drink of soda and their eyes locked instantly.

His heart pounded uncomfortably, his whole body filled with the rich dark color of her big round eyes, the smooth texture of her tanned skin, and silkiness of her long black hair. He'd never seen anyone like her. Her body was small and compact, like a cat, but not a domestic animal — a wild one, powerful and graceful. She was most certainly beautiful, but not in the way of other women. Her features were sharper, as if everyone else were slightly out of focus. And the way she looked at him—she glowed with sumptuous energy.

The dark hair. Was this the same woman he'd seen leaving Abby's a couple weeks ago? The pie woman?

The sweating cup in her hand slipped, tipped, and spilled soda all over the table. It dripped off the cliff of the table onto her white skirt. She didn't move her gaze from Henry's. When her pink lips parted, he heard the gasp as if it were the only sound in the busy restaurant.

Someone stepped in the electric path of their eyes, severing the connection. Air rushed into Henry's lungs as razor pain flared under his skin.

"Henry? Henry, you better not be having a heart attack!" Abby's voice was now loud next to his face, edged with concern. He blinked, turned to look at her leaning across the table. Her hand was on his arm—he didn't know when she had put it there. "Henry?" she asked again, voice strained.

"I . . . I'm fine," he managed as he blinked, shook his head. His chest still throbbed. He pressed the heel of his hand to his sternum.

Abby narrowed her eyes at his chest. "Liar. We better call Dr. Wells."

Henry lowered his hand, moved his eyes back to where the woman had been. The booth was empty, the soda still dripping onto the tile. She'd left her book and the soda was seeping into the edges of the pages. Panic rushed up his throat. "Where did she go?" he blurted out as he twisted in his seat to look for her.

"Who? Where did *who* go?" Abby asked. She looked around the room. "You're not making any sense, son."

"The woman!" he stammered. "Sitting right there." He pointed to the empty booth, fighting the urge to jump up and run out into the street after her. *Calm down. Don't make a scene!* "She left her book," he added quietly.

Pearl came back with drinks. "Pearl, who was sitting over there? I didn't see," Abby asked hopefully, ready to help solve Henry's problem.

Pearl turned. "Just Matilda. First time she's been in since she got back. Did you hear she's running from an abusive boyfriend?" She shook her head disapprovingly and turned. With a huff, she added, "And I guess she ain't never heard of napkins!" Pearl rushed away to wipe up the soda.

Abby took Henry's hand. "Your hands are cold." She pursed her lips. "Come on now. Talk to me." She tugged a little on his hand and he pulled his eyes from the search for the woman. *Matilda.* "What happened? Why did seeing Matilda upset you so much?"

Embarrassment rushed to his cheeks. "No, it didn't. It's nothing. I just . . . I thought . . ."

Abby leaned closer and lowered her voice. "If you're not well . . ." Her eyes widened.

"No, *no.*" Henry scoffed. He put his hand on top of hers, sandwiching it. "I'm okay. Really. She just . . . looked like someone I used to know." He shook his head, knowing that wasn't right, but he wanted to give Abby something. "Who is she—Matilda? Is she the one who brought the pies?"

Abby nodded. "Yes. Fantastic cook. Learned that from her Aunt Jetty. Matilda is one of our librarians. Sweet girl. Really knows her books; one of the best librarians we've had. She's had a rough time of it lately though. Poor thing."

His eyes moved over to the booth again. Pearl wiped the soda from the table and floor with a dingy white towel. She picked up the book. "Pearl?" Henry called out, an odd itch of urgency burning in his gut.

She walked over. "Yeah, Henry?"

Did everyone know his name? "I'll take her book." He nodded toward it. Pearl looked confused. "I'll see her at work on Monday. I'll return it to her."

"Oh, right. Here ya go." Pearl handed him the book and went off.

Henry's fingers burned where he touched the paperback; he gripped it tightly. *The Silence of the Lambs* by Thomas Harris. Henry laughed out loud. "Not what I was expecting," he said, turning the book to show Abby, who smiled.

"Matilda is many things people don't expect." Abby smiled, pleased.

Henry's smile spread. He looked back at the book. It was one of his personal favorites: bizarre, gruesome, and also somehow beautiful. He'd make sure to ask her what she thought of it when he returned it. He tilted the book to look at the soda-soaked pages, already rippling as they dried.

"Henry?" Abby asked, her eyes intent on his face. "Are you *sure* you're all right?"

He met Abby's eyes. "I'm fine." Abby frowned. "Really. Forget it. I don't want to ruin our dinner." Reluctantly, he set the book down on the bench next to his leg. A flash of warmth moved down the limb.

Abby's frown stayed and her eyes narrowed as she evaluated him. Finally, her expression softened. "Okay, then. If you're really sure?"

Henry exhaled. "Yes. I'm fine. Really. Sorry about that."

"Don't be sorry." She smiled her grandma-smile. Henry felt a pulse of comfort. Not enough though to completely erase the odd feelings still simmering in his chest. He had to fight not to look away, to search again.

What just happened?

He couldn't wait until Monday.

Matilda

*M*atilda was out of The Mad Hash and two blocks away before she stopped to take a full breath. When an empty iron bench outside Estelle's Bakery came into view, she threw herself down, pulling air into her fluttering lungs.

The wet spots of soda on her skirt were cold against her leg. Her purse was heavy on her shoulder. The air smelled of cake.

What just happened?

Looking straight ahead, out at the narrow two-lane road, Matilda saw only the man's face. He looked like something from an old movie with his long, masculine architecture and explosion of youthful freckles on pale, creamy skin. His dusty-blond hair was a casual mess on his head, unkempt and shaggy, as if that morning he'd simply ran a hand back through it and easily went on with life, unconcerned. And his eyes . . . it wasn't so much the color of them—she wasn't sure if they were green or hazel—but the *way* he had looked at her. It wasn't looking, it was more like . . . devouring. He'd consumed everything about her in an instant.

Her skin felt raw.

She tugged at the sleeves of her cardigan, tucking the ends into her fists. Closing her eyes, she felt the race of her heart and wondered what he'd tasted with those enigmatic eyes.

A loud truck rumbled past, breaking her thoughts. Her eyes dropped to her skirt. She blinked at the quaint red-brick pavers of the sidewalk. Everything about downtown Silent Fields was quaint, charming. Tree-lined streets, rows of well-maintained shops, fresh air. She touched the wet stain.

No. No, I can't have this.

Mortified, she realized she'd left her soda spilling onto the floor and ran out of the diner as if it were on fire. She'd also left her book behind. Good thing she had already paid. Swearing under her breath, Matilda looked back down the street in the direction of The Mad Hash. She couldn't go back for the book—at least not right now. Had anyone seen her flee the diner? The last thing she needed was more undue attention. Things were just beginning to calm down. Stories about her having some kind of freak emotional moment in the diner would only stir up the rumor whirlwind again.

She looked up and down the street, searching for the stares and whispers. *Did you hear about Matilda's weird mad dash from The Mad Hash? Something really weird is going on with her. She shouldn't have come back. Also, when she walks that fast, she looks like Long John Silver with that limp! Poor thing. It's a miracle Parker dated her at all.*

Matilda exhaled, dropped her chin to her chest.

What power did this stranger have? When her eyes had met his, her blood had floated in her veins, defying gravity. Her head had spun with dizziness and every muscle tensed, ready to get up and run over to him. Begging her to.

Like something out of Winston's book.

Matilda stood slowly, adjusted her purse strap, and then started walking, sluggishly. Something was wrong with this day. First the nightmares, then cleaning out Jetty's room. Touching all her keepsakes, each wafting with memories. Bagging up most of her clothes. Sweeping dead spiders out from under her fairytale bed.

Now, this stranger and her head spinning with his freckled face.

He had leaned his body toward her in those potent few seconds. She'd felt his body shift toward her as if he'd been sitting right next to her.

What did he feel when he looked at me?

The question almost stalled her stride, but she pushed on. She needed to get home to the safety of the house, to the privacy and protection of its quiet rooms.

Fumbling slightly, Matilda unlocked the front door and plowed into the living room. She tossed her bag onto the couch and dropped into the comfy blue gingham armchair. The room was silent expect for the ticking of the mantel clock. She set her mind to finding a reason for the episode with the stranger. All that came was a picture of him sitting in the booth, his long legs and knees nearly touching the under-side of the table. When she wondered just how much taller he was than her, Matilda huffed in frustration. Her eyes moved to the typewriter.

I'm losing my mind.

The typewriter had been sitting there since that first day of this bizarre, broken second life. She'd barely looked at it, though she could feel its presence almost every moment of the day. It sat there, as if watching and waiting.

Now, thinking of the stranger, she heard keystrokes in her head, echoing and haunting. Bravely, she reached out to touch the cool, smooth keys. Her stomach tightened. She pulled back her hand. Suddenly, she was heavily sad, the feeling pressing on her chest.

After a long breath, she looked around the room. "Jetty," she called out, "are you there?" When no answer came, she shook her head, angry with herself. She stood, full of purpose. "There has to be something else to clean or fix in this place."

Henry

The bedside clock read four-thirty in the morning. Henry squinted at it, the green digital numbers glaringly bright in the darkness of his room. For a moment, he listened to the lonely quiet. Sleep had teased him all night, tucking him into its arms and then shoving him awake with disturbing images of running down dark snowy streets, fear an insistent pursuer. And this woman, Matilda, standing in the shadows, always just beyond his reach. Now his body felt achy, antsy. With a frustrated sigh, he pushed the covers back and sat up. His ankle hurt, but he ignored it.

Henry pulled a random T-shirt from the brown leather couch where he'd dumped his box of stuff earlier, and tugged it on, pulling it down over his cotton pajama pants. He went to the window and lifted the blinds to look down into the empty gray street. He tried to tell himself that his trouble sleeping was due to being in his new apartment for the first time and *not* his inexplicable encounter with the librarian.

The lie didn't take.

At his feet was his box of books. A few had been upended and tossed into puddles thanks to the accident, but the police had been thorough. Every one accounted for, if some were a little worse for wear. There were so few compared to what he used to have.

He missed the books he used to have.

Buying books was his only indulgence, and he'd acquired an impressive library since his eighteenth birthday and emancipation from The System. Most of his Saturdays had been spent visiting any and all bookstores within a hundred miles. He never came home empty handed, even in the days when money had been sparse. He'd rather buy a book than a shirt or new shoes. He'd rather have a book on his nightstand than meat in his fridge.

As a child and teenager, Henry had never owned a book, but had desperately wanted to. His foster brothers and sisters always wanted Nike shoes, jewelry, more clothes, nicer clothes, their own room. All he ever wanted was a few books. Just one or two would have satisfied his unselfish soul, but in the eyes of his foster parents, books were a waste of money, completely unnecessary. After the sting of many hands and yelling rebuffs, Henry had eventually stopped asking for books and resigned himself to reading at the library. He didn't even dare check out the books and bring them back to his foster homes. Possessions, whether owned or borrowed, had a way of disappearing. And he couldn't bear the thought of being responsible for the demise of a library book.

Every book he bought as an adult was not only a pleasure to read but also a way to erase some of that childhood disappointment and affirm his freedom from that time of his life.

Stacks of books were sanity.

Of course, all those books were gone. He didn't have the library he'd collected over the years before 1992. He had no idea where all his books had gone in those lost six years. The loss made him suffer, and so he needed this small box of books bought at the used bookstore on his way to Silent Fields, and he needed more. He needed the therapy of buying books. Now that he had a steady paycheck, he needed to find the bookstore.

He bent and sifted through the box, pulling out a copy of *The Silence of the Lambs*. Did it mean something that this was one of the books he'd found at that used bookstore? Of the few books he had now, this was one? Matilda's soda-stained copy sat on his desk—its presence loud in the quiet room—next to the uninvited typewriter. True to her word, Abby had hauled the machine up the stairs and placed it on his new simple wooden desk. The two combined, Matilda's book and the typewriter, would never allow him to rest easy.

He dropped his copy of *The Silence of the Lambs* back in the box. Crossing his arms, he leaned against the window frame and stared with gritty eyes over the tops of the shadowy buildings. A few raindrops hit the glass, the beginning of another spring storm. In the distance, the open country loomed, a black swath. He couldn't erase Matilda's face from his mind, couldn't shake the odd tremor of emotions that had lingered since The Mad Hash. Both terrified and intrigued, he wished the moment of returning her book would hurry up and come. The waiting was a torture of questions and speculations. He needed to look her in the eyes and see what he felt.

Henry shuffled over to his small desk. His hand twitched to pick up her book, but he kept his arms tightly folded against his chest; he'd held it an embarrassing amount already. He lowered himself into the old wooden swivel chair found at the thrift shop, the joints squeaking loudly in the hushed morning. He moved his eyes from her book to the handsome black Remington Rand from 1937. Tipping his body forward, he released his arms and ran his fingertips lightly over the cool keys.

Words erupted in his head. Her face, her dark eyes and curvy, compact body flooded his mind. There were words all around her; seeing her had awakened a breed of words he wasn't accustomed to. The craving to write was agonizing. No way to fight it. Not now in the thin, treacherous hours of dawn.

Henry closed his eyes.

His fingers depressed the keys.

The perilous words flew out.

Matilda

$\mathcal{E}$xhaustion kindly started to pull Matilda down into sleep. She'd spent most of the night too caught up in her troubled mind to rest, but now her body relaxed into the softness of the bed, her hands loosening on the quilt. A heavy spring rain poured outside, the sound of the raindrops a soothing lullaby.

Sleep was seconds away . . .

Clack. Clack. Clack.

Matilda sat up, heart pounding.

ClackClackClackClackClackClack. DING!

Her head whipped side to side, eyes moving around the room. This was not the rain. She stiffened, body eager to fight or fly.

The noise came again. She strained her ears. "What is that?" she asked the windows. Matilda crept out of bed, listening hard. She stuck her head out the door and looked down the shadowy stairs. The noise came from downstairs. "No," she whispered. She stepped out into the hall. *Am I dreaming? I have to be dreaming.*

One cold stair under her bare feet. Two. Three. Four. Matilda stood at the bottom, near the front door and looked back at the stairs. *I'm dreaming. A new nightmare.*

ClackClackClackClackClackClack. DING!

Matilda moved into the living room, her pulse racing, her hands gripping the skirt of her pink-striped nightgown. The charming room lay washed in fractured shadows, the water drenched windows playing tricks with the soggy light. Matilda thought it looked like the inside of an aquarium. Her feet slid along the wood floor toward the source of the noise. She stopped behind the couch, keeping it between her and the room.

Between her and the typewriter working itself.

Matilda blinked, stared hard. A piece of paper had appeared in the paper table, rolled under the platen. The typebars snapped into the ribbon at top speed. The keys depressing.

She gripped the back of the couch, dizzy and confused. Pulling her eyes from the typewriter, she looked around the room for some kind of clue to explain the impossible. The mantel clocked ticked loudly. Four-fifty-one. The books sat on the shelves. The armchair stood still. The rain pounded on the roof.

And the typewriter typed.

Matilda dared to step around the couch. It had to be a dream, so why not explore? She leaned forward and waved her hand over the typewriter to no effect. "Stop that," she hissed. It did not. By now the page was half filled with words. Typed words—black and blocky on white paper. Her eyes focused on those anomalous words. She dropped to her knees.

One moment of my life, which should have been insignificant, easily forgotten in the river's flow of daily moments, has halted my existence.

I desire you.

It's madness.

I want you.

But this is so much more than lust. One look at you and I want to know all that you are made of. Your thoughts. Your strengths. Your flaws. I want to listen to you talk of pointless things, of books, of nighttime fears. I want to listen to you laugh, to cry in utter agony. To whisper my name.

It's insanity.

I am insane.

My insanity brings on the words. They will not stop. I saw your face, and the dangerous words erupted—volcanic.

So many words. They fall out of my fingertips like rain, flooding my page. Such words!

They don't come from me.

```
They come from you.
And you don't even know me yet.
Not yet.
```

The typewriter stopped, leaving only the sound of the rain. With a shaking hand, Matilda pulled the paper from the platen and dropped onto the couch. She held it between both hands, gripping so hard the edges bent. Silver light from the window spilled over the page in wavy, watery lines. She watched the shadow of raindrops slipping down the glass move over the paper.

Such words, indeed. If this was a dream, it was crueler than the nightmares of the last two weeks. These words made her feel mournful, as if she had just read her lover's obituary. Her own, perhaps. These words teased something so deep within her soul and mind that she didn't even know what to call it. These words existed on another plane. One she had no way to reach or understand.

Matilda looked from the black typed words to the typewriter. "How did you do that? *Why* did you do that?"

The row of typebars grinned silently back.

Matilda lowered the paper to the coffee table. Released it.

"Just a dream," she groaned, forcing herself to stand. She pulled away from the words and went up the stairs, the effort staggering. She dropped onto her bed, pulled the covers over her head. "Just a dream."

Henry

Henry balled his hands into fists and stared at the words he had typed. The room hummed with the power of them. His tongue felt like cotton. He needed a drink of water. He needed to sit and stare at the words forever.

Not yet.

Not yet.

The high of the words pumped in his veins, euphoric. But also depressing. He'd given in to temptation. He'd brought her to life on his page.

Dangerous. So dangerous.

Suddenly and heavily sad, Henry stumbled to his bed, burying his face in the pillow.

Matilda

Matilda woke before her alarm, the sound of typewriter keys echoing in her head. Groggy, she rolled over to look out the windows. The rain had stopped. Sunlight made the drops of water on the window sparkle brilliantly. She took a slow breath. The words of the letter in her dream filled her head. *Such words!* Stirring such precarious things inside her, like Louis Winston's words. Perhaps that was why she'd had the dream. She needed to stop reading that book over and over. She looked at it now, sitting on her nightstand. The cover was facedown. There was no author photo, only a short, unhelpful bio: *Louis Winston writes from home in Michigan.*

Matilda rolled to the other side of the bed.

It had felt so real, this dream of watching the typewriter come to life.

It was a dream . . . right?

A tug of instinct pulled Matilda from her bed. In the cold morning, she walked down the stairs, each creak of the wood loud. Her heart started to beat quickly before she turned the corner to look at the typewriter.

A piece of paper.

Words.

All real.

Her hand flew to her mouth to stifle a gasp. Diving forward, she snatched the paper off the steamer trunk coffee table. Another sharp intake of breath. Her eyes moved from the blocky letters to the typewriter. She shook her head as she eased down onto the couch. Slowly, she read the bewildering words again. All there, exactly the same.

Turning the paper over, she looked for something to identify it. But it was ordinary copy paper.

Her finger traced the words, feeling the slight indentation of each one and that overwhelming sense of familiarity again. "I don't understand," she whispered. She especially didn't understand that the words brought the face of the man in The Mad Hash to her mind as clear as sunlight. The moment replayed in her mind. She wanted to know what would happen if she saw him again.

She wanted to know what color his eyes were.

Matilda looked down at the typewriter. He'd been sitting with Abby, which meant he was probably the new editor, a stranger come to town. What had Abby said his name was? *Henry. It's Henry.* She pushed the H key. It snapped into the platen with a deft karate chop. She pushed the M key. *Chop.*

She set the paper down. She lifted the antique typewriter, examining it from every angle. Nothing out of place, no suspect modern technology placed to play a trick. Just keys and levers and knobs put together fifty-five years ago. Placing the machine back, she ran her eyes over the words again.

This can't be real.

Matilda stood quickly, stumbling a little as she backed away from the typewriter. "No more of that, understood?" she whispered, feeling foolish, but also flushed with fear. "No more!"

"What is wrong with you today?" Thea asked, standing next to Matilda as they shelved books in the fiction stacks.

"Nothing." Matilda didn't look up.

"Liar. You're in a mood. And you look terrible."

"Gee, thanks."

"No, I just mean—you look tired or sick or . . . something. Like that first day you were back."

Matilda groaned. "I'm just not sleeping well."

Thea nodded sympathetically. "You and me both, sister." She paused to rub her swollen belly. "But it's more than that, isn't it?"

Matilda sighed and turned to Thea. "Just . . . stuff. I'm fine."

Thea was quiet for a moment. And then, "Why won't you tell me the real reason?" she asked quietly. "You can, you know. Whatever it is."

Matilda wondered what Thea would say if she told her about the nightmares and the typewriter and how she'd felt in The Mad Hash and the love letter from a ghost. Not to mention six years she couldn't remember and scars she didn't know the source of. These were things she could have told Jetty, who actually believed in ghosts and inexplicable things. But Thea . . . "You're so sweet, Thea. Thank you, really. I'm just getting used to being back here. And the whispers and dagger eyes of everyone in town isn't easy to take. You know?"

"They'll move on to something else soon enough. But yeah, I'm sorry about that." Thea's eyes softened. "Something really bad happened to you, didn't it?"

Matilda looked away.

Thea accepted the silence as answer enough.

They wheeled the cart back to the circulation desk where Beverly sat perusing a stack of files. Without looking up, she said, "Miss White, the second floor needs dusting."

"Yes, ma'am." Matilda and Thea exchanged eye rolls.

"And Mrs. Reynolds," Beverly added. "The card catalogue needs to be wiped down."

Thea made a stink face, and Matilda shrugged in sympathy. The two librarians parted ways, off to complete their individual drudgery. Large feather duster in hand, Matilda climbed the grand staircase.

The second floor housed mostly reference and town history books. She started her dusting in the science section. Lost in the repetitive motion and casually reading the book spines in an effort to forget the typewriter and its words, Matilda didn't hear someone approach from behind. When the feeling of being watched pricked up the hairs on her neck and arms, she spun around, wielding the duster like a weapon.

At the sight of him she lost her breath.

Tall as a tree, dressed in easy-going jeans and a sage-green button-down shirt, the man with the freckled face stared back at her, her copy of *The Silence of the Lambs* locked in a tight grip in his long-fingered, strong-looking hands. *Henry.* Much like in the diner, her body reacted strangely: heart racing, limbs tingling, muscles ready to act. She wanted to fling herself forward and touch him. The impulse shocked her, scared her. Thrilled her.

He opened his mouth as if to say something, but didn't.

Matilda took a step back, lowered the duster and lifted her chin. "What are you doing here?"

His face flushed and his eyes dropped to the book in his hands. "I just wanted to return your book. I picked it up after you . . ."

She frowned, resisting the urge to step closer. Why hadn't he left it at the diner? She was going to pick it up at lunch, assuming Pearl had put it in the lost and found. She inhaled quietly. "You could have left it down at the desk," she said curtly. "Or at the diner."

He looked confused, like the ideas had never occurred to him. "Umm . . . yes. I guess I should have. I just . . ." He looked around the small hallway of bookshelves, uncertain energy bouncing between them. Was it always his habit to leave sentences unfinished? "Well, I . . . I wanted to thank you."

"For what?"

"The pie. It was . . . delicious."

"Oh. You're welcome."

Matilda watched him carefully, unsure what to do or say. Henry was the new editor of the town newspaper, which meant his office was on this floor, in the back. *Henry.* The man she'd brought pies to when he stayed with Abby. The man she'd fled The Mad Hash for because looking at him made her want things she wasn't sure existed. He was even taller than she'd imagined—well over six feet—and built like a runner: sinewy muscles stretched over long limbs. A sting of guilt for being rude to him tried to convince her to step closer, to smile, but she didn't like the feelings he stirred in her.

She held out her hand for the book. He stepped closer and placed it into her waiting fingers. His eyes searched her face, flickering with the words of his unfinished sentences. She noticed with a zing of excitement (which she instantly resented) that his eyes were the color of lake water: green, brown, and silver all at once. Involuntarily, she stepped slightly closer. His cheeks burned red under his handsome freckles, his posture shy, but eyes still boldly locked on her face.

When he dropped his hand, she tucked the book into her body with a desperate grip. "Thank you," she mumbled.

He nodded once, slipped his hands into the pockets of his loose-fitting jeans and turned. He was limping. Matilda noticed for the first time the big black cast on his foot. *From the accident that brought him to Abby.* At the sight of his back, she had the sudden urge to stop him, to hurry forward and place her hand on his arm. Her grip on the book tightened as she watched him disappear beyond the shelves. Matilda's breath rushed out of her lungs as she leaned her shoulder into a shelf. Her eyes dropped to the book. There she found a blue Post-it note stuck to the cover that she hadn't noticed before. It read, simply, "I hope you are enjoying this book as much as I did."

She looked back up, her bottom lip trapped in her teeth, heart taking off again.

It was signed *Henry.*

Henry

Henry hurried to the back of the second floor, cursing the awkward drag of his boot cast. By the time he made it to his office, he was starting to perspire and his lungs burned. But not from the rush to escape his own awkwardness. It had taken a great deal of will power to leave Matilda, even after her cold reception.

Dressed in a flattering pink dress that fell to the floor, the color deepening her skin tone, she was as resplendent as she'd been at the diner. Her short stature did nothing to take away from her powerful presence. Something about seeing her standing among all those books felt disturbingly right.

It had taken a couple hours of pep talks before he'd had the courage to leave his office to find her. Once on his way, he'd nearly turned and fled at least a dozen times. But then there she was, standing in the stacks. The sight of her reaching up on her tiptoes, hair swishing across her back as she dusted the books had lit a fire in his gut. A fire of longing and pleasure he couldn't explain and that terrified him to no end. Words rushed to the surface of his mind, gorgeous words about love and beauty and skin. *The sight of her was like the wind: powerful, noisy, and dangerous.* The sound of typewriter keys filled his head.

Henry had stood for nearly a whole minute, watching her, mesmerized and fighting back more words, before she'd sensed him.

Now, he went to his office window and leaned his forehead against the hot glass. The emotions of seeing her again were far worse than the first time. *I should have left the book at The Mad Hash.* More confusing than his own reaction was hers: her bitter hesitance and defensive stance. It wasn't shyness—he could recognize that—it was more like fear, apprehension. There was energy in her eyes and there'd been that one tiny moment when she'd stepped toward him instead of away. What was she thinking and feeling when she looked at him?

Henry had looked her in the eyes, her dark brown eyes, and what he'd seen and felt scared him.

I can't fall for this girl. I can't.

He'd come here to turn his back on the words, to hide from his unknown trauma. For some mysterious reason, all she did was force the words out, spike his cravings. And he certainly hadn't come here to date or . . . or anything else.

He'd have to avoid her. Though it wouldn't be easy working in the same place. But it was necessary. Matilda, the librarian, would not be part of his life. No more breathless encounters, no more thinking about her, and certainly no more letters.

Starting now.

"How was your first official day? Everything go all right?"

"Yeah. Fine. Ronnie showed me everything in about a half hour and then ran out like he'd been sprung from prison."

Abby laughed heartily. "Sounds about right. You saved his life. What's left of it anyway."

Henry smiled as he eased down onto his new brown leather couch. "It looks like nothing has been updated in about twenty years. So I think I'll look into brining the process into the present day; there's got to be a good software out there for layout and such. Do you think that'd be okay?"

"Of course. The town council would be the people to ask for the money. I'm sure they'd be open to it."

"Good."

There was a pause on the line. "Sure is quiet around here," Abby said softly.

Henry frowned. He missed her company too, though he'd never imagined that would be the case. His apartment was so quiet. "Why don't we have lunch tomorrow?" he offered.

"I'd love that." Abby's voice brightened.

"See you then."

"Good night, son."

Henry smiled as he hung up the phone. But the smile faded as his eyes came to rest on the typewriter. He stood and crossed to the desk with the intention of shoving it under his bed. But instead, as if moving of their own accord, his hands picked up a fresh sheet of paper, rolled it into place.

He sat, hands trembling above the keys.

Don't do it. Don't!

His eyes moved to a stack of books he'd unpacked the night before. On top, *A Thousand Sleepless Nights*. He still hadn't read it. Not one word. It terrified him to even touch it. He looked back and forth between the typewriter and the book. Two things he could not explain, but that felt as connected to him as his own hands.

Now, in his dark apartment, his hands begging to write, Henry groaned. He'd been unable to think of anything but Matilda all day. His earlier convictions seemed foolish now. How could he turn his back on feelings like this? Feelings he'd read about, dreamed about his whole life, but never felt. Was it some kind of betrayal to deny them?

His fingers landed on the keys and ran away with his words.

Matilda

The doorbell rang. Matilda was finishing up her dinner of fried chicken and mashed potatoes, with lots of gravy. Something about tossing the chicken in Jetty's special flour and spice mix in a big paper bag and standing over the stove frying it in coconut oil (another of Jetty's unique cooking tricks) soothed her. Not to mention the actual consumption.

She wiped grease from her fingers and answered the door.

"Parker!" Her stomach dropped. She hadn't seen him much in the last two weeks. She wasn't sure how to feel around him.

With his shoulders slumped forward, hands in pockets, he gave her a pleading look. "Hey, Matilda. Can I come in?"

"Uh . . ." *No. Go away.* "Sure. Come in. Are you hungry? I have fried chicken."

"I can't pass that up. You know how much I love your fried chicken."

The statement tugged harshly on her emotions. She shut the door and took a breath before turning. He said, "The house looks really nice. You've done a good job getting it back how it used to be."

"Thanks," she said, leading the way to the kitchen. Matilda made him a plate and set it in front of a stool at the island. He sat. She stayed behind the island, leaning against the sink. The reverse of their last encounter.

"Why are you here?" she asked kindly, wanting to get this over with.

Parker took a bite of chicken and chewed thoughtfully. "That's so good," he said and swallowed. Then to answer her question, "Thea fell asleep watching TV."

Matilda caught his eyes and looked away. "That's not really a good reason. Your pregnant wife falls asleep and you sneak out to your ex-finance's house?" It sounded harsher than she had intended.

Parker frowned, pushed at his potatoes. "I didn't sneak. It's not like that. I told you—"

"I know. Sorry. I didn't mean it like that." Matilda's throat tightened. She swallowed.

Parker wiped his chin with the cloth napkin Matilda had set by his plate. He said, "I can't stop worrying about you. Thea said you looked bad today and wouldn't talk about what was bothering you. Believe me, I'd like to stop worrying about you, but I still care. Is that wrong?"

Something about this made Matilda both heavily sad and deeply comforted. "No, no I don't think it's wrong. I appreciate that. I just don't want Thea to worry. And I don't want you mixed up in all the gossip and speculation."

"I don't care about that." He put his elbows on the sides of his plate and leaned toward her, his expression intent and receptive. "Thea told me you're not sleeping."

Matilda closed her eyes and exhaled. She shifted her weight, folding her arms. "Just some nightmares."

"Want to talk about them?"

Yes. "No, it's okay. I'm sure it will pass."

Parker's jaw tightened, his hands balling into fists. "Did someone hurt you, Tilly?" His eyes moved down to her left leg, to the scar exposed since she wore only cotton shorts and a t-shirt. She wanted to cross her legs and hide it, but resisted.

"That's just a stupid rumor."

"Is it really?"

"Yes."

"Then what happened?"

"Why does everyone need to know what happened so badly?"

"Why won't you tell anyone? They'd stop gossiping if they knew the truth. You don't have to be so stubbornly mysterious about everything."

Matilda pressed her lips together. They stared at each other for several tense moments. If she told him, he and Thea would just worry more. She'd never hear the end of it; they'd never leave her alone. She had enough attention already. She didn't want her only friends looking at her like she'd lost her mind.

The house ticked and settled.

Parker exhaled forcibly and looked back down at his plate. "Fine. Keep your secrets." He stood. "Thanks for the chicken."

When he started to walk away Matilda felt a flash of panic. "Parker?" She ran after him.

He turned, eyes wide with surprise.

"I can't talk about it." Tears burned her eyes. She felt stupidly embarrassed.

Empathetic pain crossed Parker's face. He reached out and pulled her into his arms. Sobs rose in her chest. A few escaped. Parker held her tighter. "Shh. It's okay. It's okay."

Matilda clung to him, desperate for the comfort. Not the comfort of a lover, but that of a friend. For several silent minutes, they stood there in the kitchen, the sun setting and Parker stroking her hair. Outside, some kids shouted happily to each other. Cars drove by.

Finally, he pulled back a little and took her face in his hands. "You don't have to. Okay?"

"Okay." She nodded. "Thanks." She sniffed. Parker smiled a little.

"Do you want to come stay with Thea and me? Instead of being alone in this old house."

"No, that's okay. Really. I love this place. I want to be here."

"Okay. Do you want me to stay for a bit? We could watch a movie or something. We were good at that back in the day."

"We were. We were really good as friends, weren't we?"

Parker smiled broadly, that Hollywood smile. He pushed her hair back from her wet face. "Yeah. You were my best friend. It'd be nice to do that again."

Matilda returned his smile. "I found an old copy of *Barefoot in the Park* in Jetty's room."

"Who doesn't like Robert Redford? You know, people tell me I look like him."

Matilda laughed, "No way. He's much better looking."

Parker laughed heartily as he put his arm around her shoulders. They went to the couch and sat close together. His expression sobered slightly. "When you are ready—to talk, I mean—I'm here. You can tell me anything, and I'll try to help."

Matilda's chest tightened with gratitude. She nodded. "Thanks for that."

Clack. Clack. ClackClackClackClackClack. DING.

With a strangled gasp, Matilda opened her eyes. She'd fallen asleep on the couch. Parker was gone; he'd put a blanket over her. And right in front of her, the typewriter was alive, typing more words.

She griped the edge of the cushion, not moving, her heart beating so fast it hurt. She watched, breath trapped in her lungs, as the keys did their dance.

If I called to you from the prison of the night, would you answer? Would you save me from myself? I don't know what to do with the beating of my heart, each pump of hot blood begging that I go to you.

I can't find the courage to go.

I'm frightened of what you will say. I'm terrified of the texture of the skin on your neck, the depth in your eyes. I could loose myself, fall forever, and never know where I began and you ended.

Doesn't that sound entirely blissful?

Yet there is something terrifying about reaching out for bliss because what if it's not real? What if it's impossible? What if I reach for you and my hand grasps nothing?

Please . . .

Come to me.

Seduce me.

Rescue me.

Henry

The room smelled of burning paper.

Henry pushed back from the desk and threw open the window to suck in long breaths of cool evening air. Instead of a catharsis, the words he'd put to paper only made his feelings boil. If he knew where Matilda lived, it was quite possible he'd be pounding on her door right now. If only to see her before she slammed it in his face.

You are pathetic. Perhaps the accident damaged your head after all.

He hadn't acted like himself since his car rolled in the rain. He'd let an old woman take him in, nurse him, and become a friend. He was attached to Abby. And now, this librarian. A woman surrounded by words he shouldn't think, let alone write, his desire to know her swelling in his chest.

Go back to Michigan. Right now. Go.

I can't.

Henry stared out at the quiet night.

By some miracle, Henry managed to get through the rest of the week without running into Matilda. He took the rear fire exit stairs and kept his office door shut. Abby drove in every day for lunch, and Henry spent the entire hour scanning for Matilda, begging the universe that she wouldn't show up at The Mad Hash or Estelle's. Abby pestered him about being distracted, but he brushed off her inquiries.

He couldn't remember a less productive week. Hours passed painfully slow but also vanished into the abyss of distracted thought. He would force himself to focus on a task and soon find that an hour had passed where all he'd done was stare out the window thinking of Matilda. Immediately, he'd assign himself something different with high hopes of an appropriate, productive distraction. But it never worked for more than a few moments. This was not the best way to go about a new job.

He could *feel* her, her presence in the building, like a fog seeping into his office, clouding his vision. A few times he caught himself swatting at the air around his face, trying to rid himself of it.

Saturday was salvation. He didn't have to go anywhere near the library. But he did have to fill a whole day to avoid thinking of her, or going out looking for her. First thing in the morning he dialed Abby's number.

"Morning, son!"

"Good morning. Does Silent Fields have a bookstore?"

Abby sighed forlornly. "Sadly, no, not anymore. We did. Booker's Bookshop, owned by Mr. Riley Booker. Great guy, great shop, but Riley liked to sneak out back and smoke ten cigarettes a day. He died of lung cancer two years ago. He didn't have any family and no one wanted to take on the shop. So it closed."

Henry's heart sank. "That's really too bad." *How did I move to a place without a bookstore?* One of so many offenses piling up around his rash decision to come to Silent Fields.

"Yes, it is."

"Are there any others close?"

"Let's see . . . I think there's one in El Dorado. About an hour's drive. You want to go?"

"I'd love to, but I don't want to put you out." Henry's rented Buick had been towed back to the rental company, a total loss. He hadn't thought he'd need to purchase a car, but with no bookstore in town, he'd have to get one.

"It's no trouble, you know that. I was just going to work on my quilt today, but I'd much rather go to the bookstore with you."

"Really?"

"Really."

"Okay. You are too good to me." Abby laughed, and then Henry added, "Let's also stop and buy me a car. Then you won't have to shuttle me, I can shuttle you."

"Deal. See you in a half hour."

Henry parked his used Toyota Tacoma in the reserved spot outside the Mayor House. It was a major improvement on the old Buick, though still about ten years old with over eighty thousand miles on it. But the black paint looked good, and the interior wasn't bad. So it would do. He imagined filling the entire bed with boxes of books.

He and Abby had spent a pleasant few hours in the little bookshop in El Dorado. Henry found solace in the shelves and steady comfort in the weight of each book in his arms. They'd had lunch and then found a place to buy his truck. Now, getting out of the truck, he balanced his twelve new books in his arms up to his apartment and set them on his desk.

The euphoric spell of book buying was broken the moment he saw the two letters he'd written to Matilda laying face down next to the typewriter. *Hidden sins.* It'd taken everything in him not to write another one every night that week. He moved his hands from the new books to the typewriter, feeling his restraint wavering. With a long, lonely evening yawning out in front of him, he knew he'd give in to the temptation if he didn't find something else to do. He could sit and read one of his new books, but that kept him close to the typewriter. His ankle was doing much better this week, so maybe a walk. It'd be good to do something somewhat physical. If he walked long enough, maybe he'd be too tired to want to write when he returned.

Henry grabbed his jacket and left, ignoring the dark clouds on the horizon.

Matilda

*B*aby plants all in a row, ready for planting. Matilda turned the rich soil of Jetty's large garden plot with a shovel. Her hair was tied into a messy knot on top of her head and her running shorts and faded Silent Fields Library T-shirt were spotted with dirt. Her feet were bare, mud filling the spaces between her toes.

The evening was cool and mild, a sweet spring breeze rolling through the tops of the large oaks and maples bordering the big yard. Birds gossiped and kids were laughing and yelling in nearby backyards.

For the first time all week, Matilda took a full breath and forgot for a moment about the typewriter. She'd been anxious every moment of every day, sleeping poorly, waiting for another letter. Every small noise sounded like the bounce of a key. In her dreams, the words came to life and pulled her into their warm, seductive arms. And then they devoured her whole.

With a grunt, Matilda tossed the shovel aside. She planted the two tomatoes, one basil, one parsley, one eggplant, one cabbage, one zucchini, and two pumpkins. The soft cold dirt in her hands, the breeze on her neck. *Therapy,* she thought. Then another thought: *This is the first garden I've ever planted without Jetty.*

As Matilda patted down the dirt around the last pumpkin vine, thunder growled. She turned to look at the graying sky and frowned. A small storm would be great for the new plants—soak the soil for a big drink—but any bad wind or hard rain might kill them all.

Matilda stood and stretched her back, watching the sky. The wind picked up bringing with it the smell of coming rain. She hurried to put away her tools in the tiny, sagging garage. As she finished, the rain started. Hard and fast.

She ran to the cover of the back porch. Already, her infant plants were sagging under the assault of the rain. "Oh, no. No. Stop. They don't deserve a watery grave." The garden was solid tradition. She and Jetty had planted it together every year. Something about it being ruined the first year Matilda had to plant it alone made her want to yell. Also, it felt like a bad omen. The garden *had* to survive.

After a breath, she dashed out into the downpour. The rain pelted her skin, sharp and cold. She ran back to the garage and threw up the creaky old wooden door. She gathered two shovels, a hoe, and a rake. Hurrying back to the garden, she drove the handles of the tools into the earth in the four corners of the plot, praying they stayed upright in the softening soil. Glancing down at her plants, sodden and pathetic looking, she yelled, "Don't die!"

Back in the garage she rummaged through the shelves and bins. "Tarp, tarp—there's gotta be a tarp of some kind!"

"Matilda?"

She spun around, pushing the hair out of her eyes, her heart suddenly in her throat. "Henry? What are you doing here?!"

Henry bent his tall frame and stepped into the shelter of the garage. He was soaking wet, his messy blondish hair dark with water and plastered to his face. "I was walking. I saw you running into the garage. It looked like something was wrong."

Her mind didn't want to function. Henry—here in her garage, in the rain. "Uh . . . I'm just trying to save my poor garden. I just planted it. The rain . . ."

Henry looked out the small grimy window on the side of the garage that faced the backyard. He squinted through the darkness. "You need a tarp. Two actually."

"That's what I'm looking for!" Matilda said as she turned back to the sparse piles of junk. Henry started looking too. Matilda wanted to tell him to leave. She was uncomfortable with him this close to her, but there wasn't time if she was going to save her little plants.

"Got 'em!" he yelled a moment later, already heading to the backyard, his boot cast squishing in the wet grass. Matilda followed with a length of twine. Thunder shook the ground.

"Does it always rain like it's the end of the world here?" Henry called out.

Matilda smiled. "Only sometimes."

Henry nodded, smiling back. "We need to tent the plants. One here and one here." He pointed, dividing the garden in two. Matilda nodded, seeing how that would be more effective than just a canopy. Quickly, they adjusted the garden tools to act as tent poles. Henry held out the corner of a tarp to her, their fingers bumping on the exchange; a little charge shot up her arm. She hurried to spread the tarp over the garden. Henry tugged back a little. "Do you have any stakes or big rocks?" he asked.

Matilda ran to the garage and came back with wooden stakes marked with the names of plants. She and Jetty had painted them when she was in elementary school. "These?"

"That'll work."

They cut lengths of twine, tying one end to the tarp corners, the others to the stakes. Henry urged the stakes deep into the soil. Soon the two tents were in place. The wind flapped the blue plastic, but so far they were doing the job.

A skeleton of lightning flashed overhead, close enough that Matilda felt the charge in her stomach. "Inside!" she yelled. Running fast, she bolted into the small mudroom off the kitchen, Henry only a step behind her. He closed the door behind them. Matilda hurried to the kitchen, ignoring the sound of muddy water dripping from her shorts and T-shirt onto the floor as she went. She leaned over the sink and peered out the window. The plants appeared protected, the makeshift shelter holding.

She turned. Henry stood in the doorway to the kitchen watching her, his eyes intense. She suddenly felt shy and exposed. When she ran, her limp was exaggerated. He must have seen it. His eyes moved down her body and back up. Was he looking for a deformity like many did when they noticed the limp? She pulled at the bottoms of her shorts. "Umm . . . thank you."

He nodded. "Of course."

Awkwardness had her circling the kitchen. "Sit. I'll make hot chocolate. Or coffee. Is it too late for coffee? Hot chocolate seems more appropriate with the weather and all. Or maybe there's tea. No, I didn't buy any tea. Or coffee, come to think of it. Jetty never drank it." Flustered and rambling, she didn't notice Henry approach. When she turned around, can of cocoa in her hands, he was right behind her, his body nearly touching hers. She lifted her chin to look up at him and felt her heart stutter at how good it felt to do it. As if that were the only movement her neck had been designed for.

Henry's breathing came in rapid pulls. And was he shivering? Or was she? He lifted a hand to her hair, pulled something. "A leaf," he said, his voice so quiet. He held the leaf awkwardly in his hand. She felt compelled to take it. Her wet fingers met his and she didn't pull away. Her eyes studied his face, the puzzle of freckles. Her breath caught. *Heaven help me, there are freckles on his lips!* A few dark and a few light marks embedded into his pale plump lips, like chocolate shavings on mounds of sorbet. She took her hand from his and touched the largest one on his upper lip. He closed his eyes, sighed, his warm breath moving onto her cold fingertips. A flash of heat moved down her body and a thousand emotions rocked her backward. She bumped into the counter, still gripping the cocoa tin. "Get out," she breathed.

"Matilda . . ." Henry looked at her with those sharp eyes, more brown than green in the dark kitchen. He stepped closer, hand lifted.

"Get *out*!" she yelled, the loudness of her voice startling them both.

Henry's gaze lingered for a moment. Matilda couldn't stand the hurt she saw there, the hurt she'd put there. She looked away. She listened as his shoe and cast squeaked on the tile. The back door slammed shut.

Matilda sunk to the floor, unable to stand any longer. A sickening blackness raged up inside her, turning her blood to poison. Her body shook from cold, from the broiling emotions, and from the withdrawal of Henry. She wanted him back, wanted him to hold her; she wanted to never see him again. Mostly, she didn't want to feel this way, scared and uncertain and other things she couldn't define. Being around him made her feel too many things.

Nothing makes sense anymore.

Tears came; she fought them as long as she could. Then she was sobbing loudly, the boisterous rain ensuring the breakdown didn't reach the ears of her neighbors.

Lightning flashed. Once. Twice.

She lay down on the frigid, wet floor, hugging the cocoa and hoping it never stopped raining like the world was ending.

Henry

Henry plowed out into the rain and broke into a run, difficult in his cast, and painful. His muscles defied him, stiff and unresponsive. His heart refused to cooperate, too busy beating for Matilda. He stopped under a tree and leaned forward. Her fingers on his lips. *Good grief.* It hurt to think of it, doubling him over for several minutes before he recovered. He forced himself to run again. All the way to his lonely apartment.

Pushing open the door, Henry went straight to the shower. He turned it to cold. The heat of her touch threatened to burn him from the inside out. The cold rain should have helped, but the farther he ran from her, the hotter and more uncomfortable he felt. He stripped off his wet clothes and stepped into the freezing stream. Pressing his teeth together, he took the punishment. After nearly fifteen minutes, stiff and skin tinged blue, he shut off the water.

He hurried to put on some clothes, just boxers and cotton pajama pants, and dropped into his desk chair. The words. Oh, the words. They wouldn't shut up.

Henry glared at the typewriter.

Waiting. Expecting. Demanding.

Rubbing at his cold, rigid hands, he looked at the keys. *M-A-T-I-L-D-A.* His eyes jumped from letter to letter. What had possessed him to stand so close to her? To touch her? And why had anger replaced the passion he'd seen in her eyes?

What was this unyielding hold she had on him? He'd said barely twenty words to her, and seen her for mere moments. It wasn't normal; it wasn't sane. Yet denying the feelings didn't feel rational either.

He touched his own lips, feeling the echo of Matilda's fingers, the impression of her eyes. Eyes the color of wet tree bark, dark brown, but speckled with light. Round and alert, they reminded him of owl eyes. Sharp and intelligent, her eyes reminded him of only her.

And looking down at her, her body a magnetic breath away. Good grief, was she short! Barefooted, the top of her head barely reached the bottom of his sternum. But the way she tilted her confident chin to look up at him—it somehow closed the distance, made *him* feel small.

Henry shook his head. Not that any of it mattered. He'd moved in too quickly, frightened her. She must think him an absolute jerk. *Why did I step so close, touch her hair?* He thought back to the dark kitchen. It had smelled of rain and cinnamon. He could hear her breaths as if in his ear. He'd been pulled to her, unable to keep his distance, unable to listen to normal social conventions.

He just wanted to touch her.

You're a complete freak! Who does that to a woman he barely knows? She'll never even look at you again.

Presumptuously, his hands shot forward and grabbed the edges of the typewriter. The metal was so smooth, like polished stone. Like Matilda's wet hair. He pulled it to the edge of the desk, knocking over the stack of new books. He rolled fresh paper into place. His hands hovered over the keys, hummingbirds looking for nectar, trembling.

A new letter poured out, easy, fresh as dew.

When it was finished, Henry lifted his hands from the keys, his fingertips red and tender, like new blisters. He looked at the words, feeling every letter. *Go back to her. Go back. Apologize. Make it right.* But he couldn't find the will to lift himself from the creaky desk chair.

Matilda

Matilda couldn't stop shaking. In touching Henry, she'd rattled something loose inside her. *Go back in. Go back!* she scolded. She couldn't account for the crippling fear the encounter with Henry had flushed out, forming a swamp around her heart. She had never felt anything like this. She didn't know what to do with it. It didn't have a name.

Nameless.

So she pushed it away.

After pulling herself from the kitchen floor, carefully returning the cocoa to its spot in the cupboard, she showered as fast as she could. Still trembling, she climbed into bed, pulling the covers around her. She rolled over to face the windows and stared unblinking at the rain on the glass. Her eyes filled with tears again, but she refused them. "Not allowed," she whispered. "Cease and desist."

She shut her eyes, begging sleep to come. But all she saw was Henry's lips, his hand reaching out to her after she pushed him away. All she heard was the sad sound of the back door shutting echoing in her head. The initial slam and then the softer settling. Two beats. SLAM–bump. *Stu–pid.* Matilda forced the insulting sound from her head, focusing instead on the pound of the rain, the grumble of thunder, now farther away.

He helped me, and I yelled at him. Sent him out to get struck by lightning. Please don't get struck by lightning, Henry. But having him so close, on the sacred ground of her kitchen . . . She'd wanted things she had never imagined before. She longed for him to sit in her kitchen and drink hot chocolate she made for him. So intensely had she wanted him to kiss her, to hold her. She wanted to watch him gather their wet

127

clothes from the tile and put them in the washer. She wanted him to be there in the morning and every day until she took her last breath.

What is happening?

She'd never wanted those things with Parker. Things had always been pleasant between them, but she'd never felt the need for him constricting her chest. She'd never imagined her dying moment in his arms.

For a split second, she felt a thrill. She'd wanted more from love. Was she getting it now? Was Henry the answer to her desire? The thrill quickly dissipated. Something about Henry frightened her. *Should I feel scared?* It didn't feel right to be so scared. But had anything since Jetty's death felt right?

Then, cutting into her thoughts, *that* sound.

Matilda sucked in a breath, her body stiff as stone.

The typewriter.

No, no, no. Not again. Not now.

She didn't want to go, but how could she stay away? The typewriter was working again, throwing out another letter. What would this one say? What gossamer words would it spin into existence tonight?

Matilda slipped from her bed, her feet treading softly down the stairs.

ClackClackClackClackClack. DING.

Her heart beat with an odd mixture of fear and excitement. The words the typewriter had already written had taken hold of her. She wanted more, but she knew she shouldn't. These words were unnatural. Impossible. Such impossible words.

The white paper lay back over the platen, waiting. One last key depressed, the typebar slicing into the paper. Finished. Outside, the rain fell. *Why does it keep raining?* For a long, turbulent moment, Matilda listened to it and looked at the paper. The words hidden in the shadows.

Leave them there.

Hand trembling, Matilda reached for the letter. Her heart might beat through her ribs; her own breath was now louder than the pattering rain.

```
I tear you up, a million parchment pieces. I put you
back together.
```

I blow you over, twist you into knots with my
cruel winds. I unwind you.

I destroy you, hurricane to your luscious
landscape. I regrow you.

But are you ever the same? Am I? What do we
do to each other? Can it be stopped? Would this
sucking wound in my chest close if I kissed you? If
I touched you, hand along slick skin, would we find
joy or sorrow?

The rain beats on the roof—it sounds like your
frightened heart. Like mine. The thunder speaks too
loudly. I can't hear you anymore.

But I can't let you go no matter how it rips,
twists, or destroys. I want to believe we can fix
it, smooth out our rough edges.

What do you believe?

Are you there?

Matilda dropped to the couch, a hand to her chest. *I am here. Who
are you?* The room stilled, the sound of the rain lost to the rush in her
ears. She saw Henry's lips, his freckles, in her head.

Henry?

No, not possible.

I'm losing my mind.

Matilda lowered the paper. It hurt to breathe. Her skin felt cold.
The letters had come after seeing him, after the times they had been
together. Coincidence? Her eyes moved to the keys. Her fingers itched
to type a response.

She wanted to ask one question: *Is it you?*

But what if she got an answer?

Matilda stood quickly, dropping the paper to the coffee table.

Maybe she was so alone, so sad, that she'd conjured this whole
letter thing to comfort herself. Her mind was so broken she not only
didn't remember a huge chunk of time, but now she'd created magical,
romantic letters from a mysterious stranger. Before all this, Jetty, on
her deathbed, had spoken of passionate love. Matilda had been willing
to leave everything in the middle of the night to find it.

Now six years missing and these letters.

But perhaps none of it was real. Had the want to find love forced
her mind into madness?

I've gone crazy chasing things that don't exist.

What other explanation was there?

There was no way to consider romance when her life was such a junkyard. Romance meant opening your life, your heart, your mind. What would she say when he asked about her past or her plans for the future? There was no room for passion and love when each day was a scrappy battle of survival.

Matilda gathered the three letters. She should burn them, but couldn't bring herself to destroy the stunning words, real or imagined. Folding the papers in half, she pulled one of her favorite childhood books from the shelves. *A Second Treasury of the World's Greatest Fairy Tales.* An old, large volume with vibrant illustrations that instantly reminded her of nights snuggled next to Jetty while she read the enchanted tales. Matilda opened the book, placed the letters inside, and closed it with a resolved snap.

"No more craziness," she whispered to herself. "This ends now. Get a grip. Be normal. Jetty is gone. Six years are missing. You're alone. Move on. It's okay." She looked at the picture of Cinderella running down the stairs of a grand castle, her carriage waiting. "Henry is not your prince charming. It's not real."

Matilda slid the book back into its spot.

It's not real.

Henry

So . . ." Abby said, looking sideways at Henry as they walked, a curious tone in her voice. "What's gotten into you? You've got bags under your eyes and you've barely said a word. Not that you're much of a talker anyway, but today you are . . . reserved."

"I'm fine," Henry said absently.

"Uh huh." A few steps of silence. "I stopped at the library earlier. Matilda set me up with a great new stack of books."

Henry's feet stuttered, his face contorting. He lifted his head to Abby. "That's nice," he mumbled as normally as possible.

She narrowed her eyes at him. "Yes. She's fabulous. Had on the prettiest skirt—full and long and lots of colors, like a gypsy or something. And that hair! Gorgeous. I've always thought she was the prettiest girl in town."

Henry only nodded as visions of Matilda moved through his mind. The silky wet texture of her hair. The citrus smell of her shampoo. Her fingers on his lips.

Abby pressed on. Henry wished he could stop her. "Smart too. Have you two talked at all?"

Henry stopped. "Why? Did she say something?"

Abby stopped too, facing him. She crossed her arms. "I knew something was going on. What happened?"

Henry shoved his hands in his pockets and looked at the sidewalk pavers. "Nothing."

"Hmm. Sure." Abby took a step closer. "She's had it rough."

Henry didn't look up. He thought of the scar on Matilda's leg, the ones on her arms and faint ones on her cheek. Her limp. He'd seen the embarrassment when he noticed them last night. Seeing her scars

131

felt like an accidental privilege. A secret she'd shared unwittingly, a confidence he couldn't breech. He thought of the fear in her eyes when he'd gotten too close.

Lifting his head, he looked toward the library. "Wonder what happened to her."

"You've had it rough too," Abby said quietly.

Henry finally looked at her. Abby's eyes were soft and understanding.

"I can see it," she said. "You both have *that* look. And you have scars too, old and new."

Suddenly, it smelled of rain and cocoa. *We both have scars.*

Abby tugged on his arm. "What is it with you and Tilly?"

"Nothing," he said and turned on a false smile. "I'm starving. Let's eat, huh?"

Abby lowered her hand, obviously not buying a word of his evasion. "Sometimes it takes someone else to heal our pain. Sometimes we can't do it alone."

The words smacked him hard. A knot of emotions formed in his gut. He looked over her head at the street. A few cars passed by slowly. Everything seemed to move slowly in Silent Fields. Except when he was around Matilda. Then time seemed to disappear completely. He wanted to turn and look back at the library, but didn't. To Abby, he said nothing.

Finally, she cleared her throat. "Well, I can't wait another second for some of Estelle's fresh donuts. We better get to the bakery before she sells out."

Henry nodded, still not looking at her, and followed as she continued down the sidewalk. When she wasn't looking, he glanced over his shoulder. Matilda sat on the steps of the library, eating her lunch and watching him. Their eyes met, held for half a breath. At the same moment they looked away.

In the gauze of sleep, the pain always returned with a ferocity that left Henry sweating and breathless. Tangled in his sheet, he dreamed the thing he often did, the details vague, cloudy, but the pain blindingly real. He might have been in a car—it felt like a car—but it was so hard to tell through the coagulated gray shadows. Everything looked blurry, like seeing through murky water, shapes distorted, possibly imagined. Someone was crying, another yelling. Was it him? Maybe. The voices meshed into a discordant, warbling fog.

Besides the hot pain ravaging his body, Henry felt a paralyzing need to help someone. As white and burning as the sun, that need. But who and how? Was there someone with him or was he alone? Despite the pain, he managed to reach out his hand. There was a tremor of heat, like a body just under his palm . . . and then he woke.

Ripped away.

Henry blinked at his ceiling, gasping. "Leave me alone," he whispered. "Leave me alone!" Parched, he untangled his legs from the sheet and got out of bed. He threw his soaked shirt to the floor, content to let the cool air-conditioned air assault his moist skin. He gulped down a glass of water, his heart still pounding. He set the glass down on the white quartz and pressed his palms flat to the surface. Leaning forward, weight into his hands, he let his head drop between his shoulders.

He'd never had nightmares as a kid, a point his foster parents always remarked on. The other kids often woke screaming, crying, and shaking, but never Henry. Was it because he didn't want to be yelled at or punished for one more thing? Or was it because sleep was a refuge? His waking hours were hard enough, and sleep was his only peaceful escape. Whether deliberately or subconsciously, he never let the horrors of the day follow him into his bed. What few dreams he remembered having as a child were of space and nature and books. Loving words, freely given affection.

His first nightmare came the first night he slept at Abby's house. That nightmare felt like the worst kind of betrayal, his own mind causing such fear. Twisted and wrong. In those sweaty, breathless moments after his first nightmare, Henry had wished for the days of his childhood, something he'd never done before.

The dream was always the same; since that night, it never varied. And the shock of it always equally debilitating.

Leaving the kitchen, Henry crossed to his new bookshelf and sat on the floor. He leaned back into the shelves, feeling the wood press into his back high and low, jabbing into his muscles. He let his legs flop out in front, his arms hang limp. Closing his eyes, Henry breathed in the scent of the pages. *One . . . two . . . three . . . four.* After twenty-five deep breaths, his heart had finally returned to normal pace.

Silence hovered in his apartment. Light from the moon and street-lights cut through the blinds in jagged lines. The space felt enormous; it felt like a coffin crushed by two tons of earth. The loneliness made him crazy.

Henry pushed up to his feet. His hand was on the doorknob before he stopped himself. *I can't. I can't.* He wanted to go to Matilda. It'd been a week since the night of the storm and he felt every minute of that space. The idea of walking down the sidewalk to her house felt so real in his head he could almost smell the basil in her garden.

He backed away from the door, dragging his hands through his hair.

The green glow of the clock on the oven caught his attention. *Only two-twenty. Go back to bed!* Henry's gaze moved over the rumpled bed, the windows, and settled on his typewriter. He walked to it. Proof of his last dalliance with the machine still lay curved back over the platen, relaxed and glowing, like a woman fallen asleep. In the light, the paper was the color of Matilda's skin, the typewriter her black hair. He blushed at the comparison and shook his head, feeling delirious.

Henry pulled the paper from the machine, turned it upside down on the desk. He moved to turn away, but couldn't. He sat, put a new sheet of paper in the typewriter. The silence swelled, the machine pulsed with demanding potential. The words, how quickly they came.

```
If I stand close to you, the air trembles. It begs
me to stand closer. My body demands to be closer to
yours, to feel your spiraling heat, to taste your
caramel skin. To be lost inside you for a million
years.
    It wouldn't be enough, those years.
    It is impossible not to touch you.
    Yet my fingers have known only one ephemeral
moment of connection. Is it selfish to think of
you next to me, to imagine the sound of your sigh?
It's easy to be selfish alone here in the dead of
night. It's simple to imagine there are no obstacles
in our way, that the rising sun will evaporate the
complications of the past.
```

```
    It's easy to type these words in the privacy of
the darkness. Just secret yearnings between me and
the keys.
    This desire feels like a harbinger.
    What news will it bring?
    What future does it foretell?
```

Henry pushed away from the desk with a pitiful groan. Body flushed with heat, desire so carefully kept at bay let loose. His chest hurt. He couldn't be here another moment; he couldn't be where he wanted to.

Henry threw on some shoes and a shirt and fled.

Matilda

Matilda looked down at the fourth letter. Her heart was racing, her mind spinning. The air in the living room was warm.

Stop it. Stop doing this.

She felt the sensual words in the space behind her heart; she felt them humming in her hips. She felt her hold on reality slipping away.

Hot anger rushed up her throat and she screamed, shattering the nighttime silence. She roughly threw the paper, which fluttered weakly and unsatisfactorily to the floor. She picked up her copy of *A Thousand Sleepless Nights*, which she'd left next to the typewriter, and threw it across the room too. It slammed into the front picture window and thudded to the floor.

Matilda closed her eyes, regretting her anger, but not knowing how else to feel. Determined to act, even if futile, she sat on the couch and faced the typewriter. Her hands lifted to the keys.

```
Who are you?
```

She typed the words and held her breath. Everything in the room seemed to pause and lean in to watch the keys. Waiting.

A minute ticked by. Another. Five.

Nothing came.

Something in Matilda's chest deflated. Expecting an answer was pure craziness, but what it meant that there was none was worse. *I'm making this up. It's all in my head.*

Matilda lifted her eyes and looked desperately around the room.

What do I do?

She thought of going to Dr. Wells.

She thought of going to Parker and Thea.

What would happen?

Matilda leaned forward, wanting again to cry out in agony. "Jetty," she whispered.

A sound made her startle and look up. Was that movement in the corner?

Heart now racing uncontrollably, Matilda felt dizzy, scared. *I'm hallucinating.* She looked frantically around the room, her blood pressure so high she could feel the rush of blood in her wrists and throat.

Stop it. Calm down.

Calm down.

Another movement just out of her line of sight. She choked on a scream.

"Tilly?"

Matilda jumped up and spun around.

Jetty stood in the corner, near the window, hidden in shadow.

Matilda blinked. "Jetty?" she breathed.

Jetty smiled.

Matilda turned and ran.

Henry

Henry walked along the dark streets until the pain in his ankle brought tears to his eyes. He wished he could run, fast, until his lungs burned. Walking was not fast enough. Despite the movement, his blood was still saturated with Matilda, the need to go to her as strong as before. He jerked to a stop outside of town, along a lonely road flanked by sapling cornfields. Crickets sang, fireflies glowed.

Hands on knees, dragging air into his lungs, Henry closed his eyes and scolded himself. *You're broken. Stop it. You can't have her. Why would she want you? You have nothing to offer but problems. Nightmares, panic attacks, and an orphan's emptiness.*

Abby's words came back to him to argue with his own lecture. *Sometimes it takes someone else to heal our pain. Sometimes we can't do it alone.* He had always healed himself, or at least tried. No parents, no siblings, not even a childhood best friend, made him a solitary figure. Before Abby, there'd been no one, at least no one he could remember. But Abby was still a friend, kept at a comfortable distance as friends always are. But a woman, a lover, a partner, a wife—that required an opening of the soul, exposure to the deepest levels. Or at least it should. *True love demands it; love that lasts requires it.* He wanted to write down the words.

Henry stood up, his chest still heaving hard.

Is that what I want from Matilda? Love?

He shook his head, embarrassed at such a gigantic leap. *I don't know her. Attraction is one thing . . . love is another. I'm not in love. Stop it.*

Legs unsteady, knees nearly giving way, Henry turned and walked slowly back toward home.

Matilda

Matilda stumbled out of the house and jumped onto her bike. She needed to move fast. She needed to not have seen Jetty's ghost or created letters on a typewriter she didn't know why she had.

Lost in her bike-daze, Matilda didn't see the figure walking in her path until it was too late. Two feet, long legs. Instant panic. Startled, she overcorrected, jerking the bike hard to the right. The wheels caught a patch of gravel, spun, and then stuck. She and the bike went down hard.

Matilda heard a male voice swear. She lay tangled in metal, looking up at the stars. Pain at her knee and elbow told her she had some nasty road rash. She thought, *I'm not wearing my helmet.* And then, *I don't have control of my own mind.*

"Are you okay? I'm so—*Matilda?*"

Matilda lifted her head. "Henry!" She dropped her head back to the road. Her heart suddenly flying, making her scrapes throb all the more. *Henry? Really?*

He dropped to a knee beside her, lifting the bike off her body. "Are you hurt?" he said quietly, and with such soft tenderness Matilda felt an ache rise in her chest.

"I'm okay. Just some scrapes." She sat up to inspect her wounds. "What are you doing out here? It's the middle of the night!"

In the shadowy light, she saw him smile and found herself staring, wishing she could see his freckles better. His hair was wet, spiking out in all directions. He smelled of sweat, metallic and sharp, like a child come in from the playground.

"Couldn't sleep," he said. "Went for a walk. Guess I got lost in my thoughts. Didn't see you coming. Sorry about that." He smiled again and Matilda leaned forward automatically, drawn into him. "What's your excuse?" he added.

She thought of Jetty's figure in the corner and looked away from him. "About the same, I guess." Her eyes dropped to her right knee. A large section was raw and red, already oozing. Bending the knee slightly made her wince.

"That's pretty nasty." Henry bent closer to her leg, she stiffened. His eyes moved to her other leg. "Looks like you've had worse, though." He pointed to the jagged line on her left shin. Matilda's hand instinctively went to cover it. She looked away, unable to call up words to explain the scar.

After a beat of awkwardness, he said, "I'll help you home." Henry stood and held out a hand. Like the rest of him, his fingers were long, his palm milky white and deeply lined.

Matilda started to reach up for his hand and then stopped herself. No matter how fate wanted to push them together, she refused to give in. "I got it," she mumbled as she pushed herself up to her feet. Henry nodded, stepped aside. He lifted the bike, hands on the handlebars, ready to push it. "I can do it," Matilda started.

"Don't be stubborn. I'll walk you home." He smiled at her like he knew something about her. Like he knew her.

She blinked, unsettled, but chose not to protest again. "Okay," she said and started to walk. Her knee stung, her elbow throbbed, but she tried not to let the pain show. She felt Henry watching her, but didn't return his gaze.

"We could leave the bike."

She looked over. "What?"

His eyes moved to her bleeding knee and limp, worsened by the fresh injuries. "I could carry you instead."

A flash of heat moved down from her head to the soles of her feet. An image of her cradled in his arms, head leaning against his chest invaded her mind. "I'm fine, thanks," she said stiffly.

"Okay," he said easily, looking forward. After a moment of silence, filled only with the click of her bike wheels, he added, "How's your garden? Did we save it?"

Another flash of heat from head to toe, accompanied by the feeling of his hand on her hair. She looked down at her hands. "Yeah, it's fine. Thanks."

He didn't say anything immediately. She sensed tension in him. Looking up, she saw his jaw working, a flush on his neck. "I'm sorry . . ." he started.

"It's fine," she interrupted. They could not talk about it. Talking about it made it more real between them. *Change the subject!* "Are you enjoying your job?"

The tension in his face eased. He flicked a look her way and then back to the road. "Yeah, it's good."

"I saw your first issue. Really well done."

"Thanks. It's not the kind of writing I'm used to, but I'll get better at it. And it's a good job. I like working alone." Henry blinked as if he hadn't meant to reveal such a personal detail. He cleared his throat. "Abby said you moved away for a long time and just came back. How's that going?"

Maybe it was the comfort of the dark or the pain clouding her mind, but Matilda said, "It's been really hard, actually."

Henry looked over, surprise and understanding in his eyes. "I'm sorry."

Matilda looked away from his sympathy. "How's your foot? Did you break it?"

"No. Bad sprain. It's driving me crazy." His hands flexed on the handlebars briefly before he looked up, smiling.

Matilda started to smile back and then stopped. She took a long breath. "Where did you move from?"

"Detroit," Henry answered quietly. There was a weight to the word, emotions. And something in her gut twisted.

"Do you like it here?"

Henry met her eyes. "I'm not sure yet."

Matilda nodded at his honesty, looked down the road. "What do you usually write?" Henry looked confused and she added. "You said you don't normally write for newspapers. What *do* you write?" Even in the gray darkness she saw the blush flare on his cheeks. A strange energy filled the air.

For a moment, he didn't speak and his hands flexed and released on the handlebars several times. "I have a PhD in creative writing, so fiction mostly. But nothing important or noteworthy."

Her eyes widened with surprise. "A PhD? And you're here, doing the newspaper? Why?"

Henry shook his head. "Just needed some peace and quiet." He swallowed hard and quickly added, "How's your knee doing?"

Matilda tried to read the expression on his face. "It's fine," she mumbled. They walked on in silence for a moment and she realized they were already at her driveway. She studied the shape of the house and wished she didn't have to go inside. They walked to the garage. Henry put her bike against the wall, wedged in next to the orange Beetle.

"Thanks," she said, trying not to look directly at him, to ignore the need of her neck to lift up to see his face.

He shut the garage door, brushed off his hands. Matilda stepped onto the grass in the backyard and Henry stayed on the driveway, leaving a few feet between them. The space cried out a complaint. She fiddled with her hands, not knowing what to say or do.

Henry folded his arms, eyes toward the garden. "Can I help you with your battle wounds?" He gestured to her knee and took a step closer.

Matilda stepped back. Pain flickered over his face. "No, thank you," she said softly.

Henry looked past her at the back door. "Matilda, I really do want to apologize for—"

"You don't have to."

"But I . . ."

"I know. Me too. It's fine." How many times had she said that word tonight? *Fine. Fine. Such a false word.*

Henry folded his arms again, frowned. "Okay."

Awkwardness radiated from them both. Matilda sighed. "Henry," her voice caught on his name and she hurried on to hide it, "I don't know why we keep running into each other, but I . . . I'm not . . . I can't . . ." She pushed her lips together. *Shut up.* She forced herself to look up at him, to gauge his perception of her. Her breath caught. He looked at her with a tremulous intensity, that same look he'd given her in the kitchen on the night of the storm. She found certainty and doubt in that look, strength and weakness. Mostly she saw hazardous *want.*

Henry stepped closer, closing the gap between them. He held her eyes for a moment; her skin was on fire. His face flushed red under his freckles, his jaw working, but no words coming out. Finally, he exhaled and said, "I know. I understand. Me too." He stepped back. Matilda almost reached for him. He cleared his throat. "Did you ever finish *The Silence of the Lambs*?"

She blinked, the question both surprising and somehow so natural. "Yes. I loved it."

"Me too." He looked away and ran a hand back through his messy hair. "Did you hate Hannibal?"

"No. I sort of fell in love with him."

He smiled. "Yeah, pretty genius of Harris."

She smiled back. "Amazing." Matilda stopped herself from going to him, hurt radiating through her chest.

"Good night, Matilda. Sorry again about the bike crash. Maybe we should both sleep at night from now on." He gave another weak smile.

She ached all over, unable to smile back anymore. "Yeah, okay. Good night . . . Henry."

He nodded once and walked away.

Henry

Henry didn't go up to his apartment. He pulled his keys from his pocket, unlocked his truck, and started the engine. For a moment, he only sat, staring out the windshield. He couldn't stop thinking about the look on Matilda's face when he'd asked her why she was riding her bike in the middle of the night. *Was it fear? Was it despair?* He'd had a hard time leaving her alone. He wanted to go back to her, make sure she was okay.

He looked up at the window of his apartment. He didn't want to be alone either.

He pulled out of the parking spot and onto the road, turning in the direction of Abby's house.

Henry's body felt deflated; he really needed some water. His ankle was swollen. But he didn't want to stay home, he couldn't. His stomach was in knots and he couldn't trust himself not to sit down at the typewriter again.

He'd been composing another letter in his head when Matilda's bike was suddenly there. Then her small body in a heap on the ground. If he hadn't been worried about her injuries, he would have felt extremely embarrassed. Yet something about meeting her on the road, in the middle of the night, both of them fleeing something—it felt like a bond. And he couldn't feel that.

What had kept her awake, he wondered again? She was his reason. Even here in the car, he blushed thinking of the feelings he'd awakened writing to her earlier in the night. A nightmare had started it all, and now here he was running to Abby, like a scared child.

At least he had her to run to, though the feeling of *having someone* was still anomalous.

Out of Silent Fields proper, Henry finally took a full breath, relaxing slightly. He felt stupid for leaving, but didn't turn around. A half hour later, he tapped lightly on the back door of Abby and Gill's weathered farmhouse. Memories of his first night there plagued him. After a second attempt, Abby cracked the door, eyes sleepy and gray hair a mess.

"Henry!" She opened the door all the way, looked up at him through the dirty screen door. "What's wrong, son?"

"Can I stay here tonight? I know it's crazy, but . . ." Now he felt like a complete idiot. *What am I doing?*

She narrowed her eyes at him and then pushed open the screen door. "Come in. Of course you can stay here. The spare room is always made up."

Henry stepped inside, the smell of dust and aged wood a small comfort. "I'm sorry," he muttered. He looked down at his sweat-stiff clothes, knowing he must smell and look like a vagrant. "I don't know . . ."

Abby put a hand on his arm. "I don't need a reason, honey." Her warm smile washed over him. "You look like you could use a shower though. You smell almost as bad as our cows." She chuckled as she waddled ahead of him down the hall.

"Sorry," he said again.

"Oh, stop saying you're sorry." She opened a linen closet and handed him a soft white towel. "Get cleaned up. I'll put some clothes on your bed. You go right to sleep. We'll talk in the morning."

Henry looked down at her. Impulsively, he wrapped his arms around her. "Thank you, Abby."

Surprised, she hesitated before hugging him back, but then her arms were tight around his middle. When she pulled back, she brushed at her cheeks. "Get away! I don't want your stink on me." She smiled, giving him a push toward the bathroom.

After a quick shower, Henry wrapped the towel around his waist, and stepped quietly out into the dark hall. His ankle hurt, and his mind was exhausted from thinking about Matilda. He wanted nothing more than to sleep. He didn't see Gill standing in the doorway to the spare room until he almost stepped into him. "You ever heard of coming during the daylight?" Gill grumbled.

Henry jerked back a few steps, his hand coming to the edges of his towel. He looked down at his bare chest and wished desperately to be dressed. Especially if Gill was about to kick him out. "I'm sorry, Gill. I—"

"She likes you."

Henry peered across the dim hall, unable to read Gill's expression. He hadn't seen Abby's husband since that first night, but his impression of the old farmer was the same: a rough, no-nonsense man, who Henry had to admit he was a little bit afraid of. Henry swallowed, "Yes, sir."

Gill folded his thick arms over his chest, resting them on his protruding belly. "She . . . uh . . ." He looked down at his arms, cleared his throat. "She seems happy. And it's been a while. So . . . so I hope you aren't taking advantage or nothing like that."

"No, sir." He didn't know what else to say. He wanted to praise Abby's kindness and friendship, but his throat was dry. And it seemed like Gill was the kind of man who preferred less words, straightforward answers.

"Good, good. She deserves happy." There was a softness in Gill's voice that surprised Henry. Perhaps there was something more under that gruff exterior.

"Yes, she does," Henry agreed.

Gill nodded once, let out a huff of breath. "Good night, then."

Henry stepped aside so Gill could move past him down the hall. He stood there marveling until Gill closed his and Abby's bedroom door behind him. With a small smile, Henry went into his own room to sleep.

Matilda

The corner of the living room by the window stood empty except for shadows.

Matilda took a long breath. She bent to pick up *A Thousand Sleepless Nights*. The cover was bent, so she tried to flatten it. The mantel clock ticked loudly.

Slowly, she walked over to the typewriter. Desperate, she sat down.

`Are you there?`

She typed again.

`Please answer me.`

Her only answer was her own fear.

She looked around the room once more before trudging up the stairs. She cleaned and dressed her wounds. She should sleep, but knew there was no way she could. At the foot of her bed was a small box of things she'd found in Jetty's room that still needed to be sorted.

She hefted it onto the bed and sat, resolved to put aside her fear and worry until the morning. Problems required morning clarity.

The box contained a few journals, some old letters, and random bills all marked paid. Matilda read a few journal entries, smiling at Jetty's voice on the page. One entry began, *Tilly had her first kiss and her first heartbreak.* She remembered it instantly.

Chester Boggs had kissed her after winning the school rivalry baseball game. She'd had a crush on him for most of her sophomore year, dutifully attending every home baseball game to admire him, just *hoping* he might notice her. Not only had he smiled at her during the whole game, but then he kissed her in the dugout. Her first. Matilda had never felt so excited, so grown up. She imagined dates to the movies, holding hands in the halls, school dances. But Chester never called, ignored her in the halls, and then asked another girl to the junior prom. She'd never felt so embarrassed, so used.

Jetty had hugged her and then burst out laughing. "I'm sorry, sweetie, but with a name with Chester Boggs, what did you expect? Never fall for a man with a silly name."

"It's not funny! I couldn't help it!" Matilda sobbed into Jetty's shoulder. They sat on the porch swing, chains creaking, the late spring air as crisp as fresh apple. Jetty's yellow tulips were in full bloom, the front yard an explosion of color, perfectly matched to the purple and green of the house.

Jetty made a consenting sound in her throat. "That does happen, doesn't it? Emotions are funny things, especially love. It's so hard to describe or understand that magnetic, inexplicable pull to another person. Sometimes you feel it before you even know them. That's your soul knowing something before your mind does." Jetty patted Matilda's hair. A robin landed on the porch railing, opened its throat and sang. "I loved a boy once with hair as orange as pureed pumpkin and so many freckles he looked like he'd fallen in the mud. I loved him the moment I saw that funny hair. I have no idea why. Can you imagine us together—two redheads? Our children would have been doomed." She laughed. "Poor Reggie Waters. No one deserves to look like that. And yet . . ."

"You liked him."

"Yes, I did. There are mysterious forces in the world, Tilly. We can't see them, we don't often understand them, but they are there. Some good, some bad."

Seventeen-year-old Matilda had found fleeting comfort in Jetty's existential words. But now, thinking of Henry, the words only scared her. What forces were at work now? What forces had stolen her memory and broken her mind? What forces made her want to love a man she didn't know and couldn't have and caused a typewriter to write intoxicating letters? Was it more than her soul outrunning her mind?

"Jetty," she whispered. "Forces are at work here, and I don't like it. How do I stop it?" Gooseflesh rose on her arms. *Stop talking to her. That's why you thought you saw her. Stop it!*

Matilda turned back to the box. She lifted another journal. A piece of paper fell into her lap. It looked like it had been crumpled up and then flattened back out several times. She set the journal aside and opened the folded page.

Her name was written across the top. The temperature in the room dropped.

Dearest Tilly –

There is something I feel I must tell you, but I hesitate. I made a promise not to tell. But I've never been comfortable with that promise. Even though I made it to my sweet, wonderful sister, Ivy. Your mother.

It is true that she and your father died in a car crash, but that is not the whole story. Your mother was sick. Not physically, but in her mind. As a child she had this incredible imagination. The stories she could tell! But as she got older, some of those stories started to become real to her. Dr. Wells managed to find her the right medicine and the delusions left her. That is, until she became pregnant with you. She couldn't take the medicine while she carried you; it wasn't safe for a baby. Right before you were born, things got so bad. She believed someone was trying to take you from her.

After you were born, your dad, Nash, tried to get her to take her medicine again, but her mind was so broken that she thought he was trying to hurt her instead of help her. He loved her so much! It broke his heart to watch her suffer.

That day in the car, Ivy insisted on driving and seemed to be in a good place. Nash allowed her. She drove the car into oncoming traffic, yelling that the only way to keep you safe was to take you to heaven.

You may be wondering how I know this? Nash did not die immediately. He survived for two days after the accident. He told me what happened. I think his guilt took away his will to live. He felt responsible. He loved you both so much.

Now that I've written the words, I still don't know if I should tell you. Your father made me promise to watch for signs of Ivy's sickness in you. But you're eighteen now and show none. I don't think she passed it on to you.

So the question I fight is whether you need to know at all. I don't want you to be angry at her or to blame her. It wasn't her fault. It wasn't your father's either. And I don't want you to blame yourself.

I don't know what to do . . .

Matilda's hands were shaking, the paper quivering. Her eyes were clouded with tears, the sobering words blurred.

My mother was crazy. And now I am too.

She dropped the paper, put her head in her hands, and cried.

Henry

Henry wandered into the kitchen the next morning around ten. Abby sat at the table, feet propped up into a chair, book in hand.

"Well, well. Look who decided to join the land of the living." She smiled over the top of her paperback novel. "Gill went off into the fields hours ago—thankfully—so it's just you and me, handsome." Henry smiled, thinking of Gill's tender words, his subtle but obvious concern for Abby. Despite their prickly interactions, the couple loved each other. Something about that gave Henry great comfort.

"How'd you sleep?" Abby asked.

"Good." In fact, he had slept better than in the last couple weeks. Though the unplanned, middle-of-the-night visit had proved the right choice, he still felt a little embarrassed. Gill's old flannel pajamas hanging off him only added to his discomfort. He poured himself a cup of coffee and sat across from Abby. She was reading *The Thorn Birds* by Colleen McCullough. "Any good?" he said over his steaming mug.

"Amazing!" She turned a page. "I've never felt so many emotions at once." Her eyes moved up to him and then back down. "Matilda recommended it to me."

Henry's coffee sloshed onto his hand. He swore as he set down the cup and mopped up the mess with a tea towel. "Sorry."

Abby laughed loudly, threw down her book. "So?"

"So what?" he asked, knowing exactly what she meant.

She pursed her lips at him. "So why did you grace my doorstep at four in the morning? Something happen with Matilda? What's going on with you two? Every time I mention her name you act like I've shoved you from behind."

150

Henry fiddled with his mug. After a long sigh, he said, "Honestly, I don't know." He put his forearms on the table and hung his head. He expected Abby to say something, but she waited patiently. "We've had a couple of . . . run-ins. One last night, literally. And there's this . . . energy between us." He scoffed. "That sounds so stupid."

"No, it doesn't," Abby interjected.

Henry looked up. There was no trace of disbelief or mocking in Abby's washed-out brown eyes. "It's strong, Abby. I don't understand it, and I've never felt anything like it. I didn't think it was possible to feel such a powerful connection to someone. I don't know her! And I *can't* know her. I guess that's the problem."

"What problem? Why can't you know her?"

"It can't go anywhere." The words made his heart ache.

"And for the love of everything holy, why not?" Abby raised her eyebrows.

Henry shook his head. "Because . . . I'm too broken. My life is sort of a mess. And last night she said . . . she said she can't either."

"What's her stupid excuse?"

"I don't know." Henry thought of Matilda's face when she said it: the pain, the damage. Though the exact cause was a mystery to him, he knew that look, those feelings. He looked up at Abby, whose expression was hard to read.

"Well, son, I gotta say it all sounds like chicken crap to me. Pardon my French." She smiled coolly and crossed her arms.

Henry scoffed, almost laughed. "You don't understand—"

"Oh, I understand just fine. You think you two are the first people to be damaged by life? To have terrible things happen to you and want to hide from the chance of more pain? Give me a break." Abby dropped her feet heavily to the floor and leaned forward over the tabletop. Her eyes clouded, changed. "I lost *eight* babies."

Henry's stomach clenched, the words pushing him back in his seat. The room stilled. "Abby . . ."

"Most were early on—miscarriages—but two I gave birth to. Right here in this house. One was stillborn. The other . . ." she paused, put the back of her hand to her mouth. "He took a couple breaths and then stopped. Just wasn't strong enough. He died in my arms." She looked down at her empty arms.

Henry didn't know what to say, so he kept his mouth shut. A visceral clench of pain gripped him. He felt suddenly wasted, empty. When Abby had said she and Gill didn't have any children, he had ignorantly assumed there had never been any at all, not that she'd lost so many. The revelation made him profoundly sad, her grief so real to him.

Abby inhaled sharply, "After each one, I wanted to give up. I wanted to hide from the pain I had and the possibility of more pain. But after I stopped hurting so bad I couldn't sleep, I realized something else." She caught his eyes. "Fearing the pain also kept me from the chance of having some joy. And, Henry, joy is worth the pain."

He looked away from her, emotions rising in his throat, mind fighting the logic. "But you . . . never . . ." He didn't know how to say it.

"Never got the joy? Well, not in the way I thought I would. But then you showed up on my porch, and though I can't claim you as my own flesh and blood, I can claim a bit of joy from helping you. God sent you to me, an orphan to a childless mother." She sniffed.

Henry looked up, lost for words.

Abby took a deep breath, letting go of the emotions. "There is no joy in this life like finding the one person who makes you feel at home. If Matilda is that person, then you best fight for her." She held his eyes. "If you don't, I swear I'll slap you into next Tuesday." She smiled, sunshine.

Henry laughed, the tension in his throat and gut easing. "Yes, ma'am," he said. Then he frowned. "But what if . . ."

"Uh-uh. No what-if's. Reach for the joy, risk the pain." She slid her hand across the table and patted his hand. "I'll make you a big fatty breakfast and then how 'bout a walk? It's a gorgeous Saturday, probably one of the last days before it gets too hot."

He nodded, "Sounds good."

Abby pushed to her feet with a groan. As she moved to the fridge she paused to put a hand on his shoulder. He leaned his cheek into her warm, wrinkled skin. She kissed the top of his head and then went to pull out the bacon.

Henry stepped into his apartment, tossing his keys on the kitchen counter. In his head, he replayed all of what Abby had said to him, wondering if he had the courage to reach for the joy. Was it possible to have too much pain? So much that it kills the joy before it can take form?

Lost in his thoughts, Henry wandered over to his desk. His eyes dropped to the typewriter. The earth shifted under his feet.

```
Who are you? Who are you? Are you there? Please
answer me.
```

He had not typed those words.

Matilda

"Hello?"

"I need your help."

"Tilly, is that you? Are you crying?"

"Parker, I . . ."

"What's wrong?"

Matilda couldn't say the words out loud. She bit her lower lip and pressed her eyes closed, Jetty's words replaying in her mind, loud and damaging.

"Are you still there? Matilda?"

"I need your help," she repeated.

"I'm coming."

A few minutes later, Matilda heard a key turn in the front door. Numbly, she thought, *I gave Parker a key when we were dating. He still has it.*

"Matilda?" The front door closed. "Ma*tilda!*" There was panic in his voice. She listened as he hurried through the living room and checked the kitchen. Heavy footfalls on the stairs, running. "Tilly, answer me . . ."

He stood in the doorway of her room. She couldn't look up from the letter. He rushed over to her, grabbed her by the shoulders. "Are you hurt?" His eyes scanned her body. She tried to shake her head. "What's wrong?"

All she could do was lift the letter out to him. Confused, he looked at it and then back at her. She pushed it toward him. He took it, lowering his eyes to the words. Matilda dropped to her side, curling into the fetal position. She'd been sitting for hours and her legs were numb.

She listened to Parker breathe and read.

"Oh, Matilda . . . I'm so sorry." He sat on the bed behind her and put a hand on her shoulder. She heard the paper drop into the box. *Burn it. Frame it.* "Talk to me. What are you feeling?"

Matilda closed her eyes. "She gave it to me." Parker tensed, his grip on her shoulder wavering.

"What?"

"I see things that aren't real."

"What? What do you see?" he said, his voice cautious.

"Last night . . . Jetty. I saw Jetty in the living room."

Parker was still for a moment and then he lay down behind her and pulled her against him. He didn't speak for several minutes.

With the gate to her insanity open, Matilda went on, unable to stop. "The day Thea saw me in the yard, the day I came back, I woke up in the house and couldn't remember six years. *Six years!* I thought it was the morning after we picked out our wedding cake. I can't remember leaving or where I went, what I did. Who I knew. Nothing."

"Nothing at all?" Parker asked, his voice close to her ear.

"Nothing." Matilda waited to feel better, having finally told someone, but the feeling didn't come. "I'm sick. Just like her."

"So you don't know how you got back to town? Or . . . how you got your scars?"

She shook her head against the bed. Parker went quiet again. She felt him thinking. "Are you scared of me?" she asked quietly.

"No, of course not." His arm tightened around her.

"I am," she said even quieter.

Parker lifted to his elbow to look at her. "I'm going to get Dr. Wells. Okay? You stay right here. We will fix it. Okay?"

She didn't look at him. "Okay."

"Will you be all right while I go?"

"Yes."

He pushed off the bed. "Right back."

Matilda listened to his hurried steps down the stairs. Had she been right to call him? Should she be relieved to have an answer to her delusions? She wasn't. Part of her fought it. *I'm not like my mom. I'm not sick.*

To defy her, the typewriter keys clacked downstairs.

She sat up, breathless. Ran downstairs.

I'm here.

She laughed out loud at the sight of those words pulsing on the page, and felt delirious. She sat, shaking from head to toe.

Don't . . .

But she did.

`You're not real,` she typed and held her breath.

`I am.`

`Who are you?`

There was a long pause.

`A writer. Who are you?`

`A reader. Who do you write to?`

`To you.`

Matilda smiled, her hands quaking. `You don't know me.`

`Yes, I do. You are me. I am you. I know you read my words and feel what I feel. I write for you.`

`What do we do now?` Matilda asked.

`I'll keep writing if you'll keep reading.`

The muscles in her stomach tightened. She closed her eyes. `Your words are dangerous.`

`Will you risk it?`

Matilda stared at the keys. "What am I doing?" she said aloud. "This isn't real." And yet, it felt like the most real thing she had ever experienced. But what crazy person didn't think the voices were real? That was part of the sickness.

She rubbed her hands together over the keys. Henry's face was in her head.

`Henry? Is that you?`

Henry

Henry pushed back from his desk. This was too much. He ran his hands back through his hair and looked at his name typed on the page. Typed by someone else.

Who?

I've lost my mind, he thought. *Did I just type that whole conversation?* No.

He'd seen the keys depressing, invisible hands at work. He rubbed his face, at a loss. He looked at the scars on his arms and felt a rush of fear. Seized by this fear, he snatched the typewriter off the desk and heaved it against the brick wall. It impacted with a loud metallic twang and crashed to the floor. Keys scatted everywhere, severed limbs. The ribbon lay tangled, an evisceration.

Henry blinked at the body of the machine, shocked at his own rage. He couldn't look at what he'd done. It was awful, unforgiveable. He turned several times, looking around the apartment for an answer, for the right action.

Louis Winston's book sat on the desk.

He grabbed it and fled.

Matilda

No reply came. The typewriter sat innocently quiet. After several minutes, Matilda, with a sad resignation, took the paper from the platen. She hid it away in the fairy tale book with the others. She put the typewriter up on the shelves as well, placing a few books around it like a fort. Hidden.

Parker opened the door just as she finished. He smiled hesitantly at her. Dr. Wells stepped in, black bag in hand. Matilda frowned at it, but then stopped herself. She wanted this to stop. She wanted to feel normal. She needed to. If medicine had helped her mom, it could help her. Maybe it would help her remember and cast out the darkness.

"Hello, Matilda," the doctor said kindly.

"Can you fix this?" The words sounded desperate. *I am desperate.*

He walked to her, put a hand on her shoulder. "Yes. We are going to fix this." He looked back at Parker. "Let's sit and talk for a minute."

Henry

Henry found himself outside of Matilda's house. Winston's book felt heavy in his hands. The garage was open, the funny orange car parked inside like a sleeping dog. There was another car behind it, a red Honda. He wondered who it belonged to.

He should leave.

But he didn't. Instead, tiredly, he went into the garage and sat on the ground, leaning back against the front bumper, hidden from view of the house, and the other car. He opened *A Thousand Sleepless Nights*. He didn't want to read it, but he felt he had to. And this felt like the right place to do it. He didn't let himself wonder why it felt right.

The first words:

> Time away from you, even one day, feels like a thousand sleepless nights. Exhausting, unending, unnatural. Come back to me. Let me sleep in your arms, breathe in your air, and be healed. I give myself to you, wholly. But will you take me?

The hot tears on his cheeks surprised him. Henry couldn't remember the last time he had cried. He had stopped crying at a young age. It had always made him feel so weak and tended to enrage his foster parents. But now, he didn't fight it.

He read on.

It was late afternoon when Henry finished the last page. He closed the book and stared up at the ragged wood of the garage ceiling. It was hot in the small space, musty and dusty. His back hurt from sitting so long. He looked down at the cover of the book, the moon and mountains. Each word lingered inside him, like bees in a hive, buzzing. And each one made him think of the woman inside the house next to him. His hands were shaking. He blew out an uneven breath.

Go home, you idiot.

It'd taken him most of the day to get through the two hundred pages, a ridiculously long time. But it'd been difficult, like performing a complicated surgery. Many times, he found himself staring at one sentence for fifteen minutes, trying to decode the mystery he felt lived under it. No words had ever affected him like these.

He stood, unsteady on his numb legs. His ankle throbbed in the heavy boot cast and he wanted to rip it off. Matilda's kitchen light was on. He felt like a thief in the night, like a crazed stalker. But instead of heading for home, he walked onto the grass. The red Honda was still in the driveway. Voices drifted out the screen door.

Matilda's voice and . . . a man's voice.

Red anger flashed to life inside Henry, rocket fuel and a match. He dropped the book. Before he knew it, he was through the back door and into the kitchen. A man had his arms around Matilda. Henry lost his mind.

"Get away from her!" he yelled as he grabbed the shorter man by the shoulders. Matilda screamed. Henry's arm swung on its own, smashing into the hard jaw of this other man.

"Henry!" Matilda yelled.

The man fell to the floor, cradling his face. There was blood on Henry's knuckles. *Mine or his?*

"What are you doing?" Matilda stepped in front of him, her face wide open and angry.

"I . . . I don't know." His hand hurt badly. He looked past her to the man on the floor. *What did I do?*

Matilda looked at him with pinched eyes and then turned away. "Parker? Are you okay?"

Seeing her go to him brought some of Henry's craziness back. He reached for her, pulling her away. "Did he hurt you?" Henry asked Matilda.

"What are you talking about!" She pushed away from him. "Are you crazy? That's Parker. A *friend!* And you *punched* him. Why did you do that?" She exhaled forcibly. "What are you doing here?" She looked at the back door and then at him.

A heavy wave of embarrassment crashed down on him. "Matilda, I'm so sorry."

She shook her head. "Just get out!"

The man on the floor managed to stumble to his feet, his hand on his bleeding jaw. His eyes were narrowed, watching the exchange. "Tilly?" he mumbled. "What's going on?"

Matilda, with her eyes still on Henry, said, "I have no idea." Then something softened in her eyes and she stepped closer to Henry. "Are you all right?" she asked quietly. She took another step closer and lifted a warm hand to wipe a tear from his cheek. He hadn't known he was still crying.

Henry met her eyes, wanting to disappear. But her hand on his cheek. He pressed his hand on top of hers, holding it firmly against his skin.

The man—Parker—stepped closer and Henry felt another flash of anger. Matilda pulled away. Henry balled his fists, holding back the unwarranted rage. "I think you should leave," Parker said.

Henry pressed his teeth together and kept his eyes on Matilda, ignoring Parker. His cheek throbbed where she'd touched him. "Are you okay?" he asked her.

She blinked, confused. "I'm fine."

Henry searched her face, involuntarily stepping closer. Words filled his head. He wanted to kiss her more than he wanted to breathe. Parker moved to block her. Henry humbly retreated. He looked away from her, hurting deep inside. "I'm sorry," he mumbled as he turned. Then he went out the back door. "I don't know what's wrong with me," he added to himself as he hurried down the driveway, Winston's book locked in his hand.

Matilda

*H*enry was gone. Matilda stared at the back door, her heart racing. Her hand was tingling, wet with Henry's tears. She wanted him to come back. But that wasn't how she should feel. She should feel angry or . . . maybe, pleased. Angry for the intrusion and violence, but warmed by the display of feeling from this man she couldn't stop thinking about. A betraying feeling snaked from the back of her mind. *What if my feelings for him aren't real either? What if it's part of my inherited sickness?*

Matilda thought of the typewriter.

Parker stood beside her, bleeding. She went to the sink and soaked a towel in cold water.

But Henry's actions weren't imagined.

What just happened?

"Here," she moved back to Parker, "let me see."

Parker dropped his hand. His jaw was red and severely swollen. She pressed the towel to an inch long cut. "Press that hard." Parker obeyed. He watched her closely as she went to the freezer and filled a plastic baggie with ice.

"Who was that?" he finally asked.

"Henry."

"Henry who?"

"Henry Craig. The new editor of the newspaper."

Parker's eyes widened. "And *why* did he punch me?"

Matilda shrugged and looked at the back door.

"Were you expecting him?"

"No."

Parker frowned, winced. "Then why was he here?"

162

"You better get back to Thea. I promised her I wouldn't steal her husband." She tried to smile. "Tell her I'm sorry about your jaw."

"Tilly?"

"Thanks for coming when I called, Parker. I really appreciate it. And I'm sorry to have burdened you with this huge problem. And I'm sorry for . . . whatever it is that just happened."

He sighed, shaking his head. "I've never been punched before. Hurts more than I expected."

"Yeah. The cut doesn't look too deep. I don't think you need stitches."

"Will he come back? I mean, I don't want to leave you alone if . . . is he safe? Should I call over to the sheriff's office? I really don't understand . . ."

"We sort of . . ." She didn't know how to explain it.

"Are you dating him? 'Cause that felt like a jealous boyfriend. And how you touched him . . ."

Matilda shook her head. "No. We hardly know each other." Something pulled taut deep in her gut. "But there is something."

Parker lifted his eyebrows expectantly.

Matilda said nothing. She took the bloody towel from him and went to the washer in the mudroom. When she came back Parker still looked dubious. "I'm fine, really." She took a bandage from the cupboard. Parker lowered the ice, watching her closely, the worry and concern on his face making her uncomfortable.

Bandage in place, Parker said quietly, "I can stay. It's been a rough day. Thea will understand."

"Thanks, but no. Really. I don't want to screw up your life too." She looked at his swollen face and thought of the burden of her mother's secret she'd thrown on him. And how she'd abandoned him a month before their wedding. "Any more than I already have, that is. Why are you even still talking to me?" She tried to smile.

Parker met her eyes with a significant expression. He opened his mouth to respond, then shut it. He shrugged. "I'm a glutton for punishment."

Matilda felt that was not what he'd meant to say. She watched him, sensing something. "What is it?"

Parker stood. "Good night, Tilly."

"Wait—what is it?"

Parker sighed heavily. After a long moment, he answered, "This isn't the first time I've been injured because of you."

Matilda blinked in surprise. "What do you mean?"

Parker adjusted the ice bag. The kitchen was so quiet. "About a year after you left—the day I got your note, actually—I got drunk. Really drunk. I've never been that drunk . . . before or since. I was so angry at those four completely inadequate words. 'Parker, I'm sorry. Matilda.'" He shook his head. "And I was still so scared for you." His gaze flicked to her then away. "At first, that note made it all seem worse, you know? I wanted to feel relief, but I was still so confused, so hurt. I knew you were alive but I still didn't know why you'd left." He adjusted the ice pack again, wincing as it moved against his swollen face. "So I stopped thinking and started drinking. Finally, Billy—down at The Quarry—took my keys. It pissed me off so I stormed out to walk home. Or try, anyway." He paused to take a breath. "Somehow I ended up down by the Neosho."

"The river? That's two miles out of town." Matilda felt suddenly cold in the warm kitchen.

Parker nodded. "I fell in."

A shiver moved down Matilda's body. "Parker, I . . ." Sorry didn't cut it.

"I got pretty banged up, nearly drowned. Luckily, Billy had followed me in his car, worried. He pulled me out."

Matilda leaned against the island, her legs suddenly weak and heavy. *How could I just leave and not care? How could I be that selfish, that stupid?* She rubbed at her forehead, lost for words.

Finally, Parker broke the silence. "I don't blame you."

"You should. It's my fault."

"Not really. I chose to get drunk. I could have handled it better."

"I could have not left like that. I could have called the next day, explained. I could have . . ." The fridge clicked on, humming loudly. Matilda wanted to cry, wanted to be punished for her selfishness, even if she couldn't remember it. Perhaps this was the punishment. "That was so wrong. I was hurting about Jetty, but I shouldn't have done that to you." She dared a look at Parker, who watched her closely.

He only shook his head. "Maybe that was the beginning of you being sick. Maybe Jetty's death brought it on. Maybe it wasn't really your choice."

Matilda nodded. Maybe that was true. It'd be a convenient (but still terrifying) way to explain everything. Yet something about it didn't sit well with her. "I shouldn't have called you tonight," she added. "That was selfish too. I can't keep burdening you with my problems."

Parker lowered the ice. Matilda winced at the ugly sight underneath. He said, "I can take it."

"But why?"

"Because I still love you."

Matilda frowned. "Parker . . ."

"As a *friend*, Tilly. A really good friend. And you're struggling. I was selfish after Jetty died. I'm trying to be a better friend now."

"I don't deserve it."

Parker half smiled, but the pain in his face stopped the expression. "Love isn't about what you deserve."

She looked at him for a moment, feeling slightly amazed. He really had changed. "Thank you," was all she could think to say.

He opened the back door. "Stop saying thank you and sorry so much." His tone was light.

Matilda dared a small smile. "Night, Parker."

"Good night, Tilly. And really—call me if you need anything. Promise?"

"Promise."

Henry

Henry hobbled as fast as he could away from Matilda's house. His heart was beating too fast and his hand throbbed painfully. A small cut on his middle knuckle bled profusely.

I hit someone.

A nasty tangle of emotions came to life inside him. He hadn't hit someone in over twenty years.

In elementary school, he'd been an expert at getting into, and winning, playground fights. All his orphan rage had to go somewhere. But then came Lou Smith. Foster parent, committed drunk, and strong believer in physical violence as a form of disciple. Or just plain fun when his nightly six pack was drained.

The first time Lou hit Henry, the world had turned a putrid shade of gray. Henry had never known such pain. Not only the physical burn but also the wound to his ego, the blow to his sense of safety. In that agonizing moment, hitting became repellent to him. Making another person feel that way was as wrong as it got in his mind.

Henry had never started a fight again.

Even when he'd wanted to badly, even when it'd been justified.

Now, he'd hit a stranger over a woman he hardly knew.

Words like *unstable* and *unbalanced* trotted around in his head as he hurried back to his apartment. *I am not okay. And Matilda will never speak to me again.*

Henry left the lights off in the apartment; the dark felt safer. He cleaned and bandaged his hand. Unable to even think about reading or sleeping, he stood over the messy remains of the typewriter. Gently, he gathered every broken piece and placed them neatly on his desk. Lastly, he placed the body of the machine there on his operating table

166

and started the tedious work of putting it back together. Atonement. If he couldn't fix his life or repair what he'd just done at Matilda's, he could fix this. He could put the typewriter back together and type more insanity.

Dr. Wells sat heavily in the chair across from the exam table. Henry shifted his weight and the sanitary paper crinkled loudly.

"There's nothing wrong with your head, Henry. And the ankle is healing nicely."

Henry only nodded. He had hoped there was some residual trauma to his head responsible for his behavior and delusions. Hearing that there was none was a huge disappointment.

"Stress can cause erratic behavior and actions," Dr. Wells continued, "And you've had your fair share of stress. The accident, injuries, a new town, new job." Dr. Wells folded his hands and smiled warmly. "Give yourself some time. Eat some hardy food and get plenty of rest."

Henry nodded again, thinking of his nightmares. "Okay. Yeah. I'll do that. But, umm . . ."

"Yes?"

"Do you think . . ." *Don't ask.* "I was in an accident before, in Detroit—" *Could be right—I have scars I can't explain—* "And I think my brain may have been damaged more seriously than I thought."

Dr. Wells blinked in surprised confusion. Henry wished he could take back the question. "Why do you think that? What are your symptoms?"

"Some memory loss." *Some could mean six years, right?* "And headaches, trouble sleeping, punching Parker for no reason."

Dr. Wells frowned. "It's possible. Was it a car accident?"

"Uh . . . yes."

"Well, let's do more tests then. Maybe there is some residual trauma that was missed."

Henry nodded. "Okay. Thank you."

"My pleasure. You can schedule another appointment with Fanny for those tests. Next week should work." The doctor reached back to the small counter and took a paper from a file box. "Start doing these exercises every morning and evening for your ankle. It'll help your mobility."

Henry took the paper, glancing at it but not really seeing. "Sure." He stood. "See you later, Dr. Wells."

"Yep. Have a good Monday."

Henry stepped outside the clinic. The June morning was perfectly pleasant and yet he felt gloomy, oppressed. It didn't help that he'd been up all night working on the typewriter. Using forks and knives as tools, he'd done a pretty decent job. But he still had a long way to go. He needed some super glue, black paint, and a new ribbon. Did stores even sell typewriter ribbons anymore? Maybe he could rewind the one he had.

Henry shuffled toward the library and a long day of work. He prayed he could avoid Matilda, though he knew he would think about her every moment.

Matilda

Matilda took a deep breath as she opened the large door of the library. As she'd expected, Thea stood behind the circulation desk, arms folded, face stern.

"Well?" Thea demanded as Matilda meekly approached.

"I'm so *extremely* sorry, Thea."

Thea huffed. "His perfect face. His perfect Robert Redford jaw!"

"I know. I don't—"

"Why didn't you tell me?" Thea raised an eyebrow and stared hard.

Matilda looked down at the desk. She hadn't expressly asked Parker not to divulge the truth about her mother and herself. It wasn't that she didn't trust Thea, but Thea had a way of talking. Maybe it would only be to defend Matilda's actions over the last weeks, but still. Matilda didn't want the whole town knowing that her mother was mentally unstable and had driven their family into oncoming traffic. And that now, she too, had an unstable mind.

"Thea, look. I really didn't think—"

"How long has it been going on?"

Matilda frowned, set her purse down. "Well, it's not easy to explain, but . . ."

Thea suddenly smiled and leaned in closer. "Is he a good kisser? He looks like a good kisser."

Matilda took a step back in shock. "Henry? You mean Henry?"

"Of course I do! If he likes you enough to punch Parker, it's *got* to be serious. And I want the details. So spill!"

Matilda scoffed. In some ways, Thea was still Thea. Matilda sat down in a chair. "It's not like that . . . I mean, there really isn't anything going on."

Thea plopped down in the chair opposite. "Oh stop it, Tilly. He *stormed* into your house and *punched* Parker. Which, yes, I'm really pissed about, but this is big. And Parker said there was this *thing* between the two of you, the way you looked at each other, or something. So come on!" Thea was nearly bouncing in her chair.

"Sorry to disappoint you, but I swear there is nothing to tell. I have no idea what happened last night."

"Why was he at your house?"

"I don't know."

"He just showed up? Fists blazing?" Thea put her head to the side doubtfully. "For no reason?"

"I guess."

"But there has to be something going on between you?"

"I'm not sure. We sort of . . ."

"Sort of what?"

"Keep running into each other." Matilda shrugged. "It's weird."

"Do you like him?"

"I'm not sixteen, Thea."

A scoff. "Oh, don't try to act all mature."

"Ladies!" Thea and Matilda both jumped from their seats at the sound of Beverly's stern reprimand. "What is going on?"

"Nothing, Beverly," they chorused together, like schoolgirls to a stern nun.

Beverly looked doubtful. "I need you two to go through the overstock downstairs and get things ready for the sale at the festival." She dug a fist into each hip and leaned forward. "Do you think you can pause your chatter long enough to do that?"

"Yes, of course," Matilda said. "Sorry," she added for good measure.

Beverly pointed to a stack of empty boxes. The librarians hefted them and silently headed downstairs. Once out of earshot, Thea resumed her inquiry. Matilda half hoped Beverly would stop her again.

"So do you? Like him? Are you interested? You should be interested. He's very good looking."

"It doesn't matter."

"Why not?"

Matilda shivered from the cool air of the dank basement. She took a breath of the musty air. "I forgot it was almost festival time. It was always my favorite time of year." The Bright Nights Festival was Silent Fields's best annual event. Held on the night of July fourth, it was far from the normal Independence Day celebration. It began with all the regular traditions: barbeque, small fair with vendors and rides, and kids eating too much cotton candy. But when the sky turned to navy silk, everything changed. All the lights went out. Everything. Street lights, neon signs, house lamps. All off. A moment later, a glow would appear in the distance, to the west of the fairgrounds. And then the music. Big band stuff, the happiest music, as Jetty would say. Like the call of the Pied Piper, the town came, walking down the dusty path to a field. A field rimmed in towering evergreens, all of which were ablaze with white Christmas lights. The dancing lasted until midnight. And the night ended with a grand fireworks show.

"Don't change the subject," Thea said. Then, "Those books over there, I think."

They dropped their boxes and set to the task of filling them with books to sell at the fair. Matilda asked, "Do they still serve homemade root beer at the dance?"

"Of course. And Estelle started frying donuts right there. It makes the air smell like heaven." Thea shook her head, annoyed to be pulled off the matter at hand. "He's upstairs."

Matilda gripped a book in her hands with excessive force. "I know."

"You should probably go talk to him."

"And say what?"

"How 'bout 'just wondering why you punched my friend and if you want to spend the night.'"

Matilda laughed loudly. "You *are* still in high school."

Thea grinned. "You still haven't answered my question—did you kiss? Or hold hands? Or . . . anything! A guy doesn't punch another guy over nothing."

Matilda focused on the books, trying not to feel Henry standing close to her in her kitchen. "No kiss. Sorry to disappoint. Just random run-ins."

Thea looked at her thoughtfully. "Did you date anyone or ones after you left? I know it's a touchy subject, but . . . did you?"

Matilda didn't have an answer. She'd taken her first crazy pill that morning. She couldn't pronounce or remember the medical name of the medicine Dr. Wells had prescribed her, and she didn't want to because that made it too real. He'd said it would take some time, possibly weeks for it to have any significant effect. But part of her had been hoping the memories would be coming back already. So far, only a growing headache.

"No, not really," she said as normally as possible.

Thea blinked. "Go up and talk to him."

"I can't."

Thea paused, looked over, but Matilda didn't meet her eyes. "Why not?" Thea asked tenderly. "Is it because of what you won't tell me? What happened after you left?"

Matilda looked at the books in her hand. A cheesy Western sat on top, a horse standing in the wind, a sunset in the background. "I'm sorry. I can't talk about it."

"But you can talk about it with Parker?"

Matilda looked up, uncertain if the tone she heard was curious or accusatory. "I'm sorry . . ."

"He didn't tell me. And it's okay. I know you'll tell me eventually. And I know you guys have history. I was there."

Matilda nodded. "I promise it's just as friends."

Thea shrugged lightly. "I know. I trust Parker. And I trust you."

"He told me about the river."

Thea's face darkened. She looked away quickly, blinking. "So are you going to talk to Henry or not? You better get to him before the rest of the town drives him out for assaulting our beloved Parker. I mean, Parker isn't going to go broadcast it, but these things get out. His face is hard to explain lightly. I guess he could tell people I hit him in a pregnant rage."

Matilda frowned, confused at Thea's reaction to the mention of Parker and the river. She wanted to press it, but something in Thea's stance and rambling tone stopped her. Had Parker not told her the whole story? "The town! I hadn't thought of that. They'll *hate* Henry. Almost as much as me, but he doesn't have a lifetime of living here on his side to temper the rage."

"Someone should warn him." Thea was still focused on a pile of books behind her.

"Yeah." Matilda turned to look at the old stone steps. *Go up there. I don't want to.* "I'll be right back."

As Matilda approached the back of the second floor, her heart already racing, she heard Beverly's voice. "We won't tolerate that kind of behavior in our town, Mr. Craig."

Matilda stopped, closing her eyes in sympathy. Henry mumbled a reply she couldn't hear.

"Well, I hope so. Ronnie's not dead, you know. We could easily fire you and bring the old dog back here, if it turns out Silent Fields isn't the right place for you."

Another soft reply. Matilda crept closer, wedging herself behind a shelf to keep out of Beverly's line of sight.

"You may not be my employee, but this is *my* library and I won't have a heathen working here." With that brutal honesty, Beverly stomped out of the office. Matilda watched her go. She waited until she heard the woman's low, sensible heels assault the limestone floor of the first level. Then she walked slowly to the open door of Henry's office.

The sight beyond made her heart ache.

Henry sat with both elbows on the cluttered desk, his face in his hands. His shoulders were slumped, his hair ruffled more than usual. She fought the urge to run to him and put her arms around him. "I'm sorry," she whispered.

Henry startled, dropping his hands. His eyes grew wide at the sight of her.

She took a step inside the stuffy office. There was one small wooden desk, a tall window looking down on Main Street, and one bookshelf with bound copies of past editions of the *Silent Fields Post*. It smelled of old paper. And for some reason that smell fit him perfectly. "Beverly likes to pretend she's in charge of the whole world."

Henry half smiled, his eyes never leaving her face. "She's right though. I don't really deserve to stay." A slow breath. "I owe you an apology."

Matilda stepped closer, now at the edge of the other side of the desk. She could smell soap on his skin. There was black grease under his fingernails and she wondered why. "I just want to understand what happened. Parker's the one who needs an apology."

Henry rubbed his hands over his face. He looked as tired as she. "I'd like to understand too." He shrugged. "I was walking by. I thought I'd stop. I saw the lights in the kitchen and walked back. When I heard his voice, I just . . ." He opened his hands and shrugged again.

"Decided to charge in and commit assault and battery?" Matilda said it gently.

Henry frowned, looked away. "Dr. Wells said it might be stress. Not that that is an excuse."

"What's going on here?"

Henry didn't answer right away. Silence stirred between them. "I don't know. But I think we need to do something about it."

His tone was so serious that Matilda looked up, met his eyes. "Like what?"

"I think I better walk you home tonight."

Matilda blinked in surprise. "Why?"

"To talk. To try to decode this . . . *thing*." Henry gestured between them. "Would that be okay?" He nervously thumbed the edge of his desk.

Matilda's stomach fluttered, excited, but wary. "Yeah, that's fine. I'm done at six."

Henry nodded, looked away. "Six." He stood and came around the desk. Matilda's heart pounded even harder. She lifted her chin to look up at him. She remembered that Henry had been crying when he'd plowed into her kitchen. If he'd just been on a walk, why had he been so upset? She wanted to ask him but felt too shy. He moved his hand as if to touch her but folded his arms instead. "Do you think Beverly will be back to lecture me again?"

Matilda smiled. "It's highly likely. Along with most of the town. Prepare yourself." She stepped back. "Uh . . . see you later."

Henry smiled, a blush rising under his freckles. "See you later."

Henry

I think I should cancel."

"Don't you dare!"

"But I don't understand what's going on between us. She makes me so nervous. She makes me . . . assault strangers."

"That sounds *right*, not wrong. Parker needed to be knocked down at least once in his privileged life. Real people shouldn't look that nice. A bruise on his jaw humanizes him."

Henry dropped his head to the surface of his office window. People were filling the sidewalks below, headed home. "Abby, I can't do it." It was five-thirty, and he hadn't been able to think of anything all day. His head filled with pictures of walking side by side with Matilda. He felt like a flustered moron. One moment, he wanted to run to Matilda as fast as possible and the next he wanted to leave town permanently. How could she thrill him and scare him to death at the same time? Why did she make him happy and give him nightmares? Was this normal? Maybe Dr. Wells should do those tests sooner.

"Henry, son, take a breath. It's just a walk. And it's about time. You two need to figure this thing out. Together. Not apart and brooding. Just go. Talk about the weather. Then talk about other stuff. And then kiss her." He could hear the smile in her voice.

If I kiss her, the world might implode. Henry sighed loudly. "Beverly Wilson lectured me on proper behavior today. Everyone knows I hit Parker. I might be run out of town the moment I step outside. I shouldn't have come here."

"Don't talk like that. That's just people being stupid people."

"Yeah."

"Henry?"

"It's okay to struggle."

The sentiment brought tears to his eyes. *Get a grip.* "Yeah. But what if . . ."

"Oh, no! No 'what ifs.'" There was a shuffle on the line as Abby shifted her receiver. "Now, look. Take a few longs breaths. Run out right now and grab something chocolate to give her. Not flowers—flowers die. Chocolate can be savored. And then just go. It will work itself out. Okay?"

"Okay. Thanks, Abby."

"You bet. Call me later and tell me everything. I'll be up reading, so it won't be too late. Understood?"

"Yes, ma'am."

Henry stood at the top of the second-floor stairs, looking down as if it were the precipice of an ugly cliff. In his hands, he gripped a small square turquoise box of truffles from Estelle's. He was trying not to crush them.

Walk down the stairs.

Henry tugged at the collar of his blue pinstripe button-down. He didn't own a tie. Or slacks. He looked down at his jeans.

Walk down the stairs. Now.

Henry shifted the box again. Then, bravely, his face flushed with nervousness, he descended. He listened to the murmur of voices, Matilda and Thea. He pictured Matilda's small figure, her smile and the curve of her hips under her long skirt. Words in his head. He had finished the repairs on the typewriter last night. Or at least, he thought he had. Everything looked normal, except for a few scratches and dings. The T key was a little crooked. A potent urge to try it out with the words filling his head almost made him flee back up the stairs and run to his apartment.

"Hi, Henry."

Matilda wore a long knit skirt, black and flowing, and a simple red blouse. The red made her hair and eyes appear darker, her skin whiter. She looked up at him from the circulation desk. She was alone. Thea must have slipped out; Henry was grateful for that.

"Hi." He managed as he closed the distance between them. "These are for you." He held out the little blue box.

Her eyes widened, some emotion flickering there. And then she smiled. "Are these Estelle's truffles?"

He nodded. "I ran over. Abby suggested I shouldn't come empty-handed."

Matilda's smile grew. "Abby is a wise woman. These are my favorite."

A flush of heat went through him. He'd stood at the glass counters, debating (and trying to ignore the whispers behind him). When he'd seen the delicate truffles, he knew that's what he should get. He shifted uncomfortably. *I knew. How did I know?* He swallowed. "Uh . . . ready to go?"

Matilda picked up her purse and rounded the desk. They walked quietly to the door. Henry held it open. As she passed, he got a whiff of her citrus hair.

"Did Beverly come up again?" she asked.

"No. I got lucky."

Matilda locked the doors. They descended the steps. Turning toward her street, they walked slowly, close but not touching. Henry couldn't think of a single thing to say to her. The day was warm, almost hot. The air smelled of cooking dinners.

After a few minutes, Matilda broke the silence. "How's your hand?"

Henry looked down at his red, bruised knuckles. "Sore. Stiff. But how's Parker?" He looked over. "I really am sorry."

"I know. Parker is fine."

"An old lady hit me with her purse when I went to get your chocolates."

Matilda put her hand to her mouth, smiling and suppressing a laugh. Henry couldn't look away from her face. She said, "No. Really? Who was it? I thought that only happened in movies."

"Me too. I have no idea who she is. Really short, hunched over, gray hair, a million wrinkles, and a very heavy purse."

Matilda let out a burst of laughter. "Might have been Vera Wagner. She's a mean old thing."

"Yeah, my shoulder and I found that out."

Matilda laughed again. "Of all the people to hit, Parker, town golden boy, was the worst choice. You should have hit Carl Bounder, the high school football coach. No one likes him."

Henry smiled, feeling the strange sadness that plagued him lighten. "But, uh . . . Abby told me you were engaged to him once? Parker—not Carl."

Matilda nodded slowly. "Yes. It ended six years ago. He's married to Thea now."

"But you stayed friends?"

A light shrug. "We were always better friends than anything else. How 'bout you? Any exes back in Michigan?"

"Nothing worth talking about."

"And how's the paper?"

"Yeah, it's fine."

Henry found himself walking closer to her, and she didn't move away. He was glad he hadn't run off to his typewriter. Too soon they were in front of her house. They stopped, both looking up. "This is a great house," he said.

"Thanks. It was my Aunt Jetty's. She raised me." Matilda opened the truffle box and pulled one out. "She passed away about six years ago."

"I'm sorry. Six years—same time things ended with Parker?"

"Yeah. Jetty died of liver cancer, and I ran away from him and everything."

Henry nodded. She offered him a chocolate, he took it. For a comfortable moment they savored the treats, still looking at the house.

"I really miss her," Matilda said quietly, her eyes widening as if she hadn't meant to say it out loud.

"What was she like?" Henry turned to her. He saw the sentiments on her face before she spoke.

"Wild. Simple. Loving. Artistic. She cooked the most delicious food. She fell in love with an Italian man and he taught her. She loved plants and color. She was perfect."

Henry stepped closer. "I wish I had known her."

Matilda looked up at him. "Yeah, I wish you had too." Her hand was trembling as she put the lid back on the chocolate box. Then, surprisingly, "I'm not ready to go inside. Can we walk for a bit longer?"

Matilda

The knot in her stomach had almost gone away by the time she and Henry had walked a couple blocks past her house. She felt his eyes always pulling back to her, watching her as they moved languidly through town. Those eyes which were sometimes green, sometimes gray, and sometimes turbulent with emotions.

The conversation had been simple, superficial. They seemed to skirt around the edges of things, not asking too many personal questions. She battled a peculiar feeling of enjoying every moment with him, but also wishing he would leave. Maybe it was the headache, the throbbing in her head she could only attribute to the new medicine.

"Nice night," Henry said. The evening sun brightened every color. Sprinklers swished and somewhere barbeque cooked. People waved from porches as they passed and then whispered in their wake. Matilda tried not to worry about what they were saying.

She and Henry moved from the main cluster of houses into an older part of town. Henry was so close. Matilda wished he would take her hand. Lifting her head, she looked at the sky. "Looks like a storm's coming."

Henry turned his gaze up to the dark slate clouds moving toward them from the east. "Weird weather here, huh? I didn't know it rained so much in Kansas."

"Not usually. Just lately."

Henry stopped walking. "What is that?" He stared across the street.

Sandwiched between Morrell's Auto Repair—a large garage with three bays—and the back boundary of the elementary school grass field was a tiny red brick house, Victorian in style and lovingly maintained. Matilda had always loved the two blinking-eye gable-roof dormer windows, the spindled porch railing and intricate millwork. BOOKER'S BOOKSHOP was painted in white on the large arched front window. The dust on the window made her heart ache.

"That's Booker's, but I guess it closed. How sad!"

"The bookshop? Abby told me about that. The owner died of lung cancer, I think."

Matilda nodded as she took a slow breath. "That makes sense. Mr. Booker never could stop smoking. You'd buy a book and it would smell of pages and tobacco." She smiled, remembering the many trips to the shop with Jetty. She always said, *It's never a waste of money to buy a book. Or five. Or ten.*

"What is it?" Henry asked, watching her.

She shook her head. "Jetty bought me lots of books in that shop. We came here all the time. We *loved* this place. I can't believe it's gone."

"I really wish it wasn't. I've been driving to El Dorado to buy books for weeks."

Matilda smiled at him. "Really? That's a long drive."

"I have an addiction."

She laughed. "Me too. But I have a library to feed my problem."

Henry, smiling, started to cross the street and she followed.

They climbed the creaky porch steps, shuffling through a drift of dry leaves. The front door was a fine walnut specimen, deeply grained, with a piece of stained glass set into the top third, an open book immortalized in silky white and brown, surrounded by splendid waves of vibrant blue and green. Matilda ran her fingers along the milky glass, dropping them to the matching rich-blue glass doorknob. "Jetty told me this door was magic. I think I still believe her."

Henry smiled. "I think I do too." He went to the front window, cupped his eyes to look in. Matilda joined him. Peering inside at the naked shelves and lonely tables made her ache inside. The loss seemed a grand injustice. She pictured it as it had been. She imagined she and Henry strolling in to browse books together. They could hand each other books instead of fumble for conversation.

The space was perfect for a bookshop—quaint little rooms, handsome built-in oak shelves, a narrow creaky staircase in the rear leading to the second floor with its slanted ceilings.

Thunder rumbled. A cool wind blew down the street. Right behind it came the rain, falling with fevered enthusiasm.

Reluctantly, Matilda turned away from the melancholy window to face the storm. The rain fell in thick beaded cords off the edge of the porch roof, splashing into the mud around a row of rose bushes. White roses, plump and pretty.

"Well, here's the rain," Henry said, joining her at the railing. "I guess we're stuck here for a bit. Too bad we can't go inside. I'd love to see it."

Matilda turned back to the door, wishing the same. She took a few steps forward. The doorknob was cool under her palm. She gripped it. Turned it. The door creaked open. Matilda's jaw dropped. She hadn't really expected to find it unlocked. She gasped, looked over at Henry. He quickly joined her.

The years of neglect had not cleared the smell of pages. Matilda closed her eyes, inhaling deeply. The dusty scent, mixed with the rain, took her to a hundred different places at once. Back porch nights with Jetty. Reading in bed, under the covers with a flashlight. The night with Henry in her kitchen.

She pushed the door open a little more.

"Is that a small town thing—the door unlocked like that?" Henry asked.

"No, that's weird." Matilda looked up at the underside of his freckled jaw. She had no problem picturing him meandering the aisles of a bookshop. "Let's go in," she whispered, her heart immediately kicking into high gear.

Henry looked down at her, eyes wide. She worried he was going to say no, close the door, and lecture her about trespassing. Instead, wonderfully, he smiled and stepped into the shop. Matilda nearly giggled with nervous glee, but found she could not when he reached back to take her hand, leading her inside. Closing the door behind them.

For a moment, they only stood, hand in hand, the quiet room taking in their arrival. Matilda felt Henry's own surprised tension at the joining of their hands. Perhaps it'd been impulse. Should she pull away? Even if she wanted to, she didn't have the strength. Her hand in his felt like cool sheets on a hot night. The word blissful danced in her head, and as ridiculous and traitorous as it was, she smiled at it.

Henry took a full breath, loud in the vacant room. "The smell," was all he said.

Matilda nodded, hoping he couldn't hear her heart kicking her ribs. "Is there anything better than a bookstore? Even one dead and abandoned?"

He shook his head, smiling. Every part of her warmed.

The main room, a box of a space, with four walls of shelves, hummed with the ghosts of books and book lovers. The register desk was constructed of old books, multicolored spines stacked to height and topped with a handsome slab of dark glossy wood. They walked over to it, reaching out hands at the same moment. They exchanged a smile.

From the main room they walked into another smaller room, much the same with its ceiling-height shelves. There were two tall windows between the shelves and Matilda remembered that once there had been crystals hanging in them to throw rainbows into the space whenever the sun shone. "This was the children's room," she whispered. "It's also a little magical." Henry's grip on her hand tightened. She felt a little like a teenager, sneaking around somewhere she wasn't supposed to be—with a boy. But she also felt as if she'd stepped into a richly important moment. Something almost sacred, something her problems couldn't touch. Perhaps it was only the atmosphere of an abandoned bookstore and Henry's hand wrapped around hers.

He nodded to the doorway. "Let's go upstairs."

To climb the narrow creaky staircase Henry should have released her hand to make it easier for them to ascend the low-ceiling stairwell, but he didn't. She happily angled her body to accommodate. At the top of the stairs, one large room opened up, the two dormer windows at the front.

Matilda sighed. "Wow!" she whispered, finding it hard to speak loudly. She'd always known it to be crammed with shelves and books. The surprise of so much open space and the delightfully slanted roofs made her smile. The only shelves left were those along the walls, and also one lone square table and a slouching couch under the windows.

They moved toward it. "That's the ugliest couch I've ever seen," Henry said.

Matilda laughed loudly, and then brought a hand to her mouth to remind herself of the sneaking. Henry smiled at her. It really was though—an ugly couch. Mustard yellow with an abrasive paisley design, it sat long and low, the cushions sunk in from years of loungers. It had never been in the store when she'd visited. It felt like it had appeared just for them.

"Well, then, we must sit on it," Matilda added.

Henry pulled her around and they sat, close to one another, both stiff from the contact. The couch faced the windows. Beyond the glass the sky was stone gray, the sunlight nearly gone behind the swollen rainclouds. Sitting so low, it was almost like looking up through a skylight. Matilda let her head fall back, her eyes watching the lazy water tumble down from the sky.

The only sounds were the rain and their breathing. Henry's breathing. She could feel the rise and fall of his lungs, his shoulder moving against hers. It shocked her to realize that she had never felt this at home. Not in her childhood home with Jetty, not in the library. But in this orphaned bookshop, sitting on a hideous, dust-filled couch, next to a stranger.

The idea made her want to run. It couldn't be right.

How can this be right?

Am I imagining this too?

It's an awful thing not to trust one's own mind.

Henry leaned into her a little more, relaxing his body into the cushions.

"We should probably go," she mumbled.

"Probably," Henry replied, but did not move. His grip on her hand tightened. He had not let her go for even half a second. After a moment of silence, in which Matilda agonized over how she felt and how she should feel, Henry lifted their joined hands. His energy shifted; Matilda held her breath. "Matilda . . . I am profoundly screwed up."

Matilda lifted her head to look at the side of his face. His hair was slightly wet from the rain spray coming off the porch roof; she wanted to touch it. She didn't know what to say, wasn't sure what *he* wanted her to say.

"I've tried not to want . . . this," he looked at their hands, rubbed the back of hers with his thumb. "I don't know what to do."

Matilda swallowed the knot in her throat. Suddenly, the silence was deafening and his simple honesty overwhelming. The inside of her head roared. Should she deny him again, make excuses? What was the right thing to do? The silence ticked on. Matilda knew she had to say something soon. A proper little speech formed in her head, but shattered when he turned to look at her with his lake-water eyes.

"I am also *profoundly* screwed up," she heard herself say.

Henry smiled, his eyes filling with light. "Well, as long as we start in the same place."

Matilda laughed quietly, the action releasing some of the tension in her chest. "It's a good place to start." *Oh my gosh! So is this the start . . . of us? Matilda and Henry. Together?* She had a random thought: *We've always been us.*

Henry nodded, his smile growing. His eyes moved off her face, and his expression changed. "Look at that."

Matilda turned, half expecting to see some rodent racing along the dusty wooden floor, but instead she spotted a row of books on a lower shelf. "Left behind," she said. "How sad."

Henry finally released her hand, stood. He went to the shelf and brought back an armful. She reached up to take a few. "Poetry. Short stories," she announced as she read the covers and spines. "Wonder why they are still here."

Henry dropped back into his seat, the couch protesting with a wooden groan. "Nobody likes poetry anymore," he joked. He flipped through a tattered volume. "These books need to be read. Don't you think?"

"Of course."

"But we can't do this without some supplies."

"Supplies?"

Henry popped back off the couch. "Stay here."

Confused, Matilda turned in the couch. "Wait! Where are you going?"

"Dinner. Stay." He motioned with both his hands for her to stay in her seat. "We can't survive the night on just those chocolates. I'll go get dinner. Give me ten minutes."

And off he went before Matilda could think of a response. She listened to the echo of the front door quietly closing. The euphoria of being close to Henry evaporated almost immediately. Panic closed in on her. She stood, the pile of books tumbling to the couch. She looked at the couch, the stairs, ready to bolt.

I can't do this! I can't have a romantic night in an old bookshop. I can't. I don't even have control of my own mind.

This is wrong.

Matilda crossed to the staircase. Stopped. Looked down at the narrow steps. She wanted to cry. She wanted to run. She wanted to sit back down on the ugly couch and wait for Henry. Jetty's words took their turn. *That's the soul knowing what the mind doesn't.*

What if her soul was as damaged as her mind?

What if her soul was wrong?

Henry

enry splashed through the wet streets, running despite his boot cast. He sprinted the four blocks to The Mad Hash and barreled through the doors. Pearl was there, her painted-on eyebrows lifting at his breathless entry.

"Hey, Henry. You okay?"

No, no he was most certainly *not* okay. His heart might explode; his brain might stage a full-blown rebellion. He had never felt better. "Yeah, yeah. Fine," he answered. "Just the rain."

Pearl nodded slowly. "You wanna sit?"

"No. Take out, please. And can they hurry?"

Henry placed the order for two burgers, two sodas, and a side of rosemary fries. Five minutes had never felt so long. He was both excited and panicked to get back to Matilda.

He wasn't sure exactly what had given him the courage to say what he'd said, to take that forbidden step. He hadn't been able to do it as they walked. Maybe it was Abby's words of encouragement or the security of the bookshop. Maybe it was simply the unbelievably wonderful feeling of Matilda's hand in his.

Whatever it was, now Henry had to make sure it stuck. He had to prove that it was the right thing to do, prove it to both of them.

Pearl returned with the white plastic bag of food and he snatched it from her like a hungry lion. "Thanks," he said hurriedly, and then left the diner as spastically as he'd arrived.

As he hurried back, awkward with the food and drinks, a fear gripped him that Matilda wouldn't be there when he returned. That his leaving had somehow broken the spell of the moment. The energy between them was nothing if not tumultuous, fragile. What if she changed her mind?

The rain had stopped, but thunder growled in the distance.

Hurry. Hurry.

Outside the bookshop, he paused, though his panic urged him on. What would he do if she weren't there? Go after her? Let her go? Give up? He didn't think he'd have the strength to do anything but collapse into a wasted heap.

Quietly, he snuck back in the bookshop, stopping to listen.

Henry heard nothing. The smell of the greasy food turned his stomach.

He forced himself to climb the stairs, to prepare for an empty room.

At the top step, his legs nearly refused to finish the progression into the room. He peered around the edge of the wall. The couch was empty.

The couch is empty.

Henry's eyes flashed around the room, his body tightening with despair, with disappointment. He set the food down with extreme care near the couch, next to the pile of books. He stared at the place where Matilda had sat next to him, their bodies touching along the seams. *She left. She left me.* Henry's hands went numb.

More thunder.

"Henry? Is that you?"

Henry's head snapped up so fast a shot of pain moved down his neck. *Did I imagine her voice?* He looked at the stairs. Soon Matilda appeared. *Good grief, she's beautiful.* He fought the urge to leap across the room and sweep her into his arms just to confirm she was real.

She lifted her hands. "There's an office downstairs. I poked around and found some buried treasure." There were two pillar candles in her hands, a box of matches. The feeling returned to Henry's fingers.

"Good," he breathed.

She stepped closer, emerging from the gathering shadows. "You okay?"

"Yeah, yeah. Of course. I got burgers and sodas." He gestured to the bag of food. He let out one shaky exhale before she came close.

Matilda smiled up at him. "Smells good. Rosemary fries too?"

He nodded, his heart still beating with the fear he'd felt at the sight of that empty couch. He brought his eyes to her face. The only light in the room came from her eyes. She shifted the candles to put a hand on his arm. "Are you sure you're okay? You look . . ."

Henry put his hand over hers. "I'm great." He held her eyes, wanting to kiss her. "Let's eat."

Her face lit up with a smile. She sat in her spot. Henry sighed away his remaining fear and settled next to her.

"So I thought we'd take turns reading, a little here, a little there," she suggested. "Wake up these lost books after such a long sleep."

"My thoughts exactly," he said. He reached out to smooth her hair down her back. When she leaned into the touch he finally allowed himself to smile.

Matilda

Matilda savored the weight and warmth of Henry's hand on her back. Had she imagined the fear in his expression a moment ago? He'd looked like a lost child, shocked and miserable. He must have thought she'd abandoned him. She nearly had. She hated that she'd almost left him standing here by this ugly couch, food growing cold, as he wondered why she wasn't there.

Her fear had taken her as far as the bottom of the stairs. That's where she saw the partly open office door and went inside instead of out the front door. Crammed into the small space was a gorgeous antique roll-top desk. She had rippled her fingers over the roll top, leaving smooth tracks in the thick dust. With a little effort, the cover rolled up. The space below had several pigeon-hole open shelves, rounded filing drawers, and a square section of green marble for writing. Matilda touched the porcelain drawer knobs with reverence and appreciation. She'd never seen the office in her days of book shopping with Jetty. It was very easy to imagine Mr. Booker bent over the desk, a cigarette balanced between his lips, books stacked at his elbows.

Matilda opened every little drawer, finding only the stale smell of tobacco, a few blank pieces of paper, the two candles, and a nearly empty box of matches. *Why candles, Mr. Booker?* Had he enjoyed reading by candlelight late at night, alone in his office? She smiled at the romance of it, and instantly pictured her and Henry sitting on the hideous couch, the candles burning at their feet, books opened on their laps, his body close to hers.

Lost in these daydreams, she hadn't heard Henry come back. When the sounds of footsteps finally reached her ears, she couldn't help the smile, a jolt of excitement in her stomach. The relief on his face when she came up the stairs felt like a reward. No, it felt like a sign, a confirmation. Her soul had been right after all. Thank goodness she'd seen that open office door.

Henry set out the food, while she lit the candles, placing them just as she'd imagined. "This feels like something out of a book, doesn't it?" she whispered, settling beside him. His hand came immediately to her thigh, as if to make sure she didn't disappear.

Henry smiled. "Yes," he whispered. The candlelight made flickering shadows on the wall, the dormer windows were a kaleidoscope of fat raindrops. "Kind of reminds me of *The Boxcar Children*. Did you ever read those?"

"Only one or two. But yeah, I agree. Our own little space away from the world."

"Exactly. Safe haven. But also somewhere we're not really supposed to be."

Matilda put her hand on his. "Refuge."

Henry nodded, his expression saying he thought it was the perfect description. Matilda felt he understood far more than he should, more than anyone else might. It made her feel a sense of wonder, but also comfort. Being with Henry, here like this, was *comfortable*.

He handed her a burger. For several leisurely moments, they ate in silence, glancing shyly at each other. Henry kept one hand on her thigh, never pulling it away. Matilda thought of asking him some personal questions, digging more into the reasons why he was profoundly screwed up, as he'd told her earlier. But the questions didn't want to come. Instead she craved mystery—a storybook atmosphere. She didn't really care what had come before for him or her. She wanted to embrace this refuge, live outside her problems for as many hours as possible. Here in this fictional world that belonged only to them, her mind wasn't broken, her memory wasn't lost, her life was easy. Sitting next to Henry cast the perfect spell. Sitting here not saying a word would be enough to stay enchanted. More than enough.

Wiping his hand on a napkin, Henry reached for the nearest book. It was an old cloth-bound volume, rust red and small. He flipped it open to a random page. With the book on his lap, he moved closer to her, his body pressed against hers. She laid her head on his shoulder, hooked her arm though his, and slipped her hand into his. *So comfortable.*

Henry's voice changed when he read: the shyness and nervousness dissipated, leaving a bold richness. "I am haunted," he began, "by your ghost. Apparitions of what I wanted from you, but never asked for. Specters of your touch I never felt, your voice I never heard. A million spirit thoughts of imagined moments. You exist only in my mind, outside of time. I walk the moors like Death himself stalking those about to die. Only I pursue the idea of you, the dream of us. My scythe is my fear, and I swing it at my own neck."

Matilda sighed. "So tragic."

"So dramatic."

She laughed. "I know. It's perfect. Keep going."

He kissed the top of her head and then read on.

Henry

*H*enry blinked blearily. So warm and contented, he didn't want to open his eyes. He'd dreamed of Matilda, of her tiny body lying next to his. Tantalizing words wafting off her form.

Henry's eyes flashed open to the bookstore's dormer windows, flooded with morning sunlight. He blinked quickly, his mind slow to catch up. Henry started to shift, but there was warm weight on his chest. *Matilda.* His arms instinctively tightened around her. The night came back to him in a delirious rush. The hours of reading and laughing, sitting side-by-side, books on their laps. Her hesitant touches on his hand and arm raising gooseflesh on his skin, awakening heat in his blood. Mostly they'd read from the books, using others' words, but it felt like speaking soul to soul.

We must have fallen asleep. She fell asleep in my arms.

Hugging Matilda tighter, he whispered her name. She shifted suddenly, inhaling sharply. "Henry?"

"Yeah, I'm here. We fell asleep."

She jerked to sitting, pushing hard against his chest. He reached for her, but she was already out of his grasp. "We fell asleep?"

"Yeah."

She gasped. "I gotta go. What time is it?" she said, panicked.

"I'm not sure."

"The library—I can't be late!" Matilda flew off the couch. "Beverly's going to fire me. Oh my gosh!"

Henry's stomach clenched. "I'll go with you. I'll tell her it's my fault."

"No, don't."

He was already off the couch. "I'm coming." He hurried to shove the food trash into the bag and rushed after her. They didn't speak as they speed-walked to the library. The air was balmy and heavy with the scents of wet things. The sun trumpeted brightly, pushing away yesterday's rainy gloom. Tension came off Matilda in waves. Henry didn't know what to say to make it better. So he trailed slightly behind her like a scolded puppy.

At the library steps, Matilda paused, her hands fiddling with each other. "I don't need you to save me."

Henry blinked. "I'm not saving you, I'm just helping. It's half my fault." *I can't be the reason she gets fired.*

Matilda looked over and then away. "I can't lose this job," she whispered.

He took her clammy hand and urged her up the stairs. He held open the door. With her chin lifted, Matilda walked in.

Matilda

Beverly did not look at Matilda as she approached. Matilda knew by the tense, judgmental curve of her boss's shoulders that she was in for it. Her stomach churned, acid in her throat. She wasn't sure if Henry behind her made this moment worse or better.

Matilda swallowed, licked her lips. *Inhale . . .* "Beverly, I'm so sorry."

"Forty-five minutes late. Grounds for termination," came the curt reply.

Matilda wanted to throw up. *Please don't.* "I understand, but this was a random incident. There were . . . mitigating circumstances." She winced at the stupid words. "We fell asleep."

Beverly lifted her eyes from the computer. When they fell on Henry, Matilda knew his presence would not help, but in fact had sealed her fate. *Sentence pronounced.* She braced herself. *I can't lose anything else . . .*

"It's my fault, Beverly," Henry offered gallantly. "Please—"

"It doesn't matter whose fault it is, rules are rules. I'm certainly not going to make an exception because of an amorous evening." Her frown deepened with icy judgment. "Or whatever it is you two were doing."

"Beverly, please," Matilda stepped closer. "Please forgive me. I'll work extra hours—"

"You don't work here anymore. I should *never* have given you your job back." Beverly's cold stare settled on Matilda and Matilda felt the ice in her bones. A cruel smile spread on Beverly's square face, pulling her wrinkles into an ugly grimace. "I always knew," she spat with perverse pleasure.

194

Anger flashed in Matilda's gut. "You pompous beast!" The words shocked all three of them. Henry took a step toward Matilda as if he might have to hold her back, but Matilda couldn't stop the words. "You run this library like a prison ward or, worse, a funeral home. You don't care about the books, only your stuffy, archaic rules. You're the worst librarian I've ever met."

Beverly gasped. An actual, audible gasp of surprise. Matilda grinned and then spun on her heel, flooded with bubbly triumph. *Take that!* It took only until she reached the door for the nausea to return, for reality to bite her neck and suck the life out of her.

Henry was there, putting his arm around her waist as the library doors swung shut. "Matilda . . ."

"Will you take me home?" She leaned into him, too deflated to lift her chin to look at him.

"Of course," he answered softly.

This is what happens when you listen to your soul instead of your brain. This is what happens when your brain is broken.

Matilda stumbled down the steps. One night of bliss and now she was unemployed. How was that fair? She'd taken the risk, turned to Henry instead of away, and what had it gotten her?

Quite possibly the most enjoyable, carefree night of her life. Between bites of The Mad Hash's heavenly fries, they'd thumbed the books, picking passages at random to read out loud. Words rested as easily on Henry's tongue as air. She was mesmerized each time his soft, shy voice filled the dark loft as he read love poems and ghost stories. As they read, the loft creaked sleepily and the rain *pinged* on the windows. She couldn't help but touch him and his hands wandered back to her as often as hers to him. That dusty room had felt like a private island, the worries of life swept out to sea.

And then, as the night waned and their eyes grew heavy, his long body next to hers along the length of the sagging couch. How perfectly she fit against him. His careful touches of her face, neck, and arms as the candles flickered and died. She hadn't even cared when her sleeves crept up to expose her scars.

A pile of open books on the floor, pages glowing in the silvery shadows.

Dreamless sleep in Henry's arms.

No, no. Stop it! It got me fired. Oh my gosh! I don't have a job. What do I do now?

Somehow they were already standing at her back door. Henry reached for the handle but she stopped him. "Thanks, but I need to . . ."

Pain creased his eyes. "I don't want to leave you alone. I'm so, *so* sorry. Maybe I can fix it. Maybe after Beverly cools down I can talk to her. Or maybe . . ."

She shook her head. Turned away. The garden looked good. Healthy and strong. "I think I sealed my fate with that tiny outburst."

Despite the sullen mood, Henry's lips lifted slightly. "She deserved that. And I've never actually heard someone call another person a pompous beast. It fits her perfectly."

Matilda half smiled. "It really does. I've called her that so many times in my head."

Henry laughed. The sound of it made her wince instead of laugh back. She looked away. "I better go in."

Henry put out his hand to stop her. "There are other jobs in town. I can help you find one. I happen to know the guy who writes up the classified ads."

Matilda nodded vaguely. *But what if this is a sign that I shouldn't be here, that being with you, Henry, is the wrong choice?* Her stomach revolted at the idea. "Yeah, umm, I'm gonna go . . ." She moved to the door. She had no legitimate reason to dismiss him other than that the sight of him made her chest shrink a size. She couldn't think straight with him so close, the memories of last night sparking off him like an Independence Day sparkler.

Henry reached for her hand, she pulled away. The pain on his face throttled her heart. "Okay," he said quietly. "Okay."

Sadly, she imagined what this moment might have been like if they'd woken two hours earlier. A tender kiss goodbye, a lingering embrace. She opened the door, turned slightly to say goodbye, but found she couldn't even conjure the strength to say his name. Her eyes met his in a tense, tortuous moment, and then she let the screen door slap shut behind her.

Henry

enry ran all the way back to the library, anger melting away his shyness. He plowed into the foyer. If there was one thing he hated, it was unjust punishment. He'd suffered it enough in his life; he couldn't let it happen to Matilda. Not now. "Beverly!" he bellowed, standing inside the door. A few patrons poked their heads out the ends of aisles. One woman, Lisa Pastor, a part-time cashier at Estelle's Bakery, pulled her toddler daughter away.

Two determined steps forward. "Beverly!" he yelled again.

Finally, she lumbered out of the shelves toward the circulation desk, putting it between him and her. "What do you want, Mr. Craig? I'm not giving Matilda the job back."

"You have to!" His fingers curled into fists until his stubby fingernails dug into his palms. Fear fueled his rage. Fear that the bridge he and Matilda had crossed last night was burned to ashes, he on one side, she on the other. He had to rebuild it, make it better. Make it like it was last night in the candlelight.

Beverly scoffed. "I don't *have* to do anything. She knew full well I would not tolerate one mistake. She abandoned me once. I didn't even have to give her the job back in the first place. But I did and she repays me by being late *and* insulting me. She's done. For good this time."

He plunged to the desk, gripping the edge of the wood. "Please, don't do this. Don't be . . . this way. She's good. She deserves this job. It was one mistake—one mistake that was *my* fault. She never would have been late if not for me."

Beverly crossed her arms and frowned her famous frown. "Yes. That fact is not lost on me. You've done a lot of good since you got here, haven't you?" She huffed sarcastically. "Nothing you can say will

197

change my mind. And I couldn't care less about your little *fling*." She added a nasty smirk for good measure, as if loving someone also broke a rule. "Get out, Henry."

"No!" The word echoed in the large library. Henry felt the eyes of onlookers drilling into his back. Beverly rolled her eyes impatiently as she picked up the phone. Henry watched her, confused. "Who are you calling?" he demanded. Imagining himself in handcuffs, he released the desk.

"Henry!"

Henry spun. Abby was in the doorway, holding open the door. "Abby?"

"Come on, let's go."

"Not until Beverly gives Matilda her job back." His voice had lost some of its strength.

Abby released the door with an impatient sigh. "You know that ain't happening. What happens next is Bev gets Sherriff Bailey to put you in his little cell for the night. He likes you, but Bev's sister is married to his brother, so you don't stand a chance."

"Don't call me *Bev*, Abby O'Nell!"

Abby ignored Beverly's chiding as if she'd been doing it her whole life. Henry shook his head, embarrassment edging out his anger. "But . . ."

"Yeah, I know, but you gotta go now." Abby motioned toward the door. When he didn't move she leaned toward him and lowered her voice. "Beverly's mother left when she was about five and since then Bev's been bent on making everyone else as miserable as she is."

"How dare you, Abby!" shouted Beverly.

Abby ignored her again. "We grew up together; I've watched her do it over and over. So trust me—you'll get no sympathy here, Henry. Best to leave."

Henry looked back at Beverly, the phone cradled between her face and shoulder, her lips pursed smugly, and her face red with anger. With a heavy sigh, he let his shoulders fall forward. He followed Abby out the doors. Abby didn't speak until they were at the bottom of the steps.

"What happened?"

Henry ran his hands back through his hair. "I got her fired. I held her in my arms, and now she doesn't have a job." He looked down at his empty arms. "I think I ruined everything," he added more quietly. "You said she left once. What if she leaves again?"

Abby put her hand on his arm. A car drove passed, wheels sloshing on the wet road. "It's just a job, not even a good one. Who wants to work with that woman?" Abby's eyes moved up the stairs. "And aren't *you* enough reason to stay?"

Surprised, Henry studied Abby's face. "I don't know." He shook his head, his temples throbbing with a fresh headache. "I don't know. What we have . . . it's so fragile. It was one night. I didn't even kiss her."

"Is it—so fragile?" Abby squeezed his arm. When Henry didn't answer, she said, "If it's worth fighting for then go back to her and *fight* for it."

Henry shook his head, stomach hollow and head aching. "She probably won't even let me in."

"You won't know till you knock."

Her door was the Berlin Wall. Henry wanted to climb over it, smash through it, but feared the consequences. Her doorbell looked like the spindle of a spinning wheel. Fated curses and all that. *Maybe we are cursed. Maybe I am.* He thought of going home to bash out his feelings with the typewriter. If he wrote it all out first perhaps then he'd know what to say to her. Because standing there, morning sunshine on his back, he didn't know.

He flexed his hand over the doorbell and then knocked instead. Too quietly. He knocked again.

And waited.

Matilda

Matilda came out of Jetty's room at the sound of the hesitant knock. She'd been lying on Jetty's bed, staring at the letter that Jetty had never wanted her to see. She couldn't shake the feeling that something was wrong, many things were wrong.

Matilda knew it was Henry before she saw his tall silhouette in the fogged glass of the front door. He knocked again, and she sat down wearily on the top step. She wanted to open the door and see him, let him hold her, tell her things would work out. But she didn't know what to say to him or how to feel. Too many things had gone wrong. If she opened the door, what else would fall apart?

Henry knocked once more. She watched his form shift weight from side to side. His hand lifted, touched the glass briefly and she almost felt the heat of his skin on her own. She nearly stood, but the battle in her head kept her in place. Henry dropped his hand, and walked away. Darkness welled up inside her, a pain she didn't understand; it frightened her. It was that same feeling she'd had so many times since she woke up in Jetty's ruined house with six years missing from her mind.

I'm sorry, Henry. I'm sorry.

After the fourth call, Matilda took her phone off the hook. Ten minutes later, Thea stormed in through the back door. Huffing from the hurried climb up the stairs with her large belly, she put her hands on her hips and glared at Matilda's form under the quilt on Jetty's bed.

"She fired you."

"I'm well aware."

"Because you were out all night with Henry."

"Yes. And showed up forty-five minutes late. Also, there was some name calling."

"I'm not sure whether to be angry or thrilled."

Matilda threw the quilt off her face to look at Thea who was grinning like the Cheshire. "Give me a break," Matilda mumbled.

Thea waddled to the bed and sat, rubbing her belly. "'Pompous beast.' I think we should have a nameplate made for her desk; it's the best description of her ever uttered." She laughed loudly. "And you were out all night with Henry!" She clapped her hands. "What happened?"

Matilda sat up. "You're huge. When is that baby due?"

"Couple weeks. Now, a kiss, lots of kisses . . . more?"

Matilda huffed and dropped back to the bed.

"Juicy details, please."

"Please *stop*. Depressed wallowing going on here. Not frippery kiss and tell."

"So he *did* finally kiss you!"

"I hate you."

Thea scooted closer. In a changed voice she said, "I'll miss you at the library."

Matilda looked over. "Thanks."

"What will you do now?"

"No idea."

"Are you going to leave again?"

Matilda blinked at the nervous tone in Thea's question. She sat up and leaned closer. "Why would you think that?"

She shrugged. "It happened before."

"My aunt died. I didn't lose a job."

"You can't leave again."

"I wasn't planning on it."

"You didn't plan it last time either." Thea nodded stiffly, let out a breath. "Did you start your meds?"

So Parker had told her. Matilda felt a rush of shame. She looked over at the letter half under the pillow. "Yes," she whispered.

"I'm so sorry about your mom."

"Me too."

Thea groaned quietly as she adjusted her position. "I think this kid is trying to kick his way out of me." She pushed a palm to her belly.

Matilda watched a small movement lift Thea's hand. "He's really moving."

"Yeah," Thea reached for Matilda's hand, "feel this." She pressed Matilda's palm to the spot. Almost immediately a little pop kicked back. Matilda gasped, pulling her hand away quickly. Her vision faltered, grayness welling up around the edges. In her head, she heard crying, loud and incessant, as if from a child in pain. She closed her eyes, pushing the heels of her hands to her temples.

"Whoa! What's wrong?" Thea asked, startled.

The crying only grew louder until Matilda wanted to dig inside her head to rip out the source. A baby. A baby. Thea reached out to grip Matilda's wrist. The sound stopped instantly.

"Tilly?"

Matilda opened her eyes. "The meds . . . give me bad headaches," she lied.

Thea narrowed her eyes. "That didn't seem like a headache. Do you want me to call Doc?"

"No, no. I'm fine." Matilda lowered herself to the pillow; it smelled of smoke. "I'm fine." She looked at Thea with a thin smile. "What are you going to name him?"

Thea's frown remained, but she played along. "We like Toby."

"That's cute."

"What do you want me to do, Tilly?"

"There's nothing you can do. Beverly won't give me the job back. I'll have to do something else. Though I don't know how to do *anything else*."

"I'll try talking to her."

"It won't do anything but make her mad at you too. Don't risk it."

"Why isn't Henry here?"

"Why would he be here?" Matilda thought of his foggy figure at the door hours ago, his hand touching the glass. Why hadn't she run after him?

Thea gave her a look. "Are you going to be all tragic and stay in bed for weeks?"

Matilda sighed. *Maybe I've earned that.* "No. Just today."

"Good. 'Cause the way I see it, you just got a free pass. Go spend as much time with Henry as you can. Treat it like a vacation. That's what I'd do. Someone will give you a job when you need one."

"Right." There was a beat of silence between them. "What else did Parker tell you?"

Thea smiled. "Only that you found out your mother was sick and you think you might be too. Nothing more. Though I could tell there was more."

Matilda nodded. "I think I'm broken, Thea."

Thea pushed up to standing. "Then fix yourself." She said it so simply, but it hit Matilda like a rock from a slingshot. "I gotta go," Thea added as she pushed her hands into her lower back. Matilda looked away from her pregnant shape. "Also, now you can enjoy the festival instead of standing in the library booth most the night like I get to do. Go with Henry. Eat too much, dance too close, and for heaven's sake, *get that man to kiss you.*"

Matilda smiled. "Yes, ma'am."

Henry

Henry didn't go to work. He couldn't be there without Matilda. He couldn't face Beverly's intrusive lectures or the stares of the townspeople. He holed up on his couch, staring at the repaired typewriter. Fighting the urge to write to her. By late evening he was shaking from lack of food and the temptation.

Beverly was right; he'd done nothing but cause problems from the moment he drove over the city limits. For Abby, for Matilda, for himself. Why had he followed such a thin whim and come here? Why didn't he have the strength to leave? To tuck tail and run, as he should?

Henry went to the kitchen and ate the first thing he saw, an over-ripe banana sitting alone on the counter. He didn't taste it. Standing at the island, he let his mind wander through memories. It only took a few minutes to come to the darkest one. The one he didn't want to think about. But something about the sadness inside him brought it out of hiding.

It had been March, the bleakest month of the year, and Henry was twelve years old. By then he'd grown used to the life of a foster child, and though he hated it, he'd come to accept it. To patiently wait until the day he could be on his own. For the most part, he hadn't had it too bad. No one loved him, but he wasn't on the streets.

School was both easy and hard—the learning was easy, interacting with the other kids was hard. He'd had a few scuffles on the playground that year, but nothing major. Mostly, he tried to stay out of everyone's way. And it was that mentality that brought him his deepest shame.

Late on a Tuesday night, he sat on his bed in the basement room he shared with another boy, Ronny, also twelve and bitter, prone to foul insults and rough slugs to the shoulder. But thankfully, Ronny wasn't home yet from wherever he spent his time. Henry had an old newspaper spread out before him, one he'd found sitting on a park bench earlier that day. He was half way though it when he heard the first sound that something was wrong.

His foster parents were Todd and Mavis Short. Blue-collar, scrape-by kind of people. Mavis liked kids, though she didn't know a thing about how to care for them. Henry had been with them about six months, and while he liked Mavis okay—when there were a few extra dollars she bought them the name-brand cookies at the grocery store—there was something about Todd that made him uneasy. Todd kept his distance, said very little to the boys, tolerating them only because of the State check that came every month, and also, Henry thought, because it gave Mavis something to do besides nag him.

That night Todd came home angry. Henry knew by the sound of Todd's boots on the floor above. Henry paused his reading to look up at the gray popcorn ceiling. *Stomp, stomp, stomp.* Then muffled voices. Henry's hands went cold; he held his breath.

Mavis's first scream made him jump off the bed.

A loud thud. Someone hitting the floor, hard. Henry was up the stairs before he could think. Mavis was howling in pain, pleading with Todd. Her words were slurred. Henry couldn't make out what they were fighting about. Drawn by a morbid curiosity, he followed the terrible sounds.

A slap. Another wail.

Henry found them in their disordered bedroom. He peered cautiously around the doorframe. Todd, a former football star and a house framer by trade, stood over small, smoker-thin Mavis. Her face was bloodied; she drooled blood as she tried to talk to him. Henry was repulsed by her. Maybe more than by the hulking form of Todd. She was sniveling when she should be fighting back, doing something. Henry immediately hated himself for thinking it. What chance did Mavis have against Todd?

Mavis tried to stand and Todd shoved her back to the floor. She hit her head on the nightstand and crumpled, crying quieter now.

"Stop it!" Henry yelled instinctively.

Todd rounded on him. The seething anger on his face drained all the fight out of Henry. He stepped back and hoped he wouldn't lose control of his bladder.

"Get out!" Todd hissed.

Henry's eyes flicked to Mavis. She met his look through her tears. There was such pleading, such fear; Henry felt it in his gut. She reached out a trembling hand to him. But what could he do? Todd took a step forward. Henry ran. Ran as fast as he could. He didn't stop until he found himself in the local bookstore. He ran to a back corner and pressed his face into the dusty seam where a wall met a shelf. He cried as quietly as he could.

The image of Mavis reaching out to him would not leave him. She needed help and he had run. But what could he do against Todd? The man would have beaten him to a pulp. But still, Henry felt deeply he should have done something. Maybe call the police? What would Todd do to him if he did that? What would he do to Mavis? Todd had a healthy dislike for the law—it was the one subject he spoke on regularly.

Angry and helpless, Henry wiped his face on his shirt and turned to the shelf. He pulled out the first book he saw, a random mystery with a bloody knife on the cover. He didn't open it, only tucked it to his chest and closed his eyes. *Breathe.* Then he thought of how he would write his life if it were a book. How he would write this scene so that the weak twelve-year-old boy could triumph. It was the first time he'd done that—turned his life into a story, placing himself as omniscient narrator. The hero, the savior.

He stayed lost in that world of words until the owner of the shop found him and told him the store was closing. Reluctantly, Henry slid the book back into place. He walked home. The night was cold and he didn't have his jacket. At least, he'd still had shoes on when he'd run like a coward. Hugging his arms tightly, he moved slowly, wishing he didn't have to go back and face Mavis's battered body, every cut and bruise a reminder of his failure to help. What had the fight been about? He wondered as he turned the corner.

The flashing of police lights on his street.

Henry stopped to stare, the cold forgotten. His heart started to pound. He took off at a sprint. A police officer caught him as he tried to push past the throng of people near the door.

"Whoa! You can't go in there."

"I live here," Henry whispered.

Something passed over the officer's face. "One of the foster boys?"

"Yes, sir."

The policeman, young, with sharp, intelligent eyes knelt down to face Henry. "There's been an accident. Your foster mom fell down the stairs, and hit her head. Your brother Ronny found her a few minutes before Mr. Short came home from work. I'm afraid she'd dead."

Henry blinked once. "No. I just saw her . . ."

"I'm sorry."

Henry looked past the officer's shoulder. Ronny stood by a squad car, crying. Something Henry had never seen him do. Todd stood close by with another pair of policemen, his head solemnly bent, his face sad. An act. A lie. Henry knew instantly. Todd lifted his eyes and met Henry's. Henry stepped back from the warning in them.

"Are you okay?" the young officer asked.

Henry looked away from Todd. This was the moment to help Mavis, the moment to make up for running away before. Henry looked up at the officer, then to the open door. He saw Mavis's feet near the basement steps. Disembodied by the crowd around her, already less than a person. Maybe she had never been a full person.

"What is it? You can tell me. Did you see something?"

"Nothing," Henry mumbled. "Nothing."

Now, in his apartment in Silent Fields, so many years away from that night, Henry felt the shame and regret as keenly as he had then and in the long weeks after. He had never forgiven himself. He and Ronny had been sent to a shelter that night and placed in new homes a couple weeks later. Henry never saw Todd again, and didn't get to attend Mavis's funeral. He'd made a lot of mistakes since then, but he never wanted to make one as fatal, as significant. If he left Silent Fields now, if he didn't fight for Matilda, would it be something he never forgave himself for?

From that night on, he'd wanted to be a writer. Writers could control what happened, could change it. A magician toying with fate. If he wanted, there could always be a happy ending. That night, though so awful, so haunting, had pointed him to his fate. The juxtaposition was not lost on him.

He wanted to write a happy ending for Matilda and himself. He wanted his words to make it better. But could they? Quickly, as much to clear the cobwebs of the past as to open up the future, Henry went to the typewriter.

A blank piece of paper was already waiting.

Matilda

Matilda fell asleep in Jetty's bed, the pretend tropical sun of the murals on her face. But the warmth didn't follow her into her dreams. There she found only pain, the smell of snow, and a crying baby she could never reach. And Henry standing in the shadows, calling to her.

The sound of keys woke her.

She opened her eyes and listened hard. It wasn't possible. She'd faced that delusion and moved on. She *knew* it wasn't real. Still the keys played their staccato music.

Ignore it. Don't give in to it.

But her body betrayed her, slipping from bed and padding down the stairs. The living room was warm and dark, filled with the tap of typewriter keys. Matilda went to the bookcase and pulled away the protective layer of books. The keys danced on their own, printing words she knew she must read.

```
I want to write you a story. A tale of simple joy,
of easy love. In which there is neither conflict nor
confrontation; all is blissful and sunshine. But if
I wrote that story, neither of us would read it. It
would be forgotten the moment the keys set ink to
paper.

    So instead I write you a tragedy. I write you
reality. We meet. We struggle. We agonize over what
is right and what is real. Do we turn left or right?
Do we run away?

    Do you want to run away as much as I do?
```

I feel you in my bones, in my ambiguous soul. Can that feeling be denied? What is more real than experiencing the uncertainty of love? You are real. I am real. Can we survive this tragedy? Can we survive the beginning and middle to avoid an ending?

I do not want this to end.

I would never forgive myself.

And it is forgiveness that I need.

Matilda ran to the phone. "Abby?"

"Matilda, is that you?"

"Where does Henry live?"

"What?"

"I don't actually know where he lives. I think someone said the Mayor's House? Is that right? *Please!*"

"Yes, that's right. Number three. Is everything okay?"

"I hope so. Thanks." Matilda hung up, and ran.

Running through the streets in her nightgown was not the most modest or sane thing she could have done, but the words on the page had suppressed any logic. All she wanted to do was apologize to Henry. Whether the words from the typewriter were part of her sickness or not, they had rattled a fear loose in her that letting him go would be worse than trying to figure out how to be with him.

Her left leg starting hurting about two blocks from her house, but she kept going. She briefly looked up at the library as she passed, feeling only a quick stab of regret. The town was so peaceful this time of night, the half moon keeping watch. An unexpected harmony filled her as she neared Henry's apartment.

Henry came running out of the building at the same time she started up the long flagstone path. "Are you all right?" he shouted, hurrying toward her. "Abby called." He wore only a pair of blue pin-stripe pajama pants.

Without thinking Matilda threw herself into his arms. He caught her easily, holding her forcefully. "I'm sorry I didn't answer the door," she whispered, her lips against the bare skin of his shoulder.

Henry breathed into her neck. "No, I'm sorry. The bookshop was so perfect and then . . . Beverly . . ."

"I know. But I want to try. Can we try?"

"Yes. We can. Please, yes."

Matilda laughed quietly, her face against his warm chest. She wanted to ask him to take her upstairs, she wanted to stay, her skin against his. She blushed fiercely. *Whoa, girl. Slow it down.* "Did I wake you?" she whispered, hoping her voice didn't sound shy or sultry.

"No," Henry said as he pulled back to look at her. "I was awake. What changed your mind?"

She thought of the typewriter. "I just didn't want to regret you. I'm scared but I don't want to be sorry. I think how we felt in Booker's is real, right, but it's our 'screwed up' thing that keeps getting in the way. I want to find a way to get around it."

Henry nodded, his hand rubbing gently against her back. "Good. I'm glad. I was just thinking the same thing." His eyes moved to her lips, and then back to her eyes.

"But . . . it's not going to be easy. There are things . . ." She wanted so badly to explain, but didn't know how. She still hadn't figured out a way to explain it to herself in a way that made sense. She didn't want to just blurt out that she was crazy, like actually clinically unstable.

Henry sensed her struggle, stepped in to save her. "I get it, really I do. I have things too. We will get there. We can figure it out."

She hugged him tighter. He smelled like books, like fresh paper.

"Do you want to come inside?" he whispered, lips on her ear.

She sighed, allowing her hand to trail down his chest, following a path of freckles. "I better not." It hurt to say it.

Henry nodded. "Yeah, you're right." He tucked her hair behind her ear. "You're right." He took a long breath. "Will you have lunch tomorrow with Abby and me?"

"I'd love to." She almost kissed him, but shied away. This was enough for one night. "Will you walk me home?"

"My pleasure." Henry hugged her close again. "Let me just grab a shirt. Imagine the rumors if anyone saw us like *this*." He smiled mischievously. She laughed again, more tension leaving her body. He ran back to the apartment building. She waited outside, enjoying the quiet night. He was gone only a moment before he was back, taking hold of her hand as they walked barefoot toward her house. They said very little. The hot breeze swirled around. Matilda let herself smile. Cricket song and leaf rustle filled the air.

At the back door, Matilda lifted her chin to look at Henry. She focused on a small cluster of freckles near his lips. *Like berries*, she thought, a strange sense of familiarity flushing her cheeks. *Why does it feel like I've thought that before?* "Why did you come here?" she asked before she really thought about it. "To Silent Fields, I mean."

His expression clouded. "Honestly, I'm not really sure. I was . . . a little lost, confused. I saw an old ad in a random paper and just . . ." He shrugged. ". . . came. I just came."

She nodded. "Jetty always said there are forces at work that we don't know about or understand. Do you believe that?"

He looked at her meaningfully. "I think I'm starting to. You?"

"Yeah. Kind of scary."

"Agreed."

She nodded slowly, apprehension itching at her stomach. *No, don't do that. It'll be okay. It's okay.* "Trying isn't gonna be easy. This, us . . ."

"Not easy. I understand." Henry tightened his hold on her hand. "It's okay. That's normal, right? Doing the little things every day, trusting. Otherwise you end up walking the moors, seeing ghosts, and wanting to swing a reaper scythe at your own neck."

Matilda let out a burst of laughter. "We wouldn't want that. Dramatic, and very messy."

Henry smiled down at her, his eyes softening. "Thank you for coming tonight."

Matilda stepped closer, put her arms around his neck. He held her tight. "I don't want to go inside," she murmured.

"Why wait till lunch—have coffee with me at Estelle's first thing in the morning?" Henry asked.

"Yes."

"Perfect." He released one arm from around her and pulled open the back screen door. "Good night, Matilda."

"Good night, Henry." Her hand trailed down his arm as she moved into the mudroom. Henry closed the door without a sound. Matilda didn't think she could watch Henry walk away without calling him back, so she slipped further into the house. In the dark living room, she stopped to stare at the typewriter. She wanted to feel excited, eager for what was to come, but still fought the darkness in her mind. This darkness inherited from her mother.

Matilda tried to imagine her mother yanking on the steering wheel that night in the car. Her father's certain screams of fear. Had her six-month-old self sensed the danger? *Did I cry?* Was that the crying she heard coming from the corners of the room and shifting in her dreams?

She thought of her favorite picture of her mother. Ivy held newborn Matilda in her arms, in a hospital bed. Baby Matilda was wrapped in a pink blanket, red face puckered with deep sleep. Ivy beamed, her face glowing and eyes bright. Matilda loved the picture because of the joy it had captured. *Fleeting joy,* she thought bitterly.

I don't believe she gave it to me.

Matilda still couldn't swallow the sharp barb of the idea that she, too, had a broken mind. The facts were before her and yet none of them seemed right. But perhaps that was just the denial, the fear of accepting. She had Henry now. She would heal herself and move on. She'd dutifully take her pills, looking forward instead of back. She would not repeat her mother's life.

With new determination, Matilda went out to the garage to scavenge for a box. She found one, medium size, warped and dusty, but serviceable. Back in the house, she took an old white sheet from the linen closet. She snapped it out, letting it open and flutter to the floor. Then she placed the copy of *A Thousand Sleepless Nights*, the typewriter, and all the letters in the center. She wrapped it like a present and put it in the box. Sealing the box with packing tape, she shoved it into the coat closet by the front door, and slammed the door shut.

Moving on.

PART THREE

Henry

July 1998

*Y*ou *still* haven't kissed her. I can tell just looking at your sad puppy-
dog face."

Henry scoffed. Only Abby would have the guts to say something like that before even saying hello. "Well, hello. Nice to see you
too, Abby. I'm fine. How are you?" he teased as they slid into line at
Estelle's. The smell of freshly fried donuts clung to the air. The small
bakery was abuzz with lunchtime conversation.

Abby slugged him in the shoulder. "Don't you sass me, son. It's
been a couple weeks. What's wrong?"

Henry's humor faltered. He turned away, eyes trained on the glass
display case showcasing sugary confections. It reminded him of Matilda
these last weeks. She'd placed herself behind a glass case, prettily displayed as if all was as it should be, but it wasn't. They spent each evening
together. She'd make delicious food, they'd sit outside, and talk lazily
of unimportant things. Each moment, he felt the glass between them,
smooth and cool. It made them both awkward, and though Henry
longed to reach out and take her into his arms, kiss her until they both
melted away, he couldn't do it. It felt too . . . dangerous. The reason for
that feeling completely eluded him. Each night he left feeling twisted up
inside. So naturally, he spilled his worries and frustrations onto the typewriter. Since throwing it against the wall, it hadn't tried to type messages
in response. Mostly he was relieved, but a small part of him felt lonely.

But now he knew why the typewriter had typed back and why
he couldn't remember six years. There'd been a shadow on his MRI,
on his frontal lobe, no bigger than the eraser on a pencil. Dr. Wells
said it could be the damage causing his symptoms or it could just be a
shadow. He wanted to run more tests, but Henry had been putting it

off. The explanation fit. Yet something about it didn't feel right. So it wasn't just Matilda who'd been fouling up their nights together. He'd been distracted, worried. When they'd told each other this wouldn't be easy, they had definitely been right.

Abby nudged him, pulling his attention back. "We are taking things slow," he said with a frown. *What a stupid phrase.* And by the dubious look on Abby's face, she wholeheartedly agreed. Henry braced for the impending lecture.

Abby shook her head. "Henry . . ." A considering pause. The lecture drained from her eyes. "Did she find a new job yet?"

Henry sighed. "No. I've collected applications for every opening in town." They moved forward in line. "And they are *all* sitting on her coffee table. Untouched."

"Well, I guess there's no rush. I think Jerry left her a little money. She'll be okay." Abby clucked her tongue. "Beverly's been talking too. Matilda is smart to wait for that gossip to die down."

Henry's stomach tightened. He agreed, but didn't know how to help Matilda. He wanted so much to fix things, to break through the glass, but didn't know how. They made it to the front of the line, ordered sandwiches and donuts. "Let's eat outside," he suggested, arms loaded with food.

Abby guided him through the crowd and plopped down onto a bench a little way down the street under the shade of a giant maple tree. "Maybe the festival will help pull Matilda out of her funk."

Henry handed Abby her paper-wrapped sandwich. "I hope so." Even now the noise from the setting up of the festival could be heard. Energy flowed like water through the streets of Silent Fields. All of Main Street was lined with fluttering American flags. The BBQ pits were already sizzling, filling the air with the rich smell of roasted meat. "I'm picking her up at five. I tried to get her to join us for lunch, but she said she didn't want to intrude."

"I told her she was welcome!"

Henry nodded as he bit into his sandwich. As it so often did, his mind wandered back to the night in the bookshop. He hoped to find a way to recapture some of the effulgence of that evening tonight at the festival. He wanted to hold Matilda's hand, win her a ridiculously sized stuffed animal, and wrap his arms around her as they watched the fireworks. Kiss her good night. Finally.

Abby set down her sandwich in favor of a hot donut. "Be sure to stop by my quilt tent tonight and say hi. Also, I need to talk to Matilda about one of the books she gave me."

Henry smiled. "Of course. Is Gill coming?"

Abby paid close attention to her donut. "No—old grump. Says he's feeling poorly. Same excuse he gives every year. You think he'd at least try to come up with something new."

Henry felt a tug of empathy. Abby deserved better. Where was that soft concern Gill had shown in the hall that night? "Sorry," he mumbled, unsure how to express his true sentiments.

Abby shook her head, chewed slowly. "He wasn't always this way." It was the first time she had offered explanation or reason for Gill's behavior. "Losing the babies—he didn't reach for the joy. He grew bitter. More with each one, until he . . . changed. The chip on his shoulder is cavernous." An unexpected smile. "How 'bout that word? *Cavernous.* Read that in one of the books Matilda gave me."

Henry offered a smile. "I understand how that could change a person." That phantom black sadness rose inside him.

"Yes, that's for sure. Grief and Gill did not agree. I still love him to death, and sometimes the old Gill is there, sweet and funny, but it's more and more rare as the years go on. Breaks my heart. Breaks his too—he's had two heart attacks in the last five years." A long sigh. "Getting old is extra hard when life has hurt you too many times."

Henry took her hand and kissed her wrinkled knuckles. There was nothing he could say to that. Abby sighed heavily, sniffed. After a moment, she took a sharp breath. "Look at me spoiling this perfect day." She squeezed his hand. "I'm sorry I said all that. Every year I get my hopes up that he'll come and buy me a plate of BBQ. That we'll sit by the Ferris wheel and eat it. That we'll dance under the lights, like we used to. You'd think years of experience would teach me the danger of hope."

"I'll buy you a plate of BBQ."

Abby laughed. "I know you will, son." She touched his face. "Thanks for that." She plucked another donut from the bag. "Sorrow and sugar," she mused.

Henry laughed, taking the donut she offered.

Matilda

*E*ven the weather celebrated.

The hot day gave way to a warm, vivacious evening. From her backyard Matilda could smell the food and hear the music. She closed her eyes, inhaling deeply. *Summer. That is the smell of summer.* The din of the festival rose on the air and with it her spirit.

Her eyes roamed over the fat, thriving plants in the garden. There were baby tomatoes and pumpkins, weighing down their vines. The basil plant was as big as a bush. Matilda bent and snapped off a leaf, bringing it to her nose to inhale the rich scent. Jetty used to put basil leaves under her pillow to keep away bad dreams.

I should put the whole bush under there.

Sadly, she had little influence over the night wanderings of her ruined mind. Last night, and every night since she'd run to Henry, she dreamed of typewriter keys and words. The *clack clack* almost pushing her out of bed to pull the typewriter from its tomb in the closet. But she'd stubbornly resisted, forcing the sound out of her head, fighting for sleep like an angry bear.

The medicine didn't seem to be doing anything to help. She still had no memories or clarity, only headaches. And the sound of keys, and itching fear, and a wall between her and Henry. Because how could she let him love her if she were as unstable as her mother. She hadn't even been able to tell him yet about Ivy and her own possible insanity. The secret sat between them each night, an unwanted stranger.

She fingered the smooth basil leaf, releasing its smell into the air.

"Jetty, why is it so hard to just be happy?"

"I'm sorry, Tilly." Jetty's voice, wispy and far away.

Matilda spun.

An empty yard.

And still hearing voices . . .

Matilda forced her racing heart to calm. She slipped the basil leaf into her pocket, a talisman against the waking insanity. Henry would be there any minute. She walked around to the front porch, focusing on the sounds of the Bright Night Festival. To the west, Matilda saw the top of the small Ferris wheel. Maybe tonight, sitting in a squeaky, rocking cart at the top of the wheel's rotation, she'd finally feel happy enough to let Henry kiss her. Was it possible for a kiss to erase the sorrows of the past and put hope into a bleak future?

This is not a fairy tale.

She wanted to feel different tonight, wanted to feel as normal as she had with Henry that night in the bookshop. She wanted it so badly that she had even left her long sleeves and skirts in the closet. Feeling bold (or maybe desperate), she'd opted for shorts and a tie-dye tank top. Standing on the porch in the heavy, hot air, she felt too exposed, but also exhilarated. Like she could be someone else tonight.

An urge to go to the empty bookshop twitched inside her. Over the past weeks the Ugliest Couch in the World had become a refuge. Most nights after Henry left, she found herself there, fleeing from the mixed emotions of being with him. Every time she was sure the door to Booker's would be locked, but she always found it opened. She'd hoped to find some clarity in the creaking loft, some map of direction on the dormer window glass. All she found was dust and aching sadness.

And yet, every time she'd gone back, pulled to the bookshop like a bee to nectar.

Matilda tugged at the hems of her jean shorts.

I should go change.

"Hello."

Henry always managed to approach with shy stealth, presenting himself as a surprise. A freckled surprise. Matilda's stomach flipped at the sight of his effortlessly handsome figure, dressed in khaki shorts, a Bright Night Festival 1998 T-shirt (which Matilda was certain Abby had insisted on buying him), and flip-flops. No more boot cast.

"Hello," she answered with an easy smile.

"Ready to go?"

She nodded and stepped off the porch. Her hand instinctively went to her forearm, her left leg hiding behind the right. Henry held out his hand and she took it. His eyes traveled over all her bare skin. His fingers rubbed at the scars on her forearm; she wanted to crawl away. "You look radiant," he whispered.

She laughed nervously, some of her self-consciousness fleeing. Henry flipped his arm to expose the underside of his forearm. "Shall we compare?" He smiled as he also held out his leg to show the small scar near his ankle from the accident.

Matilda warmed inside. "I think I win." She lifted her leg out in front. She'd never thought about how much they were both scared. A chill moved through her.

Henry clicked his tongue. "Yeah, I think you do."

Hand-in-hand, they headed toward the fairgrounds, an open dirt field adjacent to the pine-surrounded light theater. Tinkling, breathy calliope music floated toward them. People were everywhere, lifting hands in friendly waves. Matilda had promised to stop by the library tent to see Thea and Parker. She looked over at Henry; it'd be the first time the two men faced each other since the punch. Parker had been faithfully checking up on Matilda, but always carefully when Henry was not around. Maybe they should do that first and get it over with.

They came to the main entrance, a large wooden arch draped in red, white, and blue cloth, and strung with a thousand tiny white lights. As they stepped through, Matilda's breath caught. It was like stepping back in time to old-fashioned fairs of the twenties or thirties: wooden booths and stripped canopies, candies and pies for sale, hats and pinwheels. The energy of the night was intoxicating, the pressure of the happy sounds on her skin exhilarating. She and Henry exchanged a smile.

"Let's hit the book tent first," she suggested. "Then eat because whatever that is it smells *amazing.*"

He led her through the pulsing crowd.

"Tilly!" Thea's voice cut above the clamor, but Matilda couldn't see her yet. "Over here!"

A group of tall teenage boys moved aside. Matilda saw Thea in the library tent. Surrounded by books laid out on folding tables, she sat in a folding chair, belly protruding forward, straining the fabric of her yellow sundress.

"You made it!" Thea said. "Isn't this the best?"

Matilda smiled. "Yes, it is! How are you feeling?"

"Like a whale. Look at me! I can barely stand and I'm convinced my ankles might actually explode if they get any fatter." She rolled her eyes and picked up a paper fan to move air over her red, puffy face.

"I'm sorry," Matilda said. "Should you even be doing this? You look like you should be laying in a bed, a cold rag on your face, and something good on the TV."

Thea laughed. "I won't stay too long. Sadly, I'll miss all the good stuff. But enough about me—how are *you* two? Hi, Henry!"

"Hi, Thea," Henry said shyly.

"We're good." Matilda smiled at Henry, meaning it. "Where's Parker?"

"Right here." Parker came out of the crowd and ducked into the tent to stand behind his wife. He smiled at Matilda, but it faltered when his eyes moved to Henry. "Henry," he said stiffly.

"Parker," Henry returned. His hand tensed in Matilda's grip. "I never . . . I'm really sorry . . ."

"Don't worry about it," Parker saved him, but still the two men stood stiffly, not really looking at each other.

Matilda looked at Thea and they both burst out laughing, which instantly dissipated the tension. Matilda hadn't laughed so freely in . . . *when was the last time I just laughed?* The thought sobered her a bit, but her smile remained. She offered it to Henry and he returned it, a blush of embarrassment across his freckled forehead. She reached up to brush her fingers along it playfully. He released her hand and brought his arm around her shoulder, holding her eyes.

Feeling heat rise in her own face, she turned to Thea and Parker. "Can we bring you anything? Food, cold drinks, an epidural?"

Thea laughed, flapped a hand at them. "No way. Go be lovers in the night. Don't worry about us old, boring married folk."

They said their goodbyes, and Matilda and Henry merged into the crowd.

As the night aged, and Henry and she became more at ease with each other, Matilda felt like herself for the first time since Jetty got sick. Buoyant and carefree. Happily wrapped in the moment. They did all the obligatory fair things: ate too much food, pulled cotton candy from a white paper cone while they rode the Ferris wheel, browsed homemade fare, played impossible-to-win carnival games, walked through the fun house hall of mirrors and laughed until their sides hurt.

Around ten, they made their way to a large white tent on the edge of the fair grounds. A sign, a quilt made of red and blue with white embroidered letters, announced, *Quilts for Charity.* Stepping into the tent, Matilda took in a kaleidoscope of color. The walls were lined with various sizes of quilts, so expertly crafted they looked like paintings. In the center of the quilts displayed for purchase was an expanse of quilting frames slung with unfinished blankets and gaggles of women sitting around pulling yarn into place.

Mesmerized by the display, Matilda didn't initially notice that some of the conversations had lost volume. Henry's hand grew stiff in hers. Her eyes traveled around the tent, startled to find several sets of curious, bitter eyes trained on her. Including Beverly's, sitting next to Rosie Silverton in one of her pantsuits. Matilda blanched, blinked, and nearly turned to run. If Henry hadn't held tightly to her hand, she might have done just that. She moved to tug at her sleeves, but fumbled at her bare skin instead, hating her frivolous choice to be normal tonight.

The accused . . . the outcast . . . the unwanted. Apparently, no one had actually forgiven her for leaving, coming back, yelling at Beverly, and now dating the stranger who had hit Parker. She imagined that several of those buzzing conversations around the unfinished quilts had circled her name. Her embarrassment was soon edged aside by simmering fury.

"There you are!" Abby's cheerful announcement broke the stare down and the tent filled with chatter once again. Matilda stumbled a bit as Abby pulled her into a hug; Henry released her hand, but stood protectively close. "You ignore those nasty hens," Abby whispered into her ear.

Matilda nodded stiffly, hoping her heart rate would return to normal soon. "These are beautiful, Abby." *Normal talk. Say normal things. They don't know you or what's going on. They don't matter.*

"Well, thank you. My mother taught me to quilt. And there's plenty of time on a farm to sew." Abby moved her eyes to Henry. "Have you two had fun?"

"We have. It's quite the party," Henry said, taking back Matilda's hand confidently, as if challenging the hens to peck past his protection. It made Matilda smile and mostly forget their stares.

"And the best is yet to come!" Abby said. "Help me pack up my things. Then it should be about time for the lights to go out."

Henry

The night was both pleasure and torture, as every encounter with Matilda was. Henry's senses were hyperaware of her: each quick, graceful movement, every facial expression, the sound of her words. She'd started the night as a tight coil, but as they moved forward, he watched her unwind to that person he'd seen in the bookshop. A person free from worry.

His own emotions had started about the same: an uncertain jumble, anticipation and hope snarling in his stomach. But now, standing outside the quilting tent, Matilda's hand locked in his, and Abby crooning on about the spectacular sight they were about to see, he felt normal. He felt at peace, a sensation he barely recognized.

"This is the best spot to wait," Abby said excitedly, a large quilt tucked under her arm. Henry carried her picnic basket. "See the pines down the hill there?" she pointed. "That's the place. In about five minutes it's gonna light up like heaven." She hummed in pleasure. "You know, Gill asked me to marry him at this party. We were only sixteen." She laughed. "But that wasn't so unusual back then."

Henry understood even more why Abby wanted Gill to come. Matilda asked, "How did he do it—the proposal?"

"We stood just over there. The lights went out and when they came back on he was on one knee in front of me." She lifted her left hand. "This simple little band held out in shaking hands." She sighed nostalgically. Her smile faded a bit. "I miss *that* Gill."

Matilda reached for her hand, but didn't say anything. For a moment they stood in silence. Henry's mind wandered to the idea of marrying Matilda. He'd been careful not to think too far down that road, but now it rose so easily in his thoughts. And it felt so perfect, so

225

natural, and yet there was an itch of fear. Or something negative—he wasn't sure exactly what the feeling meant. But it was easy to picture himself kneeling down, a ring in his shaking hands—maybe in a bookshop or library—and then . . . life. Lying beside her in bed on Saturday mornings, watching TV late at night, light flickering on her face, a child, maybe two or three. Sitting on the porch, wrinkled hands joined, watching the sun set. The kind of life he'd never had, never actually witnessed, but knew existed, and wanted more than anything.

Without warning, all the lights cut out.

The world went from a whirlwind of color and light to dark indigo shadows. Raucous cheers filled the air. Henry blinked a few times, his eyes now picking up the pearly moonlight from the swelling gibbous moon high in the sky.

Matilda laughed beside him, a zing of excitement moving from her to him, and Henry felt everything would be okay between them. Whatever she couldn't tell him and all the things he couldn't tell her would eventually see the light of day and they could sort through it all. It wouldn't matter what it was. Because *this* was how they should be.

"Here it comes!" Abby called out.

In a delirious moment of anticipation, the whole town went silent, energy rising on the air like steam. Matilda leaned her head against Henry's arm. With a snap that could only be felt, not heard, the giant pines erupted with light, so blinding Henry closed his eyes involuntarily.

Matilda pulled her hand from his and she and Abby clapped, laughing. Henry watched the two women, faces flooded with light. Matilda looked back at him, smiled, and held her hand out to him. "It's amazing," she yelled. "Isn't it?"

He laughed. "It certainly is." He wanted to kiss her, but hesitated, and she turned to listen to something Abby was saying.

The big band music started, only slightly louder than the animated commotion. The three, joined again at the hands, hurried after the crowd. The square of pines boxed in about two acres of perfectly cut grass. There was a large opening at one end through which everyone passed under another big red, white, and blue arch. Each of the tall trees, at least fifty feet tall, were wrapped expertly in white lights, and so radiant as to be almost too bright to look at. The band, on a stage at the opposite end, filled the theater with their happy music. The smell of frying donuts dusted the air. A large area in front of the stage had been roped off for dancing. The rest of the grass was quickly filling with blankets and lawn chairs.

Henry had never seen anything like it; his jaw fell open in awe.

"Over here," Abby tugged on Matilda's hand. "Best spot for watching the fireworks later."

"She's right," Matilda said. "Jetty and I always sat over here too." Abby smiled appreciatively. "If you sit on the other end some of the lower ones get blocked by the trees."

Abby shook out the quilt, allowing it to flap out in the air in the satisfying way that heavy blankets do. It glided to the ground and they all sat. Henry fumbled with the clasp on the basket before handing Matilda and Abby a glass of strawberry lemonade, pink as tulle. He poured his own glass, took a long swig, and then leaned down on his elbow.

"I didn't see my first big firework show until I was sixteen," he said.

Matilda turned to him. "Seriously? How is that possible?"

Henry shrugged. "I never got placed in a family who was big on celebrating. Sure I saw some from far away—Fourth of July and such—but I never sat right under them until the summer between my sophomore and junior year of high school. A small group of us drove in for the River Days Celebration on the Riverfront in Detroit. Every year they do a big fireworks show. It's really great." Henry lifted his chin to look at her. "You know that deep *thud* in your gut each time a big one goes off?"

Matilda nodded, smiling.

"Well, that is what surprised me the most. That huge sound and how visceral it is. And I *loved* it. I was so disappointed when the show ended." Henry's eyes moved to the sky. "I could have sat there all night."

"Did you go back again?" Abby asked.

"Every year I could."

"The friends you went with—are you still close? Was one a girl-friend?" Matilda grinned, a hint of tease in her tone.

Henry laughed. "No and no. They were just casual friends. Those kind in high school who are just there out of convenience more than anything. I never really had any close friends. Abby is probably as close as I've had to a best friend."

Abby gave him a big grin. "Well, aren't you all kinds of pathetic?"

Matilda's laugh rang out.

"Yep, all kinds," he answered, smiling.

Matilda set her empty glass aside. "But I can't claim anything much better. My Aunt Jetty was always my best friend. There was Callie Burkins in junior high. We were both shorter than all the other girls and liked to read more than we liked people. So we'd sit together reading and talking about what we read. But she moved during ninth grade. Then I adopted the casual friends. Even in college. Parker was my first real friend."

Henry nodded with understanding, ignoring the little spurt of jealousy. "Favorite book as a kid?"

"*Matilda* by Roald Dahl, of course. I felt like he'd written it just for me, and not just 'cause of the name. I have three different copies of it. You?"

Henry's eyes had grown wide. He stared at her as if he hadn't heard her correctly.

"What?" she asked, almost laughing.

He shook his head. "That's a little crazy because mine was *Charlie and the Chocolate Factory* by Roald Dahl. A little boy handed a sad lot in life that miraculously gets everything he's ever dreamed of. I imagined I was Charlie so many times."

"That is crazy." Matilda shook her head, smiling at him. "How 'bout you, Abby? Favorite book as a kid?"

Abby pursed her lips. "Let's see. I think I checked out *Pippi Longstocking* at least twelve times from the library. Wore out the copy. Have you read it?"

"Of course," Matilda said. "Fantastic choice."

Henry sat up, reached into the basket and produced a plate of chocolate chip cookies. For a moment they worked on their cookies. The dance floor spun with couples. Henry let their hypnotizing movement pull him along.

Matilda said, "The cookies are fabulous, Abby."

"Thank you. I take that as high compliment from such a great cook."

"Well, it's all thanks to Jetty. And she was much better."

They chatted for several minutes, the cookies disappearing from the plate. Abby brushed the crumbs from her fingers and gestured to the dance floor. "Well, you gonna ask this girl to dance or not, Henry?"

Heat flashed in his cheeks. "I'm not much of a dancer, I'm afraid."

"You can't be worse than me," Matilda said playfully. "I'm the one with the limp."

Abby laughed heartily. Henry jumped to his feet and offered Matilda his hand. "I guess we can go fumble around and embarrass ourselves. Might be fun."

Matilda laughed as she took his hand.

They danced for nearly an hour because Henry didn't want to let Matilda go. His ankle started hurting after only twenty minutes, but he soon forgot it. The hot, sweet air and her body pressed to his—he would have stayed on the dance floor all night. Finally, breathless, Matilda said, "My legs are going to give out and I think we've left Abby alone long enough. Should we head back?"

"By way of the donut and root beer tables?"

"Of course."

Back at the quilt, they found Abby chatting with people nearby. Henry handed her a donut and glass of fresh root beer, and he and Matilda settled in for the fireworks. He placed himself behind her, scooping her into his arms.

The first firework exploded in the satin sky. The ebullient crowd erupted in cheers. Henry felt the *boom* deep in his stomach. He lowered his head a bit, and spoke near her ear, "This festival makes me think of *Something Wicked This Way Comes*. Bradbury. The fair and the carousel. The fireworks. It's October in that story, but still . . . there's something a bit mysterious and magical about this kind of thing."

Turning her head to him, she said, "That's one I haven't read."

"Really? Well, I have a copy at my place. We can get it after. And it's about time you saw my apartment anyway."

Matilda smiled. They focused on the fireworks again, Henry's heart pounding. There'd been this unspoken agreement that they would always meet at her house, but he wanted to show her his apartment, make her a part of it. Maybe her standing in the sparse room would lessen the loneliness of it. And to loan her a book—loaning out books was an intimate exchange. Here's a piece of my heart, a piece of my mind: take it, hold it, experience it.

The fireworks ended with a raucous finale. The crowd cheered until the whole world seemed full of sound and energy. The applause lasted a full five minutes before the crowd started to disperse. As the field cleared, the band played some slower, sleepier songs. Henry felt drunk on it all.

After seeing Abby to her car, he led Matilda through town toward his apartment. They exchanged few words, the silence charged with the possibility of things to come. He allowed himself no expectations; he only wanted to bring her into his world a little more. Kiss her once. Or twice.

Once they were alone on the street, he took her hand in his. So small! And yet, a perfect fit. She smiled in the dark, walking close to him. When they stopped outside the white colonial Mayor's House, Matilda's eyes lit up. "I've always loved this old building. I love that you live here."

"That one is mine." He pointed to the east corner, and then pulled her forward, after him up the stairs. The energy between them was now palatable, frantic, and unsure. He felt it, knowing she did too.

Henry unlocked the door and stepped back for her to go in first. Her body brushed his as she passed; he had to close his eyes. *Just loaning her a book,* he reminded himself. He switched on the dull kitchen light.

Matilda gasped. "Henry, your books!"

"It's a weakness," he grinned. He thought about turning on more lights, but felt it would ruin the atmosphere. The shadows complimented their energy, his mood.

Matilda crossed excitedly to the shelves, and started perusing spines. The bookshelf was nearly full now; the staff at the El Dorado store knew him by name. She touched them gently, lovingly, and Henry felt each one as if it were a caress on his own skin. He watched her, folding his arms over his chest. The tilt of her head. The lift to her toes to see higher. The muscles of her lovely legs flexing and releasing as she moved. He was glad she'd given up the long skirt for tonight. Every ounce of his loneliness skittered away. He found he had never liked his apartment more.

No longer able to resist, he crossed to her, hesitant hands on her hips. "Matilda . . ." he whispered into her hair. Citrus and cinnamon.

She turned in his grip, and now, face to face, he saw something urgent yet unsure in her movement, her expression.

She lifted to her toes, as she'd done with the books. Her fingers came to his lips, as they had in her kitchen on the night of the storm. A small smile played at her mouth, erasing all his hesitation. Henry lowered his lips to hers. The undertow of passion that erupted sent them rocking backward into the shelves. Henry's foot knocked an entire stack of books to the floor, pages crunching. The feel of her tiny body against his, the taste of her sugared breath in his mouth was beyond anything he'd imagined. Words failed him. The world existed only in her lips.

After several minutes, the kiss slowed. Henry pulled back a little to see her face, to read her emotions. To make sure everything was as right as he felt it was. She laughed. "Why did we wait so long?"

He laughed too, pulling her into a tight hug, lifting her a little off the floor, her chin resting on his shoulder. Suddenly, she stiffened. Everything about her changed from liquid warmth to frigid ice. He set her down, and she jerked away.

"What's wrong?" he said breathlessly.

She hurried past him. He turned to watch her cross to the desk. Mesmerized, confused, he waited while she lifted a quivering hand to the keys of his typewriter. Laying next to it, betraying him, were several letters he'd written to her during the week. *So many daring words!* Her fingers trembled above the pages as she shook her head slowly, and then frantically, as if flinging off an unwanted pest.

"No," she whispered once. Her only word.

Henry fumbled for what to say, wanting to explain the letters she was now shuffling across the desk. "Matilda . . ."

She bolted.

She was out the door before he could blink.

Matilda

*R*un. Running. Ran. As fast as she could. Ignoring Henry's pursuit. His slapping feet on the pavement, his calls of her name.

Matilda charged through the back door of her house and into the dark quiet. Her mind was in denial. "No," she said aloud. "No. Can't be possible." She did her best not to think of Henry's incandescent kisses, the feel of her body close to his, the perfection of his embrace. How *at home* she had felt. She *couldn't* think of that now. It would get in the way.

Plowing forward, she stumbled into the living room and threw open the coat closet. She dragged the box out, scrambling to disinter the typewriter. Sheet askew, it sat there on the floor, squatting like a predator. The black shining in the silver light. Several fresh letters lay next to it, scales sloughed off.

Sentences leaped up at her.

```
I'm terrified of what I don't know. Can you cure the
blackness . . .

    I despise my loneliness and yet find perverse
comfort in it . . .

    Can you hear the beat of my heart? I swear
it matches yours even when you are far away from
me . . .
```

Matilda backed away, crab walking, until she could tuck herself in the shadowy corner. Knees to chest, tears hot on cheeks.

"Matilda? *Matilda*!" Henry burst into the room. He saw the typewriter first, a tremor moving through him. He knelt slowly, so *slowly*.

He touched it. *Yes, it's real,* Matilda told him silently. He lifted the letters, the paper wavering in his unsure hands.

Henry dropped the pages like hot stones.

His eyes searched for her. Finding her in the corner, he approached cautiously. *Don't scare the natives.* "Matilda?" he whispered in a voice that was not his own. "I don't understand . . ." He shook his head. *No, this is not a dream. Or maybe it is. Perhaps nothing has been real since I woke up in my decaying room.* "The typewriters . . ." Henry breathed.

"The typewriters," she repeated, her own voice sounding strained and far away.

He collapsed to the floor, legs out, hands hung in his lap. "I don't . . . *the letters.*"

"Your letters."

"To you."

Matilda closed her eyes.

"Did the typewriter . . . ?" he swallowed, looked over at the black beast.

"Yes, it did."

Henry exhaled sharply. Matilda opened her eyes. His hair was a mess. She was sure hers was too. "But I don't . . ." he started.

"Understand. I . . . *we* don't understand." She wished he would move closer, hold her. But she also wished he would leave and let her stay in her corner forever. If the letters were real did that mean she wasn't insane? But wasn't this an insanity all its own?

"Matilda," he whispered carefully, "are you missing six years of your life?"

Matilda jerked, pulling her knees tighter into her chest. For a moment, she couldn't speak. "Yes." The word could have been an explosive. "Henry, do you have a book called *A Thousand Sleepless Nights*?"

Henry slouched more. "Yes."

A clock-ticking silence.

"What does it mean?" Matilda dared to ask. Henry did not look at her. He looked at the typewriter. She looked at it too. They sat in silence, imprisoned by the dark and the night's pernicious revelations.

The phone rang.

Once.

Twice.

Three times.

Henry

A tremor of white moonlight hovered near Henry's right foot, flickering with the movement of the clouds. He stared at it as if not knowing what it was, what it meant. There'd been noise and lights and happiness tonight. *Was that tonight?* It now felt so far away. His body had grown stiff and uncomfortable. The phone rang, again and again. But he didn't hear it, only hyperaware of Matilda trembling in the corner, only an arm's reach away. Every hitched breath she took was his, every confused beat of her heart he felt in his own chest. Yet, he did not have the strength or the will to move to her; the air was too charged with their discoveries. If he moved that energy would shatter the whole world.

The phone, a fly buzzing in the background.

To his other side sat her typewriter and his letters, half buried in a white sheet. Taunting ghosts of what they did not know. The impossible words swam about his head; he desperately wanted to swat them away, but felt he deserved the punishment.

Matilda sighed. The small, despondent breath tugged at him, awakening him from the haze of the night. He wanted to touch her; he wanted to run away. "Tilly?" he mumbled, his voice not his own.

She noticeably flinched. "You've never called me that."

He blinked, confused. The name had come as easily as breath. He slid closer to her, careful not to disturb the weighted air. "Matilda . . ."

She wouldn't look at him and shrank away as he drew closer.

The phone again.

"Answer it," Matilda said. She sat up, looked at him, her eyes red and tortured. Something flashed on her face. "It's Abby. Answer it!"

Henry got to his feet. "How do you . . ." But he was running to the kitchen. Henry answered the call. "Abby, what's wrong?"

Crying on the other end, muffled and broken. "Gill . . . a heart attack. He's not . . ."

"We're coming," Henry said quickly, the fog leaving his head. It wasn't a question of if Matilda would come with him or not; she had followed him in the kitchen and was headed to the door. And he could not leave her now even if his own heart stopped.

"Abby . . ." The line had grown so quiet.

"Dr. Wells's clinic," was all she said, the exhaustion and fear in her voice stabbing Henry in the gut.

"Five minutes."

Matilda opened the door. Henry took the keys from her as they hurried into the Beetle. He drove in silence, panic clogging his throat and the desire to hold Matilda's hand blurring his eyesight. The streets were deserted. The town slept soundly after the giddy exhaustion of the celebration. Burned sparklers and food wrappers lay forgotten on the side of the roads. The air still smelled of roasted meat and donuts.

Matilda stared out her window and didn't look at Henry once. Every moment of last night flashed through his mind fast, faster until he was nauseous. *The letters . . . my letters. The typewriters. Six lost years. Kissing Matilda in my apartment.* He looked at her profile, her hair slung down along her jawline. He felt he should know something more about what they'd discovered. Sitting in this car with her felt eerily familiar. He felt he should understand, but did not.

Not at all!

Henry and Matilda ran into the clinic. Only half the lights were on inside. The oak paneling glowed yellow, the white walls nearly gray. They rounded the empty reception desk and found Abby standing in the exam room hall leaning into the wall, arms hung limp at her sides. Her face was nearly as gray as the walls and looked older, more burdened than Henry had ever seen it.

"Abby," he whispered as they came near. She startled and then collapsed into his arms, sobbing loudly. Henry's guilt soured the back of his throat. Abby was the only person who had ever been there for him. Always there exactly when he needed. And now, when she needed him, he was late.

Matilda hesitated, uneasy behind them, and then stepped forward to put her hand on Abby's back. Henry's eyes met hers over Abby's shoulder. She looked away, but put her other hand on his forearm.

Dr. Wells came out of the room next to them. His thick limbs hung heavy, crumpled forward. Seeing Henry, the doctor ran a hand back over his slate gray hair and shook his head. Dropping his chin, he slipped away down the hall.

Henry's stomach dropped to his feet. He tightened his grip on Abby. Matilda wiped her cheeks.

"I turned my back on him," Abby wept. "He said he didn't feel right and I turned and walked out anyway. I was mad. I wanted to go to the festival. I should have known. He has a bad heart. I should have stayed." She took an unsteady breath. "He was alone." Her sobs became wails of agony.

Henry swallowed hard. He didn't know what to do with that kind of grief, with such raw, electric emotions. Matilda nodded to the chairs nearby. Henry led Abby to them and settled her shaking body into one. Holding tightly to her hand, he said, "I'm sorry. I'm so sorry." The words sounded so pathetic.

Matilda walked away. For a moment Henry thought she was leaving, but then he smelled coffee brewing. He wanted to say more to Abby, but words failed him. And that made him angry. *Of all the times not to have beautiful, comforting words . . .*

Abby sniffed loudly. "I found him when I got home. He must have been lying there for hours. His face was blue, but he was still breathing . . . barely. I begged him to live . . . I yelled at God." Henry put his arm around her. She fell against his shoulder, her body heaving with her crying. *Say something to her!* But his mind remained empty. Abby went on, "I told Him He couldn't possibly be so cruel as to take Gill too. He'd already let the man I married slip away after the babies, but at least Gill was still there. The house wasn't empty."

"You don't deserve it," Henry mumbled weakly as his eyes began to burn with tears.

"He never woke up. I never got to tell him I'm sorry and that I love him . . ." Abby grew unsettlingly quiet, her body stiff. Henry rubbed her arm, frantic for something to say.

Matilda came back with three mismatched mugs of steaming coffee. "Abby, here . . ." She held the mug out, Abby reached out to take it. She circled both hands around it, leaning her body forward to let the steam rise to her face. She sipped slowly.

Matilda frowned as she handed Henry his mug, avoiding his eyes. He lifted his hand to reach for her, but she moved away to sit on the other side of Abby. After a few minutes of silence, Matilda leaned close to Abby. "Before Jetty died, she told me that grief can be dangerous. I'm still so sad and angry. More angry than I thought possible. It's stuck like a bur in the side of my heart. I've felt its pain with every beat, every breath. For *years*." She sighed, shook her head. "It's the ugliest feeling. Don't be angry, Abby. Not at yourself or Gill or God. Gill loved you. You loved him."

Henry's lips parted in astonishment. Matilda had said the words he couldn't find. Abby began to cry again, but in a different, more solemn way. She nodded as she reached for Matilda's hand. Matilda finally looked over at Henry. Something in her expression tugged at him. He felt he'd seen that grief and sadness before—in her, in himself. His stomach tightened as he realized what the typewriters and letters meant. *We knew each other. BEFORE.* Henry took in a breath. And something terrible had happened. But what? Matilda nodded, as if she'd heard his thoughts. He opened his mouth to speak, but then remembered Abby sitting between them.

"Come home with me, Abby," Henry said softly. "You can rest."

Abby looked to the closed door behind which lay her dead husband. "This doesn't feel real."

Matilda took Abby's empty mug. "Did you say goodbye?" she asked.

Abby nodded, inhaled sharply. "What will I do without him?"

Matilda winced, the look so painful that an ache rose in Henry to match it. "We'll help you," Matilda answered. "Let us take you to Henry's. I'll cook—" Abby began to shake her head. "I'll cook and you *will* eat. You have to eat. And Henry will read to you until you fall asleep. Okay?"

Abby shuddered, her eyes still on the closed oak door. Matilda took her hand. After a moment, Abby looked at her, nodded. Henry helped Abby to her feet; Matilda picked up Abby's purse. Dr. Wells stepped out from behind the desk as they approached. To Henry he said quietly, "There will be arrangements . . ."

Henry cut him off. "Do what you need to do. I'll check back in the morning."

Dr. Wells nodded with understanding. Matilda handed him the coffee mugs and he retreated.

Henry eased Abby into the front seat of Matilda's car. Matilda sat behind her, leaning forward to keep a hand on the old woman's shoulder. As Henry walked around to the driver's side, he quickly brushed the tears away that finally found their way down his cheeks.

Matilda

Matilda cooked eggs with tomatoes and basil in Henry's kitchen. The basil was from her own garden, sealed in a plastic baggie and given to Henry only days ago. *Another lifetime, other people,* Matilda thought as she resealed the bag and returned it to the fridge.

Abby ate more than Matilda expected, and it made Matilda feel better. Hopefully Abby too, although Abby's face remained pale, her eyes distant. Matilda sat on Henry's couch with her legs tucked under her, staring at his typewriter as she listened to him read Abby to sleep. Matilda didn't hear the words he said, only the cadence of his voice. The only words in her head were those of the letters he had written.

He'd written them to her not knowing she read them. She knew every word was as real as it could be, every sentence unabridged, unrestrained. Raw. She found satisfaction in that. But not comfort.

Henry startled her with a hand on her shoulder. "She's asleep," he said. She didn't look up, her eyes still on the typewriter. "Do you want me to put it somewhere else?" he asked.

At that she did look up, finding the underside of his chin as he also stared at the typewriter. "No," she whispered. "We can't hide from this. Sit with me."

Henry sat, leaving space between them. Matilda hated that space, but found it necessary. The last time she'd been in this room there'd been passion hot enough to curl the edges of some of Henry's books. Part of her wanted to throw herself into his arms, kiss him, touch him, until ecstasy evaporated all the bad. She cleared her throat. "Tell me more."

"I woke up in the Detroit library, thinking it was 1992. The book and the typewriter on the table in front of me."

"I woke up in Jetty's house, in my bed, the place in shambles, and I thought it was the morning after I left Silent Fields. I thought I'd decided not to go. The typewriter and book were on the bed."

Henry ran a hand back through his hair. "How is that possible?" he whispered. Unexpectedly, he stood and went to the desk. He returned with a scrap of paper and a pen. "Write, 'For Henry.'"

Matilda's heart pounded. She took the paper, lowered it to the simple pine coffee table. With an unsteady hand, she wrote the words while Henry went back to the desk to rummage through a pile of books. He came back with his copy of Louis Winston's book. The sight of it, real and held in Henry's hands made her shudder.

He opened to the title page and lowered the book next to the scrap of paper. The air stilled. "The same," he murmured.

"Mine says 'For Matilda.'"

Henry knelt down and wrote the words next to hers on the paper.

"The same," Matilda echoed. She'd know that handwriting anywhere. "I've read this book at least ten times. Something about it . . ."

Henry shifted to sit on the floor, his shoulder against her leg. "I've only read it once. The night I punched Parker."

"Is that why you were so upset? Why you were . . . crying?"

"Yes. The words were so hard to read and they felt so . . . familiar. So blindingly real."

For a moment, they said nothing. Matilda stared at the mountain scene on the cover of *A Thousand Sleepless Nights*. "I did run away and . . . we met," she finally said, feeling dazed.

"We fell in love," Henry said. "I can't remember it, but of that I am sure." He fumbled for her hand and she took it. She rubbed his knuckles, as certain as he.

"What happened? Why is that book so important to us?" Matilda bit her bottom lip. "And the typewriters?"

Henry slowly shook his head. "Do you feel that?" He leaned into her leg. "When you think of that lost time."

She squeezed his hand. "Something terrible."

"Yes."

"I thought I had gone mad. Actually, insane. Same as my mother."

Henry looked up at her. "What do you mean?"

"My mom—there was something wrong with her mind. She . . . saw things and thought things that weren't real. She drove our car into oncoming traffic and killed herself and Dad. I was six months old." She shivered, took an unsteady breath. "I didn't know until a couple weeks after all this started. I found a letter in Jetty's room. I thought . . ."

"You had inherited her condition?"

"Yes," she breathed. "I even started taking medication. I've wanted to tell you but didn't know how."

Henry sighed, kissed the back of her hand. "I'm sorry." He shook his head. "I had no idea how to explain my memory loss. So I ran from it. I saw the job announcement for the editor here and just ran. Then when the typewriter typed back, I was sure there was something wrong with me. I threw it across the room."

"But how . . ."

"I put it back together."

"The grease under your fingernails."

"Dr. Wells found a shadow on an MRI of my brain. I thought that explained everything. I thought I'd been in an accident and hurt my head. Amnesia, you know?"

Matilda's pulse quickened. "The scars . . ."

Henry frowned, his eyes dropped to her left leg. "We both have scars. We must have been in an accident together, but amnesia? Both of us for the exact same amount of time?" He scoffed. "That sounds impossible, right?"

Matilda looked over at Abby asleep in the bed, a mound under Henry's gray comforter. "Do you have dreams?"

Henry stiffened. "Nightmares. I'm hurt, someone is crying. I'm desperate to help, but can't. I never see anything clearly."

"Me too. There is someone with me—I can feel them. I call out, but never hear the name. All I can hear is a baby crying." Another chill down her spine. Henry turned to her. "I think it was you I called to," she said slowly. His face paled, his eyes grew wide.

Matilda thought of the empty side of her bed. She thought of that moment in The Mad Hash when her eyes had found his. The air in the room now rippled as it did then, smelling of books and cinnamon.

Henry whispered. "I want to remember."

Matilda let her eyes fall to *A Thousand Sleepless Nights*. The cadence of the words, the feel of them were so similar to Henry's letters. She sat forward. "You're Louis Winston!"

"What?"

"You wrote this book, these stories. It was published in 1997, during the lost time. You wrote it!"

Henry shook his head, but the movement soon slowed. He lifted the book. "I have a PhD in creative writing. I . . . I've wanted to be a writer most of my life." The scene from his childhood of Todd beating Mavis flashed in his mind. "But I checked on this book. It's from a small publisher in Detroit. I called and they said they couldn't give me any personal information on Louis Winston. They said I could write a letter and they would pass it on. I never heard back."

Matilda knew she was right, two pieces coming together in her head. "My middle name is Louis."

Henry stilled. "Mine is Winston. Louis Winston. A pen name made from both our names." He touched the book again and opened to the dedication page. "'For my wife, who breathed life into these once pathetic stories and awakened my shy heart with her shining brilliance and sublime beauty.'"

The air in the room stopped moving, all sound sucked away in the vortex of those words. Henry's hand went cold in Matilda's grip. "For my *wife*," he repeated in a whisper.

Henry

$\mathcal{M}$atilda pulled her hand away from Henry's to cover her face. Henry, suddenly restless, stood and went to one of the tall single hung windows. He pushed it open as wide as it would go, letting in the warm, sugary breeze. He sucked in a few breaths as memories sparked in his head.

"We met at the library," Matilda said. "I ran away and didn't stop until I saw that beautiful library in Detroit."

"It took me nearly a month to find the courage to ask you to dinner."

"We went to that little Italian place, with the divine ravioli. I ate two plates, and then we had gelato. Dark chocolate. It was like silk."

"I held your hand on the walk back. The streets were so crowded with people."

"You kissed me for the first time in the stacks."

"My favorite place to be with you."

"You wrote me love letters."

"On the typewriters."

Henry did not move. His feet were rooted to the floor. He could feel the joists in the wood plank floors, the large beams underneath, the electrical wires, plumbing, dust settled between—all of it. Abby shifted in his bed. Gill was dead. And Matilda was his wife.

"But I don't remember . . ." Matilda started.

"There's more. I can't remember asking you to marry me or the wedding."

"There's more." Matilda sighed loudly as she dropped her head to the back of the couch. "My name is Matilda Craig. It felt weird when Beverly called me Miss White."

Henry shuddered, finally finding a way to move. He lowered his chin to look down into the empty street. A flutter of movement caught his attention. Someone walking. A woman in a long flowing skirt, curly hair. Henry stepped closer, looking down the length of the building, but she was gone. Something about her was familiar . . .

"Henry?" It was Abby, her voice weak and thin.

He went to her, Matilda came too. "What's wrong?" he said.

Abby shifted, sitting up against the pillows. She looked from him to Matilda. "The memories will come back."

Henry blinked. "You heard all that?"

"You think I could actually sleep?" She shook her head. "You're married!" A big smile. "I can't believe this. I always knew there was something between the two of you, something more. It's bizarre, for sure, but you're together again. I have to believe your memories will come back."

Matilda looked away. Henry asked, "But what do we do? We don't know how this happened. This kind of thing shouldn't be able to happen. How does so much time just disappear? And the books and typewriters?"

Abby shrugged. "I don't know. But sometimes it's not the how, but the why. *Why* did this happen to you?"

Matilda wrapped her arms around herself. Henry wanted to hold her. She said, "It feels like a punishment."

"Oh, Tilly. Don't say that," Abby cooed. "You found each other again. That can't be punishment. It's a miracle, really."

Henry's mind spun, a carousel of information, out of control. "But Matilda's right," he said. "It feels . . . black. Dark."

"Loss always feels that way." Abby closed her eyes.

For several minutes no one spoke. Henry dug deep into his mind, trying to force memories to the surface. A few had come, why not all? Matilda caught his eye. Henry felt the turn of her mind match his and all the words neither of them could say out loud like rocks in the gears. The despondent curve of her shoulders, the droop of her head brought a hot sting to the back of his eyes. He looked away.

Matilda lowered herself to the bed. Henry suddenly realized how bone-deep tired he felt. He lay down also, he and Matilda curled into matching positions on their sides, parentheses around Abby. He wanted to say something but didn't know what.

Cricket song drifted in through the open window.

At some point, all three of them succumbed to exhaustion and fell asleep.

Matilda

*B*irdsong pulled her from a restless sleep. Matilda blinked. Her shoulder and neck were wickedly stiff. A thick shaft of sunlight came in the open window, a square spotlight on the wood floor at the foot of the bed. She stared at the dust swirling in the tunnel of light for several long, unmoving moments.

Henry is my husband.

She could hear him breathing steadily on the other side of the bed, but didn't look over.

Henry is my husband. Lucy was our daughter. And she died. She died!

Matilda remembered it all, every terrible detail. All six years had come back to her as she slept, the worst nightmare of them all.

Somehow I did this to us. I erased those years with the fire of my grief.

She felt the power of the words she'd said in the car. *I wish I'd never met you.* How could she have such power, to actually make the black wish come true? How did she live with this? How did she face that power and not shrivel away into nothing?

What happens now?

Matilda slipped soundlessly off the bed. She stood for a moment in the warm shaft of sun, her gaze on Henry. She wanted to touch him. She wanted him to wake up and tell her none of it was true. But she knew it was, without a doubt. "I'm sorry," she whispered as she moved away. Fighting the pain, she left the apartment. It was just past dawn. The streets were still deserted; only the birds greeted the sun. She realized halfway to her house that she'd left her shoes. Her feet were starting to get raw from the rough pavement and asphalt. She sighed with relief when she stepped onto the cool, dew-damp grass of her backyard.

Glancing at the garden, a raw ache in her chest, she went into the house. She lifted the typewriter from the floor and set it on the coffee table. Slowly, she rolled a fresh sheet of paper into the platen. Her hands trembled over the black and silver keys.

```
Henry, I remember.
     I remember Lucy. Do you remember her? We had
a child. A beautiful, sweet little girl. She died,
and I wished our lives away. The power of my grief
somehow answered that sadistic wish, burying our
lives. This is my fault. Jetty warned me about grief
and I didn't listen. Now I've ruined the beauty
of what we had. Lucy is gone, and I destroyed our
memories, our love.
     I don't know how to say I'm sorry. It doesn't
matter anyway; there is no forgiveness for this.
     Goodbye, Henry.
```

Matilda left the typewriter, tears rolling down her cheeks. She packed a bag, numb and dazed, thinking only one thought: *I ruined everything.* She put on fresh clothes, good sneakers, and brushed her hair and teeth. *Ready to go.*

Stepping out in the backyard, she remembered her car was at Henry's. *I'll walk. I'll just walk until there is nothing left of me.* She went to the garden, put her duffle on the grass by her feet. Her beautiful, thriving garden. She picked a basil leaf, smelled it. An inexplicable rage burst in her chest, so hot and surprising, she reacted before she understood what was happening. With vicious hands, she ripped off whole chunks of the basil plant. Tore at the tomato and pumpkin vines, cutting the flesh of her palms. Grunting, nearly screaming, she kept going.

Ripping.

Pulling.

Destroying.

Strong hands yanked on her shoulders, pulling her back. "Stop it!"

Henry's face in her face.

"Tilly! That's enough."

"No!" she screamed, beating on his chest. "Go away!"

He didn't go away; he held her tighter, fighting her rage until she was exhausted. Finally, her eyes focused on her arms and hands pressed against him. Dirt splattered all over her. She saw it on her arms, felt it on her face and clothes, like blood at a murder scene.

"Tilly?" Henry said cautiously.

"I . . ." She looked from him to the massacred plants to her hands stained brown and green. "Lucy . . . our sweet Lucy," she sobbed, collapsing to the ground, kneeling with her face in her hands.

Henry knelt beside her. "Tilly, look at me, please."

"No, I can't," she cried. Matilda felt her chest would cave in, her body would burn to ashes. "I ruined us. I have to leave. I have to go. Leave me alone, Henry. Let me go."

Henry said nothing, and Matilda knew he blamed her.

As he should.

Henry

*H*enry's body had gone completely numb. He felt nothing, as if he floated, weightless and displaced, only a broken mind. He remembered it all, had seen it in his sleep just as Matilda had. The final nightmare. Every second of what had been missing. He'd been pulled from the final moments by the sound of typewriter keys. He dove across the room to read the words typing themselves. Her words. To him. A letter goodbye.

The moment he saw those last words—*Goodbye, Henry*—he'd run. Faster than ever before. Across town, into her yard. The sight of Matilda ripping apart her garden, the angry, foreign sounds in her chest, would never leave him.

A freak accident, a child's death, and one sentence had changed everything.

I wish I'd never met you. The words echoed in his head.

He looked at Matilda now, shaking on the grass, but hardly saw her past the white-hot anger.

All this is her fault. One errant sentence and she ruined us. How could she do that?!

Henry put his hands in his hair, pressing into his raging head. *No, no, it's my fault. I was the one driving. I killed our daughter. Matilda only erased the memories. I should thank her for that.*

In his mind, he saw Lucy, her round face and dark hair. Her eyes, the same color as his own.

The anger drained away. Only grief and confusion remained. He looked at Matilda. He could let her leave. He could leave too. They could leave each other, run away. Pretend it never happened. A rush of fear made him dizzy. *If I do that, it'll be Mavis all over again. It will be the worst mistake I'll ever make.*

I have to save us.

Henry immediately reached for Matilda, trying to take her in his arms. She thrashed at him again. "Don't touch me! I did this. *It's my fault.*"

He tightened his grip, pushing her snarling hands down. "No. No! I won't let you go away again."

Matilda stilled, stiff as stone. "How can you forgive me?"

He pushed the hair away from her tear and dirt stained face. He held her face until she looked at him. A bizarre happiness rose inside him, standing next to the pain. "I proposed to you in the stacks. It was the second of January, seven months after we met. I remember the way you looked in your wedding dress, the curve of your tiny hips under the white silk, and the smile you gave me as we faced each other to say our vows. The sound of your sigh in your sleep on our wedding night. All the words that came to me *from you.* I wrote and wrote because of you. I remember the determined, nearly supernatural look on your face as you labored to push Lucy from your body." He wiped tears from her face, ignoring his own. "I remember the horror of watching you in the backseat with Lucy after the accident. How the world ended when you said she was dead." He took a shaky breath. "And I *want* those memories, all of them."

Matilda's face broke into a thousand pieces. "But what I did . . ."

"And I drove the car that killed our daughter. We both made mistakes, but it's done enough damage. Let's fix it now. Don't make it worse. Running away is not the answer." He kissed her forehead. "Let's fix it," he repeated in a whisper. "I want to remember our baby girl. I want to hurt over her death and figure out a way to deal with it. I need you to help me deal with it. Because it's so ugly, this feeling of losing her. Stay with me, help me. And I'll help you."

Matilda held his eyes. He watched the struggle in her. He felt her body ready to run, to leave. He felt every dark emotion she was fighting and silently urged her to let them go. Finally, she whispered. "I miss her."

Henry smiled sadly, feeling the tightness uncoil in his stomach. He kissed her softly. "Me too. Yes. I miss you too. I love you. I never forgot that."

"But how do we . . ." Her lip trembled. "I don't know how. The grief . . . it's so *heavy*."

"I'll help you; you'll help me. Walking away from each other would be the greater tragedy."

"Henry is right, Tilly."

Matilda gasped loudly. They both turned to look at a woman standing behind them. "Jetty?" Matilda asked, her face turning pale. "Is that you?"

"Hi, Tilly-girl." Jetty's long skirt, made of layers of pink lace, rustled as she moved closer. She also wore a white peasant top with big angel sleeves. Her hair was ochre orange, wildly curly. Her entire form shimmered slightly, opaque and translucent. Henry sucked in a breath.

Matilda shifted away from him. "Is that really you, Jetty?"

Jetty squatted down, smiled lovingly at her niece. "Yes."

"But you're . . ." Matilda's eyes traveled over her aunt's form.

"A ghost?" Jetty laughed quietly. "Yep, that's right." Jetty reached out to touch Matilda's face. She gasped again.

"I can feel you."

"Yeah, this ghost thing is pretty groovy. I'm not bound by the laws of a physical body: I can move with a thought, I can be seen or not be seen, and I can still touch and feel." She put both hands on Matilda's face, cupping her muddy cheeks.

Henry watched a flicker of relief on Matilda's face that quickly crumpled to despair. "Jetty," Matilda cried, her voice weak and childlike. "Something bad happened."

Jetty's face tightened. "I know, sweetie. I'm so, so sorry. I'm sorry I left you before it happened, and that I couldn't help fix it. I'm sorry my death added to your grief, helping to cause this whole thing."

"How did it happen? How did I . . . ?"

"I always told you there are forces in the world we don't understand. I told you there was power in you."

Matilda shook her head. "What power? What do you mean?"

"We rarely realize how powerful our thoughts can be, how powerful our emotions are. There's tremendous energy there, and if we let it that energy can build and build until it creates its own strength, its own will. It's like when you think about someone all day and then they call you that night and say, 'I just felt like I needed to call you.'"

"But this was six years of our lives!"

"Grief is especially potent. You've heard the expression 'died of a broken heart.' It's not just a saying. Sadness has weight, and it can have power too. That's what I meant about being careful with your grief."

Matilda let out a small gasp. "I didn't realize . . ." Her eyes pulled wide. "What about Lucy? Where is she?"

"Oh, Tilly-girl. She died. That didn't change. When you two disappeared, pulled back to the places you were before you met, I helped her spirit find its way. Then I took her body to a beautiful farm. An old artist friend of mine owns the place. She has a thousand acres of corn and does gorgeous stained glass in her barn. She got the biggest kick out of me being a ghost." She laughed quietly. "And she helped me bury Lucy there in her family plot. It's a gorgeous spot, under an old maple tree, green fields, big sky. We planted yellow tulips." Jetty nodded, rubbed her thumbs over Matilda's skin. "The Bel Air and all your things—pictures, books, Henry's letters—are there as well."

"You buried her? She's there? But . . . I erased her! I—"

"No, no! Her spirit lives, just like mine. She's passed on. She's happy, safe. Her death was *not* your fault." Jetty lifted Matilda's chin to make her look her in the eye. "That was *not* your fault or Henry's." Her eyes moved to him briefly; Henry felt a chill move down his spine. "Understand me? That was an accident. Like Enzo falling off his ladder, like getting cancer. That's just life."

"But I took those years from Henry and me. I screwed up everything!"

"It can be fixed—if you want. Would you rather face the grief of Lucy's death or never have known her and Henry?"

Matilda stilled, looked briefly at Henry, and then back to Jetty. "But it hurts . . ."

"I know, honey. But Lucy is happy and free. You've imprisoned yourself in the loss. It's time to set yourselves free as well."

"Jetty . . ." Henry said hesitantly.

Jetty turned her bright green eyes on him. "Hello, Henry. Nice to meet you."

He smiled shyly. "And you." He swallowed, nervous and amazed. "The typewriters and books . . . did you?"

"I did. I made sure you had the typewriters and the books to help you remember. I used some of my ghostly powers to send the letters from one to the other. I thought of simply appearing and telling Tilly everything, but I was worried about her mind."

Matilda sucked in a breath. "Mom's disease? I do have it?"

"No, I don't think you do. But they say it can be brought on or aggravated by a tragedy or extreme shock. I was trying to find the right time, the right way."

"So it was all real, not my damaged mind? And I did see you that night?"

"It's all been real, sweetie. And yes, I was testing the waters, but the way you ran, how scared you were—I didn't want to push it again. And then you found my letter. I had to know your mind was stable before I tried again."

Matilda reached for Henry, he pulled her into his arms. Her arms tightened around him. "What if we had never found each other again?" she asked.

Henry looked at Jetty. "I think we have Jetty to thank for that too." Matilda pulled away to look at her aunt.

Jetty smiled. "An old newspaper in the right place at the right time."

Matilda shook her head. "You saved us. Thank you, Jetty. It's . . . it's so good to see you again. Have you been here the whole time—since you died?"

"I have. I knew you still needed some help. So I stuck around, I watched. I was so happy when you found Henry." She smiled at him. "But I still sensed something. One of those pesky feelings I always got. Guess those pass on with you."

Matilda smiled sadly. "You always believed in magic."

"And you always wanted to. Now you see, don't you?"

"Yes, I do. Will you stay, Jetty? Help us get through this?"

Jetty took her hand. "No, Tilly-girl. It's time for me to go. You and Henry are all you need to get through this. Help each other."

Matilda leaned forward. "You're leaving?"

"It's time I be with Enzo and Lucy and my parents. They're waiting." Her hand came to Matilda's face again; Henry's heart ached for her. "Enzo's waiting."

Matilda nodded. "Of course. Go to him."

"Thank you, Jetty," Henry said.

"My pleasure, handsome. Take care of my girl."

"I will."

Matilda sniffed, "Tell Lucy we love her. We *miss* her. Tell her . . ."

"I'll tell her *everything.*" Jetty kissed them both on the forehead. She reached into her right pocket. "Here are the keys to the Bel Air. The address for the farm is written on the keychain; it's not far from El Dorado. And here," Jetty reached into her left pocket and pulled out a rolled piece of paper. "A little parting gift."

Matilda opened the paper with a gasp. In soft, cottony watercolors, Jetty had painted Lucy, sitting in the grass surrounded by yellow tulips, and smiling. Matilda's hand came to her mouth, and Henry's heart tugged hard. They both looked up to thank Jetty, but the yard was empty.

Henry pulled Matilda into his arms and held tight.

Matilda

Matilda closed her eyes and clung to Henry. She looked at the spot where Jetty had been, marveling at her appearance, her help. All the pain felt a little less awful knowing Jetty had been there, doing what she could to guide them back to each other, back to the truth. *It's not my fault. We can get through this.*

In her head, Matilda heard typewriter keys and Lucy laughing: her two favorite sounds. The ache of Lucy's loss swelled in her chest. She knew it would never go away. But maybe she could make it stop burning.

Opening her eyes, she looked at the remains of the garden. She felt ashamed at the senseless display of emotion and mourned the loss of the thriving plants. "I ruined my garden," she whispered.

Henry brought his chin over her head to look at the garden. "I think we can save some of it. Come on."

Together they went to the edge of the plot. Matilda set Lucy's portrait nearby. Henry pulled away some debris and she saw that some of the basil was intact and one tomato plant. Their hands went to work.

A short time later, as they were finishing the rescue mission, Matilda heard a car pull into the driveway. A door opened, but didn't shut. Henry and she exchanged a look. Parker's voice came from the front of the house.

"Tilly! Tilly, are you home?"

Matilda ran around the house, Henry behind her. "Parker?" He nearly collided with her by the red Honda. "What's wrong?"

"Thea!" he huffed and bent to look in the backseat. Thea was there, in obvious pain, her face even more swollen than before. "She wanted you with her," Parker went on, voice frantic. "But I'm worried. Something's not right."

"Let's go!" Matilda said. "Henry, you drive. Parker, passenger seat. I'll sit with Thea."

They piled into the car and Henry raced off toward the clinic. "Thea? What's wrong?" Matilda said, quickly scanning her friend. "Tell me what's wrong."

Thea, sweating badly, red faced, and breathless said, "I can't catch my breath. And the contractions—" She doubled over, groaning as one hit hard. All her memories now intact, Matilda remembered that all-consuming pain of labor. And the fear of the unknown inherent to a first birth.

"Okay, okay," she said. "Take my hand, hold as tight as you need. We'll be with Dr. Wells in just a minute. Hey, look at me." Thea's wide, scared eyes lifted to Matilda. "You're having a baby." She said it with tender awe and excitement.

Thea grinned. "I'm having a baby."

Four hours later, Matilda sat in a chair next to Thea's bed, tiny pink Toby in her arms. "He's perfect, Thea."

"Of course he is." She smiled sleepily and then sighed. "Doc said I had that toxemia or whatever. Blood pressure through the roof! But we got here just in time. Thanks for being with me, Tilly. I needed that."

"My pleasure."

"Where's Henry?"

"He went to get Abby. Gill died last night. Heart attack during the festival."

"What?" Thea opened her eyes. "No. Is she okay?"

"She's about how you'd expect. But she wants to see Toby. I think it will help her to see him, to hold him. New life, you know?"

Thea nodded. She looked at Matilda for a thoughtful moment. "How did you know so much about having a baby?"

Matilda's eyes instantly filled with tears. She looked at the newborn through the mist and only saw Lucy's face. "I had this."

Thea started. "What do you mean?" Parker opened the door, back with some Mad Hash food for Thea.

He looked between them. "What's wrong?"

Thea waved him forward, snatching the food from him. "Sit down," she said. "Matilda is going to tell us her story."

Matilda launched into the whole story, feeling a tiny catharsis as she told it, but also feeling a strange hope bloom in her heart. When she had finished, she looked up at Thea and Parker, not sure her friends would believe it.

Thea's eyes were narrowed in thought. "I can't imagine how you must feel. That little guy is not even an hour old, but if I lost him . . ."

"It hit me like a train. I didn't want to feel the pain of it." Matilda touched Toby's warm face. "And I had never faced the pain of my parent's death or Jetty's. It was so much."

"Grief hits us all differently. You've had more than your fair share, so I can't blame you. When my grandma died I didn't want to leave my bed for days. When you left Parker he jumped in the river. And you—"

"What?" Matilda said, her stomach twisting. She looked to Parker, "You said you fell."

Thea sighed. "No, he jumped. He was sad and drunk and he jumped into the river."

Matilda went cold from head to toe. "I . . . I can't . . ."

Parker raised a hand. "I didn't jump to kill myself, I jumped to *feel something*. I'd gone so numb from the pain that I needed a shock to the system. I jumped in that stupid river and got pulled out a recovered man. The next day, I stopped wallowing in the pain, started living again. Jumping in that river was a *good* thing."

A sigh of relief. "Why didn't you tell me that? Why the story about falling in?"

"It's hard to explain. The falling in story is what I tell everyone."

Thea cut in. "Everyone thinks he's covering up a suicide attempt with the falling story. Most still believe he did want to kill himself. That's the more dramatic story. Much juicer than wanting to reset, refresh himself. That's part of the reason you got such a warm reception." She smiled. "I mean, it is pretty crazy to get drunk and jump in a river."

"But you understand crazy, don't you, Tilly?" Parker smiled, a glint of humor in his eyes.

Matilda laughed quietly. "Too much, I'm afraid."

"So what now?" Thea asked. "What will you and Henry do?"

Toby stirred in his sleep, Matilda bounced him a little. "We move forward. This is our jump in the river, I guess. Now we let the anger and the blackness wash away."

"That's sorta beautiful." Thea closed her eyes again. "Maybe you should have another baby."

A kick in her heart, a flood of warmth in her blood. "Maybe."

A quiet knock on the door brought all their heads up. Henry pushed the door open for Abby, who hurried in, tears on her cheeks but bearing a smile that filled the room. "Hand over the goods," she said, opening her arms.

With a laugh, Matilda stood and shifted the baby into her waiting embrace. Abby adjusted the baby into the crook of one elbow and then lifted her free hand to Matilda's face. She didn't say anything, but Matilda knew everything she meant from the look in her eyes. Abby nodded once. Turning to Thea, she said, "Have mercy, he's so handsome, Thea. But of course, you and Parker would have a beautiful baby." Abby turned. "Parker, well done. Although, what did you do, huh? Thea did all the hard work."

Parker frowned in mock insult. "I gave him that full head of blond hair and perfect nose. It was hard work."

They all laughed.

Matilda went to Henry who took her into his arms.

Matilda

*M*atilda pulled back the paper from the window. The new white letters read, *The Typed Page. A Bookshop for Book Lovers.* The Remington Rand typewriter shape stood in as the shop logo, placed below the words.

Abby clapped her hands. "Praise the Lord! Silent Fields has a bookstore again." She looked up at the sky. "Thank you, Gill, for taking out life insurance."

Henry put his arm around Matilda's shoulder. He kissed the top of her head, and warmth washed down her body. The time since their discovery had not been easy. Matilda struggled with the guilt every day, but Henry never gave up on her. He moved into the house with her, and they started the painful process of healing. The memories were not as forgiving as he. Every moment, she felt the space where Lucy should be and the consequences of what she'd done. At times it was abrasive, leaving her feeling stripped of all her skin.

Opening the bookshop had become a sort of redemption, as well as a distraction. They all needed it—Abby, Henry, and she. So they took it on with vigor, using the money from Gill's life insurance to pay for the stock and new business costs.

Henry had started work on a new novel as well as continuing his duties as editor of the newspaper. The clack of keys often filled the house and the bookshop, a typewriter placed in each location. His letters to her, the ones that had come miraculously, were framed and hung on the wall of the bookshop office above the roll top desk. And a new shoebox was quickly filling up with fresh love letters.

"There's one more sign you need to put up." Abby smiled mischievously, nodding toward the door.

"What sign?" Henry asked.

"Follow me!" Abby led them to the children's section in the small room off the main area. Matilda couldn't help but smile at all the full shelves and especially the children's space, bursting with colorful decorations. Twenty crystals hung in the windows. She'd even managed to fit in a small table with two chairs. She imagined Lucy sitting in one of the chairs, flipping the pages of a picture book.

Abby lifted a pink gift bag from behind the small table and presented it to Matilda. There were tears in her weak-tea eyes. Matilda smiled as she exchanged a look with Henry before plunging her hand into the bag. Tossing the tissue paper to the floor, Matilda revealed a small pewter plaque. Her own tears came instantly.

Henry looked over her shoulder, his hands coming to her hips. "In loving memory of Lucy Jetty Craig." He smiled with emotion. "Thank you, Abby."

"Felt right, you know," she said, wiping at her wet cheeks.

"It's perfect," Matilda said. "We can hang Jetty's painting of Lucy with it."

"There's one more thing in there." Abby gestured to the pink bag.

Matilda pulled out a framed picture. It was a beautiful photograph of Lucy's grave. The plot was nestled under the shade of an old maple tree, rolling hills of vibrant green cornfields beyond. The sky above was brilliant azure and marked with cotton clouds. Just as Jetty had described it.

"I took it last time we were there," Abby said reverently. "It was such a lovely day."

Matilda, Henry, and Abby had visited the gravesite many times now. Milly Baker, the owner of the farm and Jetty's friend, had welcomed them with open arms, quickly becoming a dear friend. She'd even been here to the shop to expertly clean the stained glass in the front door. This place on Milly's farm—Matilda touched the glass of the frame over the simple granite headstone that marked her daughter's resting place—was peaceful and beautiful and perfect. Every time they went she felt closer to Lucy.

"Thank you, Abby," Matilda whispered through her tears. "This will go home with us. I want it on my nightstand, next to my favorite picture of me and Jetty."

"Sounds right." Abby gave her a long hug.

Henry took the plaque, removed the sticker covering on the back, and pressed it to the space of wall next to the doorway to the children's room. "It's perfect," he repeated quietly. He looked at Matilda, eyes brimming with emotions. She reached up to touch his freckled face. A flash of guilt threatened to ruin the happy moment. She still struggled to understand the power inside her that had erased their lives. But she clung to something Henry had told her late one night when she woke crying and thrashing. He'd held her in their bed, whispered in her ear. "We are stronger now. You gave us that."

Abby said with a happy sniff, "I can't wait to see the new little one running around in here. I'm betting on a boy." She leaned forward and spoke to Matilda's slightly rounded belly. "Are you listening, little man? Auntie Abby can't wait to meet you."

Henry smiled. "Should we name him Gill, if it's a boy?"

Abby scoffed as she stood up. "Of course not! Awful name. A fish's name. You find him a good strong name, like his father's."

Matilda laughed. Henry shook his head, leaned down to kiss her forehead. Then he went off to his office to write, Abby trailing behind him listing off boy names.

Matilda touched Lucy's name on the plaque with one hand as she touched her belly with the other. A new baby. What had Jetty told her? *You need a reason to live after tragedy.* Matilda smiled to herself. *I have you, little one. And I have Henry, and Abby. And this bookshop.*

Matilda went to the big front window and flipped the sign to *Open.*

Discussion
Questions

1. Grief is a major theme in the book. Discuss the different ways characters deal with death and loss.

2. What thoughts and theories did you have when Matilda and Henry woke up in different places after the accident?

3. Who was your favorite supporting character and why?

4. Weather is used as a symbol several times in the story. Recall when and discuss the purpose of this technique.

5. Books play a major role in this story. How do books help the characters?

6. Which one of Henry's letters was your favorite and why?

7. How do you feel about the idea that our thoughts and emotions have energy and power?

CREATIVE BOOK CLUB SUGGESTIONS

1. Take your book club to a local bookstore. Spend time browsing and sharing and then hit a bakery (like Estelle's) for donuts and discussion.

2. Take your book club to a local antique shop. Spend time browsing old things or see if you can find some of the items mentioned in the book, such as a rotary phone, an old Chanel purse, a steamer trunk, and old typewriters. Major bonus points for finding a 1937 Remington Rand 5.

3. Serve some of Matilda and Jetty's favorite foods: pasta, pie, cinnamon rolls, or fried chicken and mashed potatoes. Or serve food inspired by The Bright Night Festival: BBQ, cotton candy, cookies, pink lemonade, donuts, and root beer.

4. Track down a working typewriter and have everyone write/type a love letter to his or her favorite person.

Acknowledgments

This novel had a little bit different of a writing process in which good books and the luxury of time deserve the most thanks. I worked on it in the background while I wrote my first three books, so it had lots of time to evolve and get better. I also read some very helpful books on writing, namely *Story* by Robert McKee, *Writing the Breakout Novel* by Donald Maass, and *Save the Cat!* by Blake Snyder.

Many thanks to the crew at Cedar Fort and Sweetwater Books. To Melissa Caldwell for her insightful editing. To Jessica Romrell for sharp-eyed copyediting. To Breanna Call Herbert for the perfect typesetting. To Shawnda T. Craig for the gorgeous cover design. To Kaitlin Barwick for editing coordination. To Vikki Downs for marketing help. To Erin Tanner who read it first and said yes. And to those of you whose names I don't know, thank you for your work.

A big thank you to my family for your support and love. Thanks Kenneth and Natasha for some last-minute opinions. The most thanks goes to my husband, Matt, who is always there to provide a practical insight, a late-night fried egg, and endless encouragement. He also inspired the typewriter idea by giving me a 1937 Remington Rand 5 for one of our anniversaries. It sits on the shelves next to my desk, and I adore it.

Finally, a big, warm thank you to *you*, the reader, for picking up this book.

About the Author

*T*eri Harman has believed in all things wondrous and haunting since her childhood days of sitting in the highest tree branches reading Roald Dahl and running in the rain, imagining stories of danger and romance. She's the author of three previous books: *Blood Moon*, *Black Moon*, and *Storm Moon*. She also writes about books for ksl.com and contributed regular book segments to "Studio 5 with Brooke Walker," Utah's number-one lifestyle show. She lives in Utah with her husband and three children.

Scan to visit

www.teriharman.com